death comes for the trophy wife & other stories

death comes for the trophy wife & other stories

Karen M. Vaughn

BRAIN MILL PRESS
GREEN BAY, WISCONSIN

Published in the United States by Brain Mill Press.

Print ISBN 978-1-948559-69-0

EPUB ISBN 978-1-948559-72-0

MOBI ISBN 978-1-948559-70-6

PDF ISBN 978-1-948559-71-3

www.brainmillpress.com

contents

death
comes for
the trophy
wife & other
stories

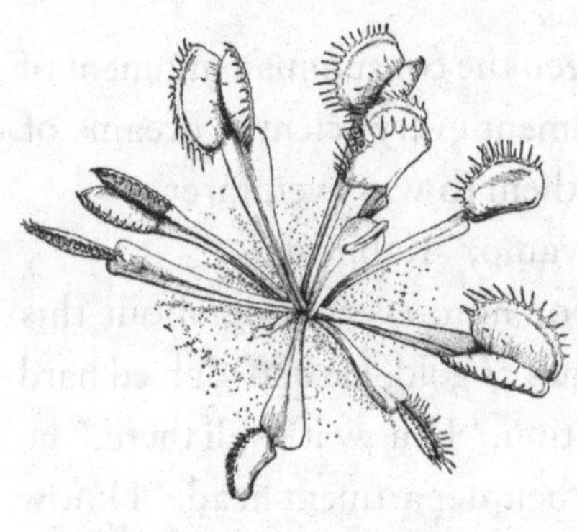

bird watching

For the second time in eight years, Kabir and Ismael found themselves in the heart of the Florida Panhandle, camped beside the murky Choctawhatchee River. Their binoculars were trained on the branches above them. With great care they examined the crown spread of blushing red maple; of river birch with its curls of peeling bark, exposing nerve-soft membranes beneath; of pond cypress draped with a funereal fringe of Spanish moss. Just as before, they sought something elusive, something thought to have vanished entirely from the modern world—the ivory-billed woodpecker, believed by most ornithologists to be extinct. And they had found it, oh yes. They had found it and they had lost it. Still, its appearance had been the consummate moment of their careers, the moment every scientist dreams of. And what it had led them to was even rarer.

"God, I hate the swamp," Kabir said.

Ismael flinched. For him, everything about this place was etched in lines of gold. He had lobbied hard for this return expedition. "I know it's still there," he had told Dr. Carver, their department head. "I know it as sure as I am standing here. If we could just obtain proof this time, think what a coup it would be for the university." In the intervening years, Dr. Carver had sent four different teams to the Choctawhatchee to investigate, and when each of those came up short, she had at last agreed to dispatch the original pairing, in the hope that lightning might strike a second time. But four days in, Ismael and Kabir had no more to show for this trip than the first one. The swamp was positively swarming with life—scrub jays, egrets, wood ducks, flora of every variety—just not the variety they were looking for.

If only they hadn't been so reckless the first time. If only they hadn't been so caught up in the exhilaration of discovery that they dropped their compass while running and then didn't stop to retrieve it. How would they ever find the place now?

But then, they had been about to give up that time, too. They had been conducting their final sweep of the southern bank when the woodpecker at last materialized on a branch just beside them, taking sudden shape where there had been nothing, at least nothing that they had seen, as if conjured from the matter of the swamp itself. They had gazed at it in stunned silence. Truly, the bird was the very emblem of evolved beauty. It was huge, for starters. Its slender body was nearly twenty inches long, with a wingspan that was probably double that. It boasted jet-black plumage veined with stark ribbons of white. Its eyes were wild, yellow, prehistoric-looking. The signature beak was a gleaming prong of ivory, while the scarlet crest bobbed in concert with its movements, at times seeming to flicker in midair like a flame. The woodpecker was like a watcher out of time, like a great bird from myth.

"Beautiful," murmured Ismael.

"It's just like the photographs," Kabir said. "Better even."

The last undisputed photograph of an ivory-billed woodpecker was from the 1940s. For decades, the American Birding Association had deemed it a class 6 species, meaning 'definitely or probably extinct.' As such, their trip had been framed as more of a postmortem. They were to conduct a last-ditch survey, purely to confirm the bird's absence, while also searching for clues to what might have led to its extinction. But now here was the specimen itself, alive and well, tossing its fiery head in chastisement of their presumption. This discovery would change everything.

"Get your camera," said Ismael, holding perfectly still so as not to startle it.

Oh-so-slowly, Kabir reached into his backpack and withdrew the camera.

It was then that the woodpecker took off, winging swiftly away from the river and toward the interior of the swamp. In horror they watched it disappear behind a cypress, slipping into the green as if into an envelope, and without a thought they had plunged into the woods after it, running at full speed through tangles of vines and pools of standing water. Kabir had always had a slight limp, arising from an untreated childhood infection, but here he raced as if his life depended on it, his imbalance not slowing him down at all.

The men ran side by side for what felt like hours, forging on even when their lungs ached from the exertion. Several times the bird seemed to evaporate and then re-emerge behind them, so that they felt they must be retracing their steps, though they couldn't have said for certain because of the uniformity of the terrain. Before long, they were hopelessly lost. With no time to orient themselves, they clung to the spider-silk thread of the bird's trail. Indeed, the woodpecker seemed to know precisely how fast it could fly and still be pursued. It remained just near enough for them to catch the occasional glimpse of it, a seductive blur of ivory and black, or hear the faint tattoo of its drumming, as if summoning them to some ancient war council.

Siren song, Ismael thought, with a tiny, wary part of his mind. He watched the compass tumble from Kabir's backpack, along with their protein bars and half of the batteries, and again there was that pang of concern, a flare sent up by his amygdala. But it was quickly extinguished. The only thing that mattered in the short term, he assured himself, was capturing proof of the bird's existence. If they could do that, the world as they knew it would be remade. They could always retrace their muddy footprints later, or even navigate by the stars, if needed.

When the woodpecker finally halted its flight, Kabir and Ismael had found themselves in a particularly dense part of the swamp. They pushed aside a heavy curtain of vines and entered a small clearing, where they found the bird perched on an enormous plant, consisting of two broad leaves and a fringe of feathery cilia. In this setting the bird looked even larger. More primitive. Its yellow eyes peered at them without blinking, its avian thoughts pondering god only knew what, though Ismael theorized that it was cross-checking them with images in its archives, that knife-sharp mind leafing through a taxonomy of ghosts.

Throughout his life, Ismael had formed many such conjectures about the thoughts of birds. As a boy in working-class Cardiff, peering over the stonework wall to watch blackbirds in his neighbor's garden, he had tried to imagine what they might dream about. Flying? Hunting for bugs and worms? Being enfolded once more in their mother's wings, and hearing the rapid flutter of her heartbeat? Later, after a dissertation's worth of research, he had had to broaden his suppositions. Here, after all, were creatures capable of complex communication, of tool-making, of play for its own sake, of deception and even empathy, all while displaying a host of other qualities that were entirely foreign to humans, chief among them a faultless sense of geolocation. They were literally never lost. They could be sedated and carried on a plane to the farthest reaches of the planet, and somehow, with the pull of magnetic fields like an ache in their bones, they would always, *always,* find their way home. Still, the same question kept returning that had haunted him under that gray dome of sky, the stone wall cool against his chin. If he could peek into the brain of a bird, what would he see? Would it be in some way familiar—if not akin to, then at least adjacent to human thought? Or would he be sent reeling by the strangeness of it, his senses adrift in an alien landscape?

As Kabir readied the camera, snapping countless photographs, Ismael began to furiously scribble notes in his field journal. He tried to detail every aspect of the bird and its environs—precise shape, colors, behavior, flight pattern, preferred tree species, etc.— making several sketches for later reference. Soon, though, an additional data point seemed to creep into his awareness.

"What is that smell?" he whispered.

"I don't know. Must be decaying organic matter from the bog."

"It's making me feel a little unfocused."

"Yes, me too."

After a few minutes, the bird hopped to a branch slightly farther away, and the men took a step closer. By then Ismael's fingers had started to tingle. He flexed his hand several times, trying to restore circulation, and kept writing. Once they drew nearer, the woodpecker again flitted away a short distance. Several times this process was repeated: the men would take a step forward, while the bird retreated a commensurate interval. Soon they had reached the gigantic plant where the bird had been sitting when they first entered the clearing. It was directly in their path, and Ismael was just about to thread a course between the leaves, straining to observe the precise pattern of the plumage, when something by his feet happened to catch his eye.

A jumble of white objects lay before them. Some short and stubby, some elongated and delicate-seeming. Among them was an array of curved planks, as well as what looked like a pair of tapered bottles, deeply pitted and lined with small, blunt protrusions. Because Ismael's mental acuity had been impaired by the mysterious odor, it took him a moment to understand that what he was seeing was not the remains of one large creature, but two. Here were the skeletons of what had probably been deer—white-tailed deer, if his memory of the indigenous wildlife was correct. Their rib cages were so close as to be conjoined, intersecting really, as if the animals had been caught in the act of mating. There was no hint of skin or muscle tissue anywhere. Only the bones themselves, bare and elegant and gleaming.

"What the…?" muttered Kabir.

In his dazed state he stumbled forward to look, his foot coming to rest on the very edge of one of the plant's broad leaves. Then something had happened. There was a sudden blur of motion. A rush of wind. The world shifted, and Kabir could only gape as the two sides of the plant came swiftly together, closing like a clamshell around the mound of bones. Around him. Ismael had just enough time to grab Kabir's starched collar and pull him to safety. They fell back into the mud together, and when they dared to look up again, they saw that the leaves of the plant had fully sealed, the feathery cilia interlocking in a zipper pattern. Like teeth, Ismael realized.

For a long while, the two men sat sprawling in the mud, too astonished to speak.

"It can't be," said Kabir finally, his breath returning at last.

Ismael didn't seem to hear him. "I must be dreaming. That bastard is the size of a Volkswagen!

I think the biggest one ever recorded had a rosette of around eight inches. This," and here he gestured weakly at the plant, "...this is just absurd."

"Oh, it's absurd, all right," Kabir agreed, and without warning, he began to giggle. "We almost got swallowed whole, like Buddha and the Rainbow Fish. Only we are not gods, so I don't think we would have fared as well." His mirth at this thought grew more intense until soon he was doubled over, clutching his broad knees to his chest and convulsing with laughter. Tears streamed down his cheeks.

Ismael was nonplussed. He had never seen Kabir emit so much as a guffaw. Even among ornithologists, a famously stoic breed, the man was notable for his seriousness. But the combination of adrenaline and the pervasive odor was clearly taking its toll, and before long Ismael found himself laughing right alongside his colleague—huge, bellowing laughs that belied his small frame. In the space between fits, he managed to gasp out, "But Buddha? I thought you were some kind of Hindu."

Kabir laughed even harder at this. "I *am* some kind of Hindu!" he said, delighted. "Oh Izzy, you are a riot. In Hinduism, as you know, Buddha was an incarnation of Vishnu."

"Oh, that's right," Ismael said with a snort at his own idiocy. "I don't think I'm operating at peak capacity here. My head feels like scrambled eggs."

"And mine feels like sizzling bacon," Kabir cackled, elbowing him in the ribs. "Together we'd make a splendid breakfast."

After some time, the men began to recover from the episode. They expelled a few final giggles and wiped the remaining tears on their sleeves.

When he was sure there would be no more, Kabir gave Ismael a small, sly smile. "You won't tell anyone about this, will you? Wouldn't want to jeopardize my reputation as a humorless academic."

"I won't tell a soul," Ismael said.

"Swear on your crazy Welsh god?"

Ismael grinned. "I swear."

They turned again toward the scene of the almost-crime, marveling anew at the plant's monstrous dimensions. No doubt the nutritional requirements for a plant this size were substantial. Ismael felt something like regret that it had come so close to garnering a meal, only to be thwarted at the last second. As they looked on, the two massive leaves slowly fanned open again, as if on a hydraulic hinge, and reset to their prior position. As they did, the bones of the unfortunate deer came back into view, the gleaming white of their surfaces now slick with membranous fluids, likely secreted in anticipation of imminent digestion. Kabir shook his head, as if dismissing the reality of the tableau. "A colossal Venus flytrap in the midst of the Florida swamp. It's impossible."

But deep down, Ismael felt that nothing was impossible here. Wasn't it in places like this where life as they knew it had begun? Where microbes had first surged and foamed in a burgeoning tide and ambitious lizards had come lumbering out of the muck? From his nearby branch, the ivory-billed woodpecker still thrummed with primeval purpose, hammering home the point. Nature was unpredictable. It lurched ever forward, making false starts, spinning out wild experiments that sometimes took hold and sometimes petered out, never to be repeated. Others lingered far beyond the point of viability, enduring, perhaps, out of some sort of evolutionary stubbornness, some fabulous defect that would not allow them to countenance defeat. In his mind Ismael could still see the plant's prehensile teeth as they had swung toward them, the relic of an ancient hunting mechanism. Long ago these movements had been encoded into the flytrap's DNA, and it would continue to carry them out for as long as it was able, without malice or understanding. Trying to recreate a world that was gone.

Ismael had a sudden flash of understanding. "Do you realize what's happening here?" he asked excitedly. "The woodpecker is working in tandem with the flytrap. I think what we're seeing here is cooperative hunting between species, like coyotes sometimes do with badgers. Like moray eels and groupers."

Kabir's eyes were brighter than he'd ever seen them. "You might be right, Izzy. And don't forget the scent generated by the bog, to disorient and distract." He gripped Ismael's shoulder, arresting his attention. "But how could it possibly know to herd us here? Or rather, how could that be a successful strategy when hunting the other animals that live here? It's not like the deer were chasing the bird, hoping to publish their findings in a scholarly journal."

Ismael placed his hand over Kabir's, clutching it with the force of this observation. Increasingly, he was feeling breathless, as if the amount of oxygen reaching his brain was no longer sufficient for normal functioning and the bulk of it was being routed elsewhere. Most of it, in fact, seemed to be going to his skin. It was often said that the skin, not the brain or the liver, was the body's largest organ, and right then he could feel the truth of this. Every part of him tingled, alive with the flashing of tiny stars. Every one of his mammalian hairs was converting itself into a receptor for sensation. He was attuned to the slightest stirring of air, the shifting of his body within his garments, the rough texture of Kabir's hand beneath his own. From within this haze of tactility, his scientific brain struggled to reassert itself.

"Maybe the woodpecker carries the scent of the bog with her," he suggested after a moment, "and there's something about it that's irresistible to native wildlife. Maybe it only worked on us incidentally."

Kabir's eyes seemed to have gone out of focus. He was opening and closing his left fist, trying to jolt himself back to normal. "Makes sense. But it did work on us eventually, as we're seeing. Probably just took longer for us because our bodies are bigger."

"Well, whatever it is, it's a magnificent process," Ismael exclaimed. "We're witnessing something that may not have been seen since the Mesozoic era."

"Oh? And who exactly was around to see it the first time?" Kabir had the wherewithal to ask.

Ismael laughed. "I don't know. A T-Rex?"

Kabir smiled and turned back to the plant. His right hand still rested on Ismael's shoulder, while his left began to make an undulating motion, the way he did when the car window was down and he was enjoying the pulsing of air around him.

In a dreamy voice, Ismael continued his speculation. "Maybe no one has ever encountered a flytrap like this it because it can only flourish in a highly specific set of circumstances. Maybe it's the only one of its kind, the only one that has ever grown. Every so often it would have to reproduce—asexually of course. It would have to bear and then become its own child, casting off the husk of its former self, like how cells replace themselves in a human body. That would mean this plant represents an unbreakable line reaching back through the ages."

The scent in the air was becoming stronger. Ismael found he was wholly intoxicated by it now. It was as if he had a large orb in the center of his brain, and all his efforts at rational thought were sliding off the rounded sides, unable to gain traction. He could not imagine how he had lived this long without smelling this particular odor signature. It seemed to contain so many answers. It was unbelievably complex: so sickly sweet and pungent, so suggestive of death, but also somehow teeming with life. It was like the smell at the start of the world, the olfactory distillation of all biological existence. Ismael's sense of professional euphoria remained, lighting up his frontal lobe like a Christmas tree, but it was rapidly losing ground to the gauzy fog of sensations. The latter formed a kind of force field around him, within which his skin floated free of muscle and bone.

All at once a bright pulse went spider-webbing through his chest. It shot through his neck and arms. Shot through the veins that ran up and down his legs and exploded into the fenestrated space of every capillary. By the time it reached his groin, he was at last able to recognize what it had become.

"Jesus," he breathed.

Kabir's eyes were already on him, his expression unfamiliar. "I know."

"Kabir…"

"I know."

And so, in a frenzy of movement, a whirlwind of undressing, the two of them had bedded down there among the ferns and buttonbush, their hands clasped and pressing into the viscous mud. There was Kabir's mouth, hungry upon his neck, his chest. There was the surprising smoothness of his skin. The half-moon curve of his buttocks. The earthy almond-and-ginger smell of his hair oil, which at times rose above the general bog miasma and at other times was like an underlying current nested within it. Moreover, there was the palpable sense that the swamp itself comprised a living body. The forest inhaled and exhaled around them—not rapidly, as with their own urgent breaths, but steady and slow, according to its own unhurried rhythms. The Choctawhatchee River flowed along its prescribed arteries, passing life into every sector of its domain. Overhead, the canopy of maple and birch was woven into a protective layer, holding them fast beneath an epidermis of leaves. And at the center of it all was the woodpecker. Its latest gambit having failed, it had resumed its predations, and the sound of its drumming carried through the trees like an erratic heartbeat.

A persistent buzzing began to build in Ismael's ear. At first, he thought it was only the mosquitoes, excited to madness by their presence, but then he came to realize that the disturbance came from within, as if his senses were so overloaded that they could not keep up and had to discharge the excess as static. He found himself wondering if any of it was happening at all.

He remembered the dream he had had as a child, the night before his father lost his leg in a crane accident at the steel plant. He had seen his father's heavy work boots, disembodied, pacing circles on the wooden floor beside his bed. They had a peculiar rhythm to them, which soon turned into an Irish reel, and though Ismael had felt a vague sense of unease at the preposterousness of the spectacle, he couldn't help laughing and dancing along with them. He had woken just like that, dancing in his nightshirt and his bare feet. Alone.

When they were finished, Ismael collapased back against Kabir, his unbuttoned shirt falling to the sides. Glimpsing his own boyish, freckled torso, he suddenly felt a vulnerability greater than any he had known in his life, even greater than after his first awkward fumblings with another man. He stared at the flytrap in wonder, as if it were the architect of all of this. And really, he supposed, it was. A strange, herbaceous matchmaker, making mates because a plant of its size needed to economize its efforts: why subsist on one meal when it could have two? And then his thoughts returned to his own position. He felt again his nakedness, felt the significance of their act without the benefit of the narcotic haze that had first induced it. He was afraid to speak. Anything he said might shatter the moment, might cause him to wake from the dream and find himself alone.

Kabir, perhaps sensing this, had sought to reassure him. He had dipped his finger in the mud and, with a firm hand, traced slow, looping whorls along Ismael's arms. At once, Ismael's panic began to dissipate. He allowed himself to be held, to be ornamented and adored. He watched the pattern emerge on his body like coils from a knitter's needle. Each convolution felt self-evident, as if it had always been there just beneath the surface, a hidden language of skin. *I will draw you back to earth*, it seemed to say. *I will anchor you.*

Soon Ismael had relaxed enough that he felt safe teasing his lover. "Look what a romantic you are," he said.

Kabir had laughed at this. "That's a very serious accusation, Izzy."

"Hasn't anyone ever told you that?"

"No, never," said Kabir. "I suppose you must bring it out in me." And lifting his finger to Ismael's lower lip, he had languidly drawn it across the inside rim.

(Much later, Ismael had thought, were it not for this single action—this unthinking impulse on Kabir's part—he might have been able to let it all go. He had not yet been so far gone. His reasoning faculties were still in view, still capable of being marshalled to the cause of prudent judgment. But that minor gesture had doomed him. It had imprinted the taste of mud in his mouth for years to come, so that even now it lingered like a persistent secret: rich and loamy and faintly sweet.)

"You know," Ismael had said, venturing as close as he dared to the heart of the matter. "I'm glad I saved us from almost certain digestion. But I want you to know that if I *were* to be eaten by a giant plant, I don't think I'd mind it so much if you were there with me."

Kabir laughed again and closed his teeth playfully around Ismael's neck.

The two had eventually found their way out of the swamp, despite the loss of the compass. They had joked and knocked against each other as they walked, Kabir with his slight limp, Ismael unconsciously matching his pace, until they happened to discover again the river and follow its serpentine trail back to the station wagon. For a while they had even held hands, and their combined warmth made each one feel that he was holding a brilliant light in his palm, a tiny sun known only to themselves.

Driving back to the airport, they had not been able to get enough of each other's voices. They had talked nonstop, regaling each other with stories from childhoods spent in their respective homelands, stories of parents and brothers and sisters, stories from young adulthood, stories of former lovers and their idiosyncrasies, and from their careers before they knew each other. The stories were told in no particular order and without concern for relevance.

They were together now, after all. They would have a lifetime to fill in the gaps. And in a strange way, the thrill of their burgeoning relationship came to commingle with the thrill of their professional success, came to be part and parcel with the prospect of tenure, the certainty of speaking engagements, the funding that would never run short or dry up. Having emerged separately, these joys coalesced to form an inextricable whole. It all became one to them.

As they moved farther and farther from the swamp, into the heart of the city, the smell of the bog still lay curled in Ismael's nose, like hoarfrost hanging upon the hairs and skin. The scent was reassuring. It confirmed that what had happened was real, and furthermore that it had happened to *him*, and not to some carbon copy from a neighboring universe. For once, everything was on a glorious upward trajectory. He was soaring on a monochrome-feathered wing, lifted to heights he would not have thought possible.

But when they had gone back through the airport, things began to go wrong. The handlers took one look at Kabir and refused to do a hand check of their film. They were forced to send the canisters through the scanner, where the machine, apparently miscalibrated, had subjected them to twenty times the expected radiation. All of Kabir's gorgeous photographs had been ruined. Everything had been ruined.

They had thought at first that a few of the images might be salvaged. Back in Kabir's personal darkroom, they had pored over the film like desperate parents, seeking signs of life in the space of every frame. Nearly all the photographs displayed the usual effects of excessive radiation. There was fogginess, a grainy appearance, and ethereal streaks of light that bisected and obscured their subjects, rendering the woodpecker and the flytrap all but unrecognizable. But they had found three that were mostly clear of such artifacts. Two focused on the bird itself, while the third showed the bird perched just beside the great plant, the juxtaposition providing a much-needed sense of scale for the subjects. Here, the bird was in profile, its features identifiable to any ornithologist worth his or her salt. The photo was crisp and clear. Perfectly framed. In short, it was made for the journals. Ismael could imagine it printed alongside the article they would write, in splendid full color, with a small caption reading, "Photo credit: Kabir Acharya."

But their excitement was short-lived. Within minutes, these photographs, too, began to deteriorate. One by one, they were overtaken by a creeping fog, which appeared first in the corners, then bloomed inward until it had encompassed the full frame. The men could only watch as their precious images were reabsorbed into darkness. There was nothing to be done.

Ismael had presented his field notes to Dr. Carver anyway, but without photographic substantiation they were of limited value. It wasn't that she hadn't believed them, exactly—she believed they had seen *something* extraordinary—it was just that she saw no utility in expending more time and money on results that were unpublishable. Better for them to cut their losses and move on to the next project. Kabir was charged with traveling to Monomoy National Wildlife Refuge to study localized breeding patterns, while Ismael stayed close to home, researching the impact of climate change on the birds of New York State.

Ismael would ordinarily have relished his new assignment. He had published a paper on birds as the harbingers of environmental shifts—they are true bellwethers, he had asserted, oracles in the purest sense—and he had always hoped to examine the birds of his home state in such a context. But the failure of the Florida expedition had left him distracted and dispirited. When the time came, he could take little pleasure in it.

And then there was the fact that, back in Ithaca, he and Kabir no longer knew how to relate to each other. The closeness, the camaraderie they felt in the swamp had evaporated. Ismael now began to perceive a faint overlay of vines growing around and between them, wholly invisible to Kabir or to anyone else. Wherever they went, the vines followed, licking at their heels like a surging tide. They sprung from earth and concrete alike, twining across walls and dropping from ceilings. The matted barrier they formed, when they became dense enough, proved to be impenetrable. Even face-to-face the two found themselves at an unaccountable remove. It was as if they stood on opposite sides of a canyon, and though each could see the other's mouth moving, the words themselves were indecipherable, muted by an indifferent wind.

For the better part of a year they had tried to make it work. When Kabir was not traveling, they met at late-night cafes, attended gallery openings, and took leisurely strolls through the botanic gardens. They camped in autumn forests saturated with gorgeous yellows and oranges and reds, and in winter, they went to view the mostly frozen waterfalls—cascades that were transformed by the cold into alien architectures of ice. There was a spring road trip to New York City, painstakingly engineered by Ismael, in which they followed a lovers' map from one romantic spot to the next. But here, too, the barrier of vines was evident. It rose up between them as they picnicked in Central Park, rogue coils falling like ropes across their laps. It manifested its surreal presence at the Guggenheim, the vines moving in slow revolutions past them, past de Chirico and Pollock and Miró, past the gift shop and the oblivious docents, seeking out the support points as if to reclaim the entire structure. It surged after them on the ferry, rising out of the choppy bay like the tentacles of some ancient sea monster. Admitting defeat at last, they had driven back to Ithaca in uncomfortable silence.

Naturally, the bedroom was where it was at its most profuse. Each time Kabir and Ismael were together, just as they were beginning to shed their inhibitions, to see and hear one another with some clarity, the vines would surge up from the mattress and fill the room, fully occluding their faculties. Once, in desperation, they had attempted to banish the barrier through chemical means, but this had only resulted in an emergency room trip for Kabir and a massive, lingering bruise where the IV had been inserted.

Often, Ismael found himself envious of the birds he studied. These creatures were subject to a thousand daily dangers, true, and their short time on the planet sometimes ended violently. But on the whole, their existence was a far simpler one. To a bird, everything was instinct. It sang the songs its mother sang. It built the same type of nest. It used the Earth's magnetic field to navigate to the same far-off climes, year after year after year. A bird was not capable of overthinking, or shame, or self-sabotage. In the Florida swamp, under the influence of the bog matter, he and Kabir had been just like this. They had acted purely out of instinct, and it had been beautiful. But how to reclaim that sense of freedom when the human brain was itself a kind of animal, feral and untamable, insisting at every moment upon a thousand contrary paths?

One weekend, Kabir's parents had flown in from India, and the four of them had had dinner at an expensive restaurant just off Fulton Street. The meal had been an awkward one. From the start, Kabir would refer to Ismael only as his work colleague. Whenever Ismael began to talk about a trip they'd taken or something they'd done as a couple, Kabir derailed him by interjecting that the department had gone as a group. "It's like you're all a family," his mother had said, clearly pleased. "How wonderful."

But it was only when she asked if he had a girlfriend that Ismael at last caught on.

"I'm not really looking for anything like that," he replied, as honestly as he could, given the sudden ache in his head. In that same moment, the vines had returned. They had come surging in a great mass out of the kitchen, wending their way through the servers' legs and making a beeline for their table. Soon they were so plentiful they formed a kind of roiling carpet beneath his feet. They crept up the table legs, circling like boa constrictors around their prey. Ismael felt that if left unchecked, they would drill a hole in his chest and envelop his spine.

Kabir would not meet his eyes across the table.

"Mind you don't take too long," Kabir's father had said. "A man should have a woman to keep him grounded. Otherwise he may just float off into space," he added, with a wink at his smiling wife.

Afterward, Ismael had been unable to hide his sense of betrayal. "I don't understand what just happened," he said. "Why the hell did you invite me to dinner with your parents?"

Kabir looked more tired than Ismael had ever seen him. "I don't know, Izzy. I guess I thought you'd like to meet them."

"Don't be disingenuous. You know very well I thought this was going to be a proper introduction. But they don't even know you're gay, do they?"

"I'm not anything," was Kabir's stubborn reply, and though he was too kind to say it, the subtext was clear: *We are not anything. Or at least not anything that I would risk my family for.* "I'm sorry dinner didn't work out."

"But…why was I even there?"

Kabir sighed. "I suppose I was hoping for a miracle."

After that, they had given up. Or Kabir had, anyway.

No more road trips. No more late nights at the café. Just two coworkers avoiding each other whenever possible and nodding their heads in silent greeting when it wasn't.

From time to time, Ismael overhead Kabir talking on the phone to someone or other, speaking quietly in that unmistakable way that people do when conversing with a lover. He even brought a date to the office holiday party one year, a beautiful Indian woman, although Ismael noted with some satisfaction that he did not seem particularly affectionate with her. Still, it was clear that Kabir was moving on. Ismael pledged to do the same.

He went out with a series of men, each more unsuitable than the last. One had a career in high finance and was an obvious bully. Another would not shut up about his thoroughbred cat. A third claimed to be a burlesque dancer, and Ismael found this quite exciting until he discovered that the man was also a Flat Earther. Several were cruel and distant, making rough use of his body and then vanishing into the wallpaper afterward. A few were kind, armed with sad eyes and inoffensive backstories, but these either had no intellectual life to speak of, or it was focused on such far-flung subjects that he could find no common parlance with them. One wore a toupee so unkempt that, over the course of the beer they shared, Ismael fancied he saw a handful of baby robins emerge from it, winging their way to freedom with the sudden blast of the air conditioner. Better to be alone, Ismael told himself, than to be with one of these.

He settled into his solitude, letting it fall over him like the folds of a loose-fitting garment. The years blew past in a gust of leaves. Holiday followed fast upon holiday. And every time it rained, there was the ineffable reminder of what was lost. The loops that Kabir had drawn on his arms would reappear, as dark as if they were just inked, curling out from his shirtsleeves like the wheels of a circus train. No amount of scrubbing could rid him of them.

And now here they were in Florida once more, the promised land of Ismael's dreams, with its marshes, its wildlife, its fertile landscapes virtually unchanged. It was just the way they had left it eight years before. Kabir stood before it all like an actor before a backdrop, the scene almost artificial looking, and Ismael had a fleeting sense that Kabir was the only thing that was real. Here he was, with more gray in his hair but still so handsome Ismael could hardly look him in the eye. He had put on a little weight in the intervening years, and yet somehow it suited him. He looked like a man almost regally comfortable within his skin. Ismael's own slim frame, meanwhile, had grown more angular than ever. The bones were discrete and pronounced, as if they were pushing up through the earth at an archaeological dig. As if they were crying out to be discovered, brushed clean, and cataloged.

Loved.

His body transmitting the message his words could not.

And here was Kabir, after all of Ismael's efforts, after all the things that had passed between them, lowering his camera in defeat. Waving the white flag and readying himself for the march home. *You never did try hard enough*, Ismael thought bitterly.

You were always too willing to cede the ground. He watched in silence as the camera was returned to its cushioned case—its sarcophagus of partitioned foam—to await its summons at some future date. He had once thought of Kabir's camera as a kind of ally. It had seemed a secret avenue to the man himself, like a best friend to be won over, or at least a willing party who would abet their love with a wink. The evidence it provided would validate everything they held dear. But with the incident at the airport, it had proven itself an enemy, or worse: indifferent. Like so many best friends before, it would outlast him, the lover. Ismael watched Kabir sling the bag over his shoulder and kick the mud off of his boots. He watched him check his watch and hold up the compass like an offering to the swamp. Watched him prepare to leave.

"Don't," Ismael said at last, his throat constricting with despair. "Please."

Kabir turned to look at him. His expression softened. A hint of the other Kabir flickered into being again, the one from before, and for a moment it hung suspended between them like a mote of dust, held aloft by the egrets' keening and the earthy smell of cypress on the wind. Just as quickly, though, it disappeared. It gusted away between the branches of the river birch, which was still molting, still laying itself bare, uncovering without discrimination its knotted heart. "It's over, Izzy," he said gently. "Maybe we were wrong before."

Ismael shook his head. "No. We weren't wrong."

"Look," Kabir said, taking his hand. Ismael felt a shiver pass through his body. "What we experienced wasn't real. Can't you see that? It was only some kind of plant hypnosis. Just a weirdly potent aphrodisiac emitted by the decaying swamp matter. I mean, we tried, didn't we? We tried for a whole year. There was just nothing for us to hold onto back in the real world. No essential chemistry, although I despise that term. If we're being honest, I don't think the flytrap was even real. I think it was another hallucination. I mean, how would something like that exist in this day and age without anyone knowing about it? It's not possible."

Ismael felt the ground falling away from him. "Okay, and what about the coelacanth?" he demanded, retreating to the safer realm of the scientific. "Thought to be extinct for as long as the dinosaurs, just another lost species, then bam, they find a whole school of them swimming off the coast of South Africa. Six feet long, and two hundred pounds. Armored like a Sherman tank. What about Omura's whale in the Sea of Japan? The Lord Howe stick insect? All Lazarus creatures. All very much alive. All very much oblivious to our theories about their nonexistence."

"Yes, Izzy, but at the time we already had evidence that all those species existed. No one has *ever* seen anything like what we saw."

Ismael felt a sudden glimmer of hope. He thought he detected in Kabir's argument, in his willingness to meet him on his own deliberative terms, a sense of wanting to be proved wrong, to be out-argued. To be won over. In a fever, he forged ahead.

"Of course they have! Just on a smaller scale. And if you think about it, it's far more plausible than the other examples. A larger version of something familiar, something thoroughly documented…how many times throughout history has something like that been encountered? So many I couldn't begin to enumerate them."

"You're not being objective. You're bending truth to fit a predetermined outcome."

"The world is constantly reinventing itself, Kabir. People discover things all the time. It's almost banal."

"Yes, and sometimes they don't!" Kabir blurted out, giving in to his exasperation. He stopped and rubbed his forehead like he did when he was getting a migraine. When he spoke again, his voice was barely audible. "Sometimes, Izzy, nothing is there. I wanted it, too. But you're chasing a dream."

"No. It was more than that."

Kabir sighed. "If only we had the pictures. With pictures, you know what's what. Memories aren't like that, you know. They're always changing. Every day they alter their fundamental shape, color, texture. They mutate."

Ismael was silent. How could he explain that, regardless of the truth of the incident, for him it *was* real? Had *become* real? Love was at its core a chemical process, and it didn't much matter whether it occurred naturally or was externally manufactured. The resulting experience was the same.

Kabir walked away, limping just a little as always. And this time, Ismael let him.

On the drive out of the swamp, Ismael was sure he heard a final echo, a tantalizing tap-tap-tapping off in the distance. And it occurred to him that perhaps they hadn't escaped the flytrap after all, or that only Kabir had, and that he himself was still trapped there within the dome of that green cavern, the pitiless velvet teeth like a crown across his brow. Perhaps everything since was only a dream cast up by his ebbing consciousness, a flutter of dying cells, as his body was eroded to better nourish the plant for its next hunt. If so, he could hardly object; it was, after all, the way of things. Appropriate, even, for a man who had decreed nature the icon of his secular faith. Such a fate would not be so bad. At least he would have the pair of deer as his companions, their gleaming bones still fraternizing suggestively, still enveloping each other like the doubled fronds of a fern, or like a zipper folding in, their long legs intertwined in love.

Or perhaps, just perhaps, there was another Kabir. The Swamp Kabir. The Kabir of memory, who did not lower his camera while simultaneously raising his defenses. Who did not walk away. Who, instead, curled toward Ismael like a smile. Who summoned him deep into the moss-strewn trees, the mud, the naked river, the woodpecker's holy habitat, and lay down with him among the coiling vines.

And Ismael dozed off thinking of things that were too lovely, too exotic, too astounding to last. Things that could only flourish in a highly specialized set of circumstances, and were impossible to bring to bear a second time, the results irreproducible in a lab. Things that were definitely or probably extinct.

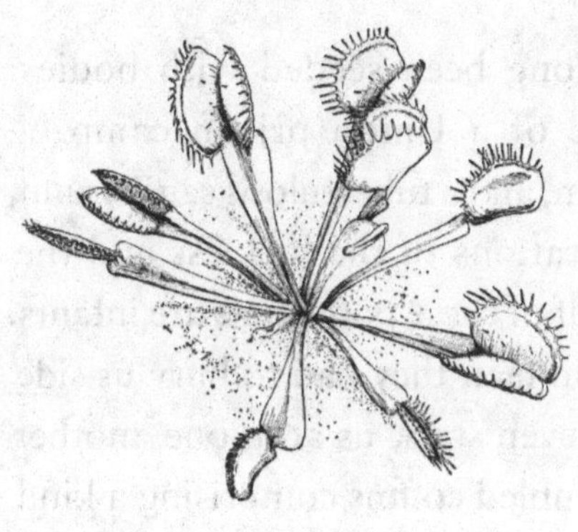

hart island

FIVE DOWN, TWELVE ACROSS, SIX DEEP.

From inside my tiny coffin, I can see everything. The sprawl of this desolate potter's field. The tumble of ruined buildings. The occasional fringe of trees—feeble installations that cannot hope to challenge death's hold on this place. And beyond the shores, across the choppy waters of the channel, the dazzling, sun-bright world of the living.

A litter of kittens is born on the steps of the public library. A woman from Africa solves the Hodge conjecture.

This island has long been seeded with bodies. Alternately the site of a Union prison camp, a workhouse, an asylum, and a tuberculosis sanatorium, it has claimed generations of the luckless and the destitute. At least half of these poor souls are infants. There are so many, in fact, they had to bury us side by side in trenches, even stack us atop one another like bricks, our assembled coffins comprising a kind of inverted tower. Hundreds of these structures proliferate in the darkness, their combined effect that of a shadowy cityscape. My particular borough houses infants who died from pneumonia. Another was dug after an epidemic of scarlet fever. Still others hold the remains of those who died of unknown causes, or who perished in fires, or of exposure, or from simple neglect.

Two boys steal a kiss beside a blue windmill. A new type of influenza circulates the globe, killing thousands.

My pneumonic brethren and I have been here a hundred years, and we are prophets, all. There is a timetable, you see, for the distribution of our powers. At one year, you become self-aware. At ten, you may travel to nearby islands to observe the whims and machinations of the living. At a hundred, you can see the future. And at a thousand, you are able to create wormholes. You may shape your consciousness into a vehicle for flitting between galaxies, bearing witness to supernovas in progress, the birth of nebulas, and other scenes of unthinkable beauty. It is the universe's small recompense for dying so young. No one has reached this stage yet, but it is something to look forward to.

When it rains, and it almost always rains here, we rise up like steam from the earth. Our souls are buoyed up on the wind and ferried past the brown scrub bushes, past the ruins of the old asylum and the workhouse, and out over the waters, skimming the whitecaps on our way to the other islands, to the places where our corporeal selves held only the briefest residence. But a connection always remains: a thread vibrating within us like a homemade compass, signaling our true north.

A woman with long black braids walks up a green mountain path, her child strapped to her back. She pauses to watch a hang glider as it slowly descends into the valley.

Our mothers. Oh God, our mothers. Before I reached the century mark, I spent most of my time in the shabby tenement where my mother lived until her own old age and death (by heart failure). There was a crack in her cornflower blue table lamp, and I fitted myself into that gap so that I could watch her while she ate her breakfast or read her paperbacks in the evenings. She had other children, but I felt no particular envy toward them. In fact, I took little notice of them at all, so deep was my fixation on her. With all my strength, I radiated love at her, or at least my notion of what love was. As if sensing this, she seemed to gravitate to the lamp. She often returned to the room for no discernible reason and then would look around, puzzled. At times her hand fell upon it as she walked by, and I would see a flicker of cognition cross her lovely face, a sliver so small it was nearly subliminal.

When she died, I followed for a time the progress of her children, my erstwhile brothers and sisters. I rotated between their households and made note of their domestic milestones, but I never again experienced the same feverish adoration I had felt when observing our mother.

A woman falls through the ice of a northern lake and is unable to climb out.

For a period, I became enamored with an old man who slept on a bench in the subway in upper Harlem. From inside his tattered scarf, I reveled in his spontaneous recitations of original poetry. He was a genius, I believe, nearly hemorrhaging with unacknowledged brilliance. I learned from him that words could be manipulated to create wounds in the listener, and then to seal those wounds with beauty.

Even when I did not understand the meaning of the man's words I was enthralled by their musicality, and by the strange, hypnotic fury with which he delivered them. His poems felt inevitable somehow. They were like skeletons that had been lying in the earth for eons, only waiting to be discovered. I did my best to repay him for his great gifts. I imbued him with warmth when it was cold, and when he slept, I whispered pleasant images into his dreams.

Next there was a middle-aged woman in Chinatown. I chose her because she was a greengrocer, and I was enthralled by the colors of the fruits and vegetables she sold. I stowed away inside the lenses of her glasses and took it all in. There were vibrant reds and oranges. Gorgeous, stripy greens. Pinks and purples that gleamed like deep-sea treasure. Yellows that I had never seen in nature or within the realm of human creation. Coming from an existence filled with so much rain, so much gray, I could not get enough of this sudden infusion of color. It almost seemed that the produce was too vivid to be a part of this world at all, that it must have bloomed through the cracks of some richer, lovelier dimension. For her part, the woman seemed to share my fixation. She spoke to her wares as if they were her children. She called them beautiful, and luscious, and sublime, and she described in intimate detail the savory dishes they would one day be a part of. She sometimes refused to sell them to a customer if she didn't like their looks. She was truly a marvel.

There were others. A chemist. A rabbi. A shoeshine girl. A Wall Street financier (I hid myself inside his ruby tie tack pin). Each one contained wonders. Each one opened up an unknown corner of the city to me.

The sky opens over a school playground, dropping hailstones the size of blueberries. In a remote mountain cabin, a little boy opens a book of plays by Ibsen.

Most recently, I visited a series of young children. They were a source of endless fascination to me, having grown only slightly beyond the point I did when I died. I loved their wondrous contradictions. They exhibited all the wildness of our primate ancestors, paired with a modern intellectual curiosity. They were keen to organize the world into taxonomies by day, while at night they still dreamed animal dreams. Fantasy and reality coexisted in them without conflict. As for raw emotion, it was in such abundance it nearly leaked from their pores. They were just as likely to burst into laughter as to fall into a sudden spasm of rage, and who could say what tipped the scales in either direction? The color of the shirt they were wearing. An unfamiliar object glittering on the sidewalk. The flight of a flock of pigeons overhead.

I swung on the hinge of their shifting moods, riding each one like The Whip at Coney Island.

And there was one more thing. They were *radiant*. I could locate a small child in a crowd of thousands because there was something of the eternal about them, a shimmering aura that could not but command my attention. They disturbed the air around them, sending out ripples that were like waves of heat. Perhaps it was purely a physical phenomenon—say, a bioluminescent chemical that was manufactured only for the first few years of life—but to me, their bones appeared starry with light. The sun glinted off them like mirrors.

I expected to continue this pattern in perpetuity, visiting child after child until my spirit-matter had degraded and there was nothing of me left. I thought I would never find anything so compelling again.

Then everything changed. This morning, I looked out from my shoebox-sized coffin and discovered that I could see the future.

A blue and red fishing boat passes beneath a bridge in a strange harbor. Two pregnant women stand at the bow. Though the flags along the riggings are battered by wind, the women themselves are unmoving, their feet planted in a posture of grim defiance.

This scene fell like a banner across my vision. It was as if a ribbon of negative space had materialized before me, onto which these forms were being projected. The world behind it softened, went out of focus. It might as well have ceased to exist. The vignette was brief, but there was something about the crispness of the images, their hyper-real vividness, that made the import clear. None of this had happened yet. The gliding boat. The fluttering flags. The women, sisters maybe, standing proud in their act of rebellion. I was watching a moment slivered from the fabric of the future. I wondered if such moments had always been in the air around me, free-floating like radiation. Perhaps the events depicted were of such epochal significance that they could not help but reverberate back through the ages, delivering visual echoes into the past, toward me and my spectral kind. I suppose I will never know for certain, just as the ones living in that moment could never know such a thing.

How far into the future was I seeing? Had these women already embarked on their fateful journey? Had they become pregnant yet? Had they even been born? There were no answers imminent, and truly I felt that it did not matter. What I did feel was a frisson of something electric, unlike anything I had yet experienced. I had felt love before. I had felt sadness. I had felt curiosity, amusement, and even disgust. But this was new, like a sensation from an organ I never knew I had. It forked through me like lightning, its expression keening and laced with a kind of primitive ache. Ecstasy is the only word for it, and even that is woefully insufficient. I was left reeling. When the vision faded, I despaired, fearing I would never have occasion to feel such bliss again. I needn't have worried; within the hour there was another. And then another, and another after that. Each one carrying with it a blinding surge of pleasure. Each one bringing the satisfaction of a piece fitted into a puzzle, a fragment of the strange and rich human experience I had missed. Sometimes it was just a single vision; sometimes they came in pairs. In the afternoon there was a coursing river of them, so densely populated with images that I could scarcely make sense of them.

A dignitary tumbles into a koi pond, pushed by the famished child who will later start a sprawling war across continents with falling skyscrapers and love that blooms in the ashes—great swirling flowers of it—in defiance of the darkness, skip to countless rockets with passengers/settlers/pioneers taking to the skies to establish camps on a nearby planet followed by settlements then villages then cities with streets and libraries and museums and cathedrals and yes, cemeteries, all supported by air converters that transform existing molecules into configurations that are more benevolent to humans, their fierce will like a fire that turns a plane of death into a gleaming sphere of life…

What a revelation these visions were! I saw that before long I would no longer be bound by the concrete connection of these islands, saw that little by little I would be free to explore so much farther, haunting new continents, oceans, even planets. I saw a time when my birth and the tragedy of my untimely death would be a distant memory, so far in my past it might have happened to someone else. And of course, I saw myself at the thousand-year point, traversing the universe on stolen passageways of space, a glowing pulse delivered between two points like a drop of dew along a spider's thread. It is not such a terrible fate, I think.

One thing I could not see: if, after this period of exploration, there would be a conclusive end to my existence. The not-knowing is a gift. It allows me a sense of greater kinship with those I have observed, and those I will never know, and all those who live out their years scattered along the dazzling shore. It brings me closer to my beloved mother, who is both long gone and still alive within the rounded bowl of time.

A sprawling jazz funeral moves through a crowded street, the casket draped with beads and orange blossoms. Pausing mid-song, the trumpet player turns toward a small child and smiles.

And so, for the time being, I remain tethered to the heart of this barren island, with its derelict buildings and overflowing graves. But I have glimpsed the truth: namely, that the place where I reside is not a single island at all, but a never-ending ribbon extending out into space. It ladder-threads around the living world like half of a double helix, both sides necessary to the other, both holding together the rich DNA of the universe.

There are more than a million souls here, each one dreaming and ready to burst forth with their own stories.

And I am just one.

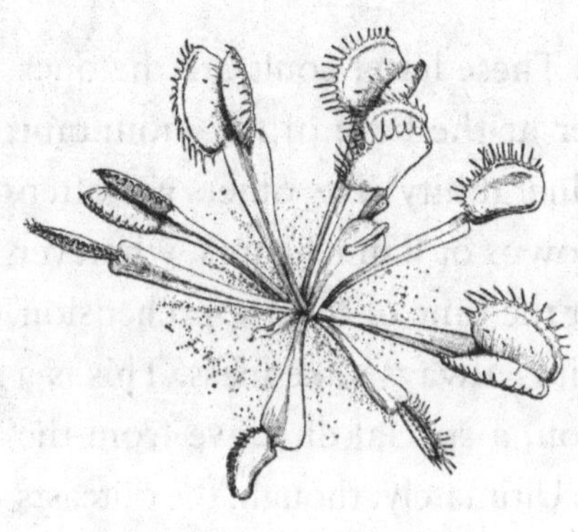

the climbers

EVERY YEAR THEY COME TO THE MOUNTAIN. THE ONES WHO HAVE BEEN LABELED DIFFERENT, VOLATILE, NONCONFORMING. THEY ARE MARCHED BY THE guards to the outskirts of the city, prodded by bayonets, and pierced through the abdomen if they fail to comply. It is a huge, prosperous city, but they have to maintain order somehow, and so they choose the ones among themselves who are agitators, or could potentially be so. They choose the ones without whom the city can better flourish. Sometimes it is the activists, sometimes it is the artists, sometimes it is those with different gods or those whose skin is dark enough that it is thought to harbor treacherous secrets. Sometimes it is merely those who have transgressed in love. These latter souls are the ones who huddle together at the base of the mountain, clad only in their vulnerability. The others are often taken in their nightgowns or flannel pants, whatever they were wearing at the time of their apprehension, but with the lovers, it is always nakedness. This is a calculated humiliation, a special directive from the Most Worthy Mayor. Ultimately, though, the outcasts must all meet the same end. Every year they come to the mountain. They are given a pickax and a rope. And they are forced to climb.

THE ANCIENT PEOPLE KNEW THE TRUTH OF MOUNTAINS. Somehow, they sensed the primordial spirits that breathed and murmured within. Such a view now falls squarely into the realm of mythology, but that does not change the facts. The mountain spirit we speak of has endured epochs. It has felt the ache of shifting continents. It is real.

Like any god, the mountain is dangerous. It is haloed with storms. It is crowned with rocky outcroppings and a persistent glory of clouds. Snow falls upon its upper regions without ceasing, so that over the years, many unfortunates have been dazzled blind during their climb. They have fallen, frozen, been impaled, become trapped inside crevasses, or suffocated beneath avalanches. They have even walked right off the side, their brains withered to a husk from lack of oxygen. Yes, the climbers have died upon the mountain in myriad ways: some swift, some so prolonged and terrible they can scarcely be imagined.

In the old days, the mountain's solitude was unbroken. It dreamed alone. Then came the climbers, only a few and far between. An occasional straggler, a visionary, a religious fanatic already sky-high on plumes of opium. Back then, the mountain was unforgiving. It saw those tiny bodies break against it and felt nothing, save a surge of contempt at the arrogance of those who would dare to dominate it. Back then, it often killed the intruders outright, snapping their spines or devouring them like Cronus. Now, things are different. Thanks to the Most Worthy Mayor, the climbers appear like clockwork every spring. Slowly, the mountain's antipathy has been transformed, has reshaped itself into a kind of mercy. Perhaps it resents being conscripted into the role of executioner. Perhaps it has simply been too long on this earth; it has gotten soft.

THIS YEAR THERE ARE FIFTEEN SUBVERSIVES. FIVE OF them are artists (a singer, a poet, a weaver, a potter, and a dancer), all of whom have been accused of working anti-government themes into their creations. Three are distressingly dark of skin and have been branded infiltrators, though they have lived in the city their entire lives and cannot conceive of what lies beyond those walls. Four were discovered in their homes worshiping nonsanctioned gods. One is an activist, who painted a radical graffiti picture of a dove on the wall that faces the city council. The final two are lovers: caught, of course, in the act of loving.

The lovers are a pair of women, and this is one of the transgressions set out as particularly damaging to the moral character of the city. They are married, as all women of childbearing age must be, with two children apiece, and they are neighbors, their tenement-style homes sharing a single pinewood wall. Their families are friendly. They celebrate name days and feast days together. But in the evening the women send their dreams out across the space to find each other. Like curls of smoke they pass between the planks in the wall, tracing ornate shapes against the spreading darkness.

One day, the women meet in the corner of the neighborhood garden. Discovering that a pair of garden shears has been left behind, they decide to open narrow embrasures in their chests and exchange hearts. With great ceremony, each woman plucks the organ from its red cavity, placing it into the other's body like a love note, a gold bar tucked into a vault. When they have finished, they stitch up the wounds and retie the laces on their bodices. They allow themselves a single kiss to seal their bond. For just a moment, lips and tongues coalesce in the most intimate of protests. Then they return to their homes, their preordained domesticities.

But of course there is no real privacy in the city. The Most Worthy Mayor has placed cameras everywhere. They are to be found between the stones that keep the various neighborhoods divided. They can be seen winking from church eaves and shop windows, and in less likely places as well, strapped to the heads of birds or installed in the glassy eyes of stray cats. Add to this the scads of informers, who scour the streets in exchange for bits of silver, and the outcome is predetermined. The ritual in the garden was witnessed many times over. Truly, the women did not have a chance.

One Sunday, while their families are at church, they stay home baking bread together. The kitchen is bright and warm. Shafts of gold pour through the windows, bathing them both in a hazy glow, and the shimmering envelope of dust lends them the aspect of titans amid a sun-filled galaxy. The women laugh, enjoying the momentary simulacrum of married life. Like children they playact, calling each other "wife." When the pans of dough have been placed between the bricks, they at last disrobe, falling easily into each other's arms. A lovely and highly illegal ivy tattoo can be seen spreading across the first woman's shoulders, while across the second's, there tumbles lush skeins of chestnut hair. As they move they are aware of the electrical field generated by each other's skin. They can feel the tug of their expatriated hearts, trying to burrow homeward. By the time they have reached the apex of their passion, they are perfectly sequestered—islanded, like a yolk. And it is then that the guards pour in. Sneering. Armed with crude taunts. Wrenching the women apart and making a mockery of their coupling.

So now they stand before the mountain among the other subversives, the tattooed woman curving her body like a shield around her lover, though both are helpless against the bitter cold. The activist is defiant. She shouts blistering words at the guards, raises her fist to the sky. Clouds of profanity rise like balloons on the wintry air. The four heretics, all men, pray aloud to their idolatrous gods. The dark-skinned family—for it *is* a family: a man, a woman, and a boy of about ten—are mute with terror. So is the singer. The weaver weeps. The potter shapes empty pleas in the space before him. The dancer hops from foot to foot, trying in vain to stay warm. The poet begs for mercy, her fine mastery of language applied to an act of self-abasement.

The guards, as is their reputation, are unmoved by any of this. One of them reads aloud from a dog-eared manuscript, a statement of condemnation written many years ago by the Most Worthy Mayor, who regrettably could not be present today, too pressing are his duties to the city. The speech is dedicated to the grave necessity of preserving order. There is an anecdote from the mayor's childhood, the import of which is that a too-lenient punishment is worse than no punishment at all. There is also a passage praising the many splendors of the city, and the prisoners are asked to take solace in the fact that their neighbors will still thrive without them. At the end of the speech, one of the guards presents each prisoner with the tools of his or her demise. One pickax and one rope. The smallest pickax is given to the child, who accepts it with trembling hands. "If you can reach the summit, you are free!" the guards laugh, and elbow one another in the ribs. But of course, this is nothing but a cruel jest. No one has ever reached the summit. This mountain is the tallest in the world.

When they have tired of making sport, the guards press the points of their bayonets against flesh. The prisoners wince and stumble forward. Weeping or silent, pleading or wrathful, they all must begin their arduous climb.

THE MOUNTAIN NOW LOOKS UPON THE CLIMBERS with sympathy. It sees them all, these tiny, distinct souls. Sees the baby the heretic man will never meet and the two babies another has already lost. Sees the cherry-blossomed stream that channeled past the activist's childhood house, the wordless beauty that once inspired her to action. Sees the fine rugs and wall hangings wrought by the weaver's fingers, the pulse at the temple as he worked, the fingers grown tender and bruised with the effort of his art. Sees the dark-skinned family as they sit down to a meal, the serene gazes of total belonging, the convulsions of laughter at shared jokes. Sees the dancer, the singer, and the poet, each caught at the peak of their separate reveries. Sees the lovers' switched hearts irradiating their chests, light seeping out from the seams where they made their incisions. Sees farther still, into their thoughts, the mothers and fathers that will be missed, the friends, the children, the dreams unlived, the sumptuous gardens unplanted, the books never read and the art unseen, all those things that are lost, that are mourned in the final moments, as these fragile creatures cling to one another, scrabbling up the snowy slopes. Despite the cold, the mountain can feel them burn. That these tiny creatures should have such intensity in their hearts—how can it not try to save them? How can it not, at least, do what it is capable of?

THE CLIMBERS ARE BEGINNING TO STRUGGLE NOW. They have walked as far as they can, and now are awkwardly employing the pickaxes and the ropes to continue their ascent. They try not to look at the bodies of the fallen, though they cannot help but recognize them from years past, from their childhoods sometimes. The schoolteacher. The rogue clergyman. The neighborhood boys who dared to hold hands beneath a willow tree. The librarian who maintained a secret cache of forbidden books. These corpses flank the path like silent sentinels, though their mouths are often open, frozen into the shape of warnings.

The mother and father hoist their child above their heads, helping him to the next handhold, and though they know that each step forward brings him closer to death, they tell themselves that they are lifting him out of darkness, toward a place of undiminished tranquility. With every labored breath, the mother says, "I love you." The singer hears it and, at last, finds strength.

The poet remains terrified, urinating on herself as she traverses a particularly treacherous patch of ice. She cannot find the words to make any of this okay, or even to render it less abhorrent. The creation of poetry requires a certain stillness of mind that is unthinkable now.

Before long, the potter discards his tools, preferring to use his hands, to grip the earth directly as he has done so many years in the warmth of his kiln room. With every contact of his hand, he can smell the clay deep within the rock, can sense the potential for loveliness and utility, the yearning to take shape. The dancer, meanwhile, finds the courage of her feet. She imagines herself shooting upward like a meteor, her toes barely touching the slopes as she rises. Her legs are lean and muscled. Of all of the subversives, she is able to climb the highest.

The others do the best they can. The activist climbs alone. It is the most natural thing to her, though it is lonely, even now. The heretics work as a group, each one taking the lead in turn and joining their ropes so that they are able to belay one another. They take turns, also, telling stories of their wives and children, though the telling is intermittent and punctuated by long periods of ragged breathing. Some distance away, the lovers make much slower progress. Naked, frostbitten, they are unable to keep a firm grip on their ropes. Soon the one with the chestnut hair falters, and the tattooed one stretches out an arm to catch her, cradling her back just as she did the first time they kissed. As she pulls her in to relative safety, she is struck by the vastness of the panorama below. Objectively, it is a beautiful view, but even the capacity for experiencing beauty has been distorted by the Very Worthy Mayor. On a gusty ledge, the women decide to make their final stop. They squat down, wrap their arms around each other, and whisper their confessions: how they miss their children, how they never wanted to hurt their husbands, who, after all, are kind. They say good-bye.

When the climbers have passed out of sight, the guards largely disperse, leaving only a few to make camp and keep watch for possible escapees. It does happen from time to time. A runner, chased through the brush like a rabbit, eventually halted by the resolute thrusts of bayonets. Secretly, they hope for it. It breaks the tedium.

The potter is the first to fall, his skilled hands frozen into useless claws. He closes his eyes and feels the uprush of air, hears the sharp whistle of wind in his ears. Anticipates the impact and, with the narrowed tunnel of his thoughts, thinks, this is not so bad. This life that has revolved around the shaping of earth—he has always known that it was a temporary arrangement, that the clay of his body was a gift to be given only for a time, and then gently reclaimed. So now here he is, returning to the earth as expected, albeit more rapidly than he would prefer.

It is then that the mountain makes its move.

It plucks the spirit from the potter's flesh, replicates the body after a fashion. It cannot return him to his home, or to some far-off haven across the sea, where he could, perhaps, live out his remaining years in peace. Though a god, the mountain is not omnipotent. It merely preserves him as one preserves a plant in a terrarium. A pocket universe, you might call it. The potter is not dead. Or rather, both dead and undead. The duplicate abides in a dewy bubble, still tethered to his ruined body like a balloon attached by a thread, like a final thought conjured by the body, a dream of immortality.

One by one the mountain takes the others. It captures them as they stumble, fall, pass quietly into slumber or perish from agonizing internal hemorrhages. Some are placed in a single pocket, while others inhabit a shared one. All are hidden away, though, folded into the seamless fabric of space. They exist parallel to eternity. Where they are, the city cannot reach them.

The climbers are not precisely conscious in this form: their eyelids flutter as if in sleep, as if living the sedimented history of the mountain itself. But their thoughts are purely human—they are, first of all, back in their homes. They are basking in the warmth of a summer's day, or rapturing in the lushness of a spring rain. They are small children again, their parents beaming at them with pride, and a moment later they are grown and playing with their own sons and daughters. They are laughing, loving, making art, worshiping as they please, and saying wonderfully scandalous things without fear of arrest. The heretics are still lighting a path for one another in the darkness, no longer defined by the gods they pray to. The family is taking a stroll through twilit gardens, holding hands as a curtain of purple falls across the flowers. The lovers once again lie enmeshed in each other's arms, their transplanted hearts pulling together like magnets; in the next room their children doze, blissfully unsevered from their mothers. The singer belts out whatever songs he desires, sacred or profane, and the threads of silver curling from his throat put the ancient bards to shame. The poet writes in a fury, or not at all, no longer afraid of her words or the absence of them. The dancer luxuriates in her strength, in the fluid motion of her lovely limbs.

The artists, the activist, every one of these cloistered souls is free to do everything in the world or nothing. To live large or to quietly subsist in a region of utter peace.

There are no spies where they are. Birds and cats do not haunt their steps with cameras. They are finally, finally safe.

And so they will remain, held like so many jewels upon the mountain's surface, until such time as people are no longer cast upon its crags to die. Already there are so many, the slopes fairly glitter with them. You see, this is not the first Most Worthy Mayor.

The mountain is as generous a god as the city is likely to see, its troubled arc at last bent toward justice. It will keep watch eternally, if it must. It is vigilant even now, marking the wounds that make a mosaic of the people's hearts, of their radiant, multiform bodies, and hoping to heal them.

It cannot do this alone. Even a mountain cannot fix all the broken things of the world.

Ultimately, it does what it can.

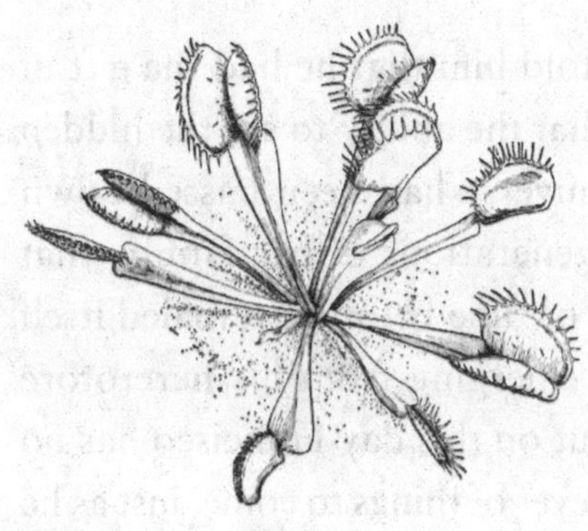

the prison guard learns of his past lives

ON THE DAY THE ANOMALY APPEARS, FRANCISCO EATS HIS BREAKFAST LIKE USUAL. IT IS THREE THIRTY IN THE MORNING—HE HAS TO BE TO WORK BY FIVE— and the darkness still hangs like a papery shroud over the windows of his shabby apartment. The character of the darkness seems to change from day to day. One day it manifests as a spontaneous gathering of crows, a virtual roiling cloud of them, while the next day it is as still and deep as an underwater lake. Either way the darkness has a way of getting inside him, of resonating within the bowl of his belly and making him feel that he has somehow floated free of the world, that he has become an organism without mass, held to earth by the barest tether.

His mother once told him that he had the gift of prophecy. She said that the ability to see the hidden framework of the universe had been passed down through numerous generations of her family, that it was only a matter of time before it revealed itself to him, a third eye emerging from his heretofore unblemished skin. But on this day Francisco has no presentiment whatsoever of things to come, just as he had no presentiment on the day she left. As he walks the ten blocks to the bus stop, the stars above him are as inscrutable as ever, and if there are mandalas of meaning buried within the beer bottles and fast food refuse, he cannot decipher them.

FRANCISCO HAS WORKED AT THE MEA CULPA WOMEN'S Prison for nearly six years. In that time, he has been in love countless times, always with one of the inmates or other. Black, white, young, old…it makes no difference. He finds some ethereal spark within each of them and then rhapsodizes about it until her image is wefted through the warp of every thought. She might be present in a flash of silver from the cooks' knives, or in the gloss of the polymeric floor tiles. She might appear in the wood paneling of the chapel, or within the gleam of the cell block skylights. She might even be revealed in the suggestive curvature of the laundry bins. She fully inhabits him, so that at times it feels as if she is the only true thing about him, that his love for her is a floating orb moving through the world with his body dangling, puppetlike, from the center.

When at last this love begins to falter, flickering to ash, another quickly springs up to take its place, roaring into being like a god in a burning bush. Love, and the continuity of it, is an abiding fixture in his life. It is his lodestar. More than that, it is in some fashion a bodily requirement for him, like food and oxygen, though the precise organ that demands it is harder to pin down.

Right now he is in love with a middle-aged Black woman named Clover. She is large-boned and loud and oh, so beautiful. He cannot get enough of her raucous laugh, her bawdy, Baptist-gone-bad stories. He loves the way she sometimes rubs her index finger against her left wrist while she is thinking, as if worrying a gem that has been sewn into her skin. He adores, too, her intricate sketches of wildlife, executed on napkins and concealed from the other inmates so as to maintain her reputation for toughness. Naturally, he cannot let her know of his feelings for her. He is unfailingly professional with all of his secret loves. He does not flirt. He does not bring them flowers or other contraband (he would be fired in a heartbeat for doing so). Aside from what is required for breaking up brawls, he does not permit himself any physical contact with the women, though of course he is often occupied by such thoughts. At night, his dreams sprawl wide with the raptures of bodies, his mind dilating like an aperture to accommodate a Kama Sutra's worth of possible couplings.

He knows many of the women's histories intimately. As a neutral fixture of the facility, not unlike a lamp or a table, he is privy to the copious sob stories that are poured out in the visitation room, the chapel, the library. Sometimes these confessions cause him to inwardly kindle with wonder, emerging as they do from even the most obdurate of prisoners. They are as tiny miracles to him, the tears that accompany them as improbable as those issuing from a stone Madonna.

Francisco often thinks of what it must be like for these women, their whole existence shrinking to fill the mold of prison walls. Some are perforce diminished by it. Some burn bright within their confinement, fierce as lions, though captivity hangs like lead weights from their necks. Some have simply placed themselves beyond reach. Peering into their eyes reveals nothing; like a nautilus, they are chambered deep within. It is only in the courtyard, with its salt breeze and intoxicating stretch of pale sky, that the truth of their condition can be glimpsed. The women often fix their gaze upward, past the spiraled wire of the crenellated wall, and he knows that in those moments they are lobbing their hearts like bombs across the battlements. They are casting them into the world beyond and praying for the tender sprout of wings.

It could so easily be him in a place like this, he knows. He too had a troubled childhood—motherless, penniless, drug-addicted at times, entering and exiting the orbit of the various gangs of East Los Angeles. Though he does not believe that any of the women at Mea Culpa have been wrongfully imprisoned, he sees the injustice of their circumstances, of mandatory sentencing that separates mothers from their children after a single indiscretion. It is clear to him that at best the justice system is wildly arbitrary; at worst, it is cruel and unusual. Privately, he feels that he may be too soft for this line of work. If it were not for his imposing appearance, his pervasive tattoos and heavily muscled arms, he is certain that his empathy would shine through like a beacon, making him an object of suspicion, an easy mark in this place of judgment.

ABOUT AN HOUR INTO FRANCISCO'S SHIFT, THERE IS a major altercation in the cafeteria. What begins as a dispute over biscuits soon evolves into full-on internecine warfare, as rival gangs take the opportunity to vent their hostilities toward one another. He knows he should wait for backup, but, seeing Clover in the mix, he dives into the fray anyway, hoping to prevent bloodshed, offering himself as a target so that the women cannot do too much damage to one another. As he reaches the epicenter of the conflict, the violence falls over him like a blanket. He feels acutely the contact of fists against flesh, the kicks to his shins, ankles, even groin. He has a sudden image of himself as a medieval castle under siege, battering rams at every gate. All that is missing is the flaming arrows, until one of the women puts her cigarette out on his arm, and then he thinks, of course.

A sharp blow knocks him to his knees—it is delivered by a blond bruiser named Sunny, ironically one of his former loves. For a moment he cannot think clearly. He can only marvel at the organic swiftness with which the fight spreads into the spaces above him, fists bridging the void like the unfurling boughs of a tree.

It is then that he sees it. Winking in the air before him is what looks like a tiny, iridescent seed. It hovers impossibly, no more than two feet from his bloodied and rapidly swelling nose.

The room shifts.

His skin crawls in the most spectacular way.

RIGHT AWAY HE CAN SEE THAT IT IS WRONG, THAT IT is a thing out of sync with the workings of the natural world. It is not even possible to look directly at it. He can only deduce its diamantine shape through the ribbons of air warping strangely around it. His mind tries to classify what he sees, offering him words like *hummingbird, butterfly, raindrop*. But the anomaly resists any attempt at taxonomy. As the fight rages on around him, Francisco is shoved from behind.

He lurches forward, and before he can catch himself, tumbles face-first into the thing. The cool, metallic sensation that greets him is the first shock. A sheet of liquid silver seems to slide across his features, enveloping him centimeter by centimeter until it at last it closes, cocoonlike, around him. *Like falling into a mirror,* he thinks.

For a moment there is nothing to see. There is only a kind of dim lull, a soothing pocket of darkness that holds him like a marble in a velvet pouch. And then he explodes outward into light.

The glare, at first, is unbearable. His eyes ache with the strain of it, though he is squinting, and he marvels at the way they feel rolling around their sockets, how the sensation is both familiar and brand-new, as if he is merely a test-driver in someone else's head. In fact, his whole body feels like a strange receptacle that he has somehow been stuffed into. He becomes aware of a far-off droning sound, like a bee probing a windowpane. The sound grows louder, filling his ears, until he realizes that what he is hearing is not an insect at all, but some kind of engine. The glare at last recedes, and he is astonished to find himself wedged into the cockpit of an airplane, a small one, swooning so low over a verdant hill that he is nearly brushing the tops of the pines.

What the hell is happening to me?

He glances down at himself, spies the drab green cuff adorning his wrist. Though he has no prior knowledge of such things, he recognizes the insignia as belonging to the Imperial Japanese Navy. He looks up to see his fellow pilots dotting the sky ahead. They fly single file, forming a staggered line into the distance like the *shimenawa* on a Shinto shrine.

How do I even know what that is?

Because he has no feeling of danger, he guesses that he must be participating in some sort of training run. Again, a thought strikes him, and he instinctively knows himself to be inside an A6M Zero, called thus after the last number of the Imperial Year 2600, the year it was first introduced into service. All of these facts come to him as naturally as if they have always been there, lying dormant, embedded in some forgotten fold of brain tissue.

And then, with a kind of mute terror, Francisco begins to sense his thoughts giving over to those of the pilot. He feels himself slipping behind the boy's consciousness, becoming shadowed, as in an eclipse, until there is not enough of him left to protest. All that remains of his mind is a pearly film, a second whispered skin. A ghost layer.

He is besieged by emotions that are not his own. He feels the exhilaration of ascent, feels the burden of duty to army and empire lessening with every moment he is airborne. He feels the expectations of his demanding father falling away, left to ink the sky behind him like so many condensation trails. Most of all, he feels weightless, as if he has been transformed into a slender and elegant bird. As he flies he imagines a cormorant cutting across the water, its jetty wings outspread, perhaps dipping its neck for a fish then rising again. From the first, flying has come naturally to him. It has felt like an expression of something he always knew how to do, a biological imperative threaded through the spongy marrow of his bones. Even his superiors marveled at how quickly he took to the craft.

A command crackles through the radio, and the pilot does as instructed, arcing wide to intercept the line and assume the position of leader. His chest swells with pride. If only Yoshi could see him now! Yoshi, the family favorite, who, gods take him, is already a seaman first class. His own name, Hiroto, means "to fly far," and he fully intends to. He will fly as far as he has to, as far as it takes to persuade his stubborn family to let him marry Yumi, so beautiful in her powder blue coat, with her hair falling over her eyes and her delicate hands shyly outstretched to his. Ah, sweet Yumi. He can feel his love for her like a wound spreading in his chest. It is so capacious that the golden skyline ahead could not absorb the whole of it. It populates the air around the plane, creating a perfect envelope of possibility in which he is free to forge his own bright destiny. Family blessing or no, he will find a way to marry Yumi. Beyond that, he has no other thought but to keep flying, to be a glorious speck upon the rising sun, the pulsing muscle of his heart replaced with a bright, beating wing. If he has to, he is even prepared to die flying.

With the sliver of Francisco's consciousness that remains, a single thought emerges. *A past life. What I am seeing is a past life.*

Suddenly, there is the sensation of being yanked backward by invisible cords. He can almost feel the points of entry where these cords are attached, glowing like LED lights on a circuit board and forming a luminous constellation on his back. The plane, the skyline, all of it, begin to recede rapidly into the distance. It telescopes away from him until there is only a far-off pinpoint picture, a painted landscape rendered impossibly small. Soon that, too, blinks out.

And then he is back on the hard floor of the cafeteria. His fellow guards have formed a covered-wagon circle around him. They are eyeing the scattered inmates warily, while Dr. Sternberg, the prison physician, pushes her way through to him.

"Hello? Hello? Can you hear me?"

The doctor is practically shouting at him, and the authority of her voice begins to root him once more in the reality of this place, this self. He can feel Hiroto's love for Yumi begin to ebb away from him. It seeps out as if from a sieve, as though his heart has suddenly sprung a thousand leaks, and though he tries, he cannot recover the fullness of it. In his desperation, he imagines saving a pool of it in his cupped hands, so that at least this small portion will not be lost. But soon enough this, too, dissipates. His hands are once again empty. He can remember the whole experience vividly, can remember Yumi in particular, but the fierce love he felt for her as Hiroto has vanished, in its place a series of benignly pleasant impressions. The ache of this absence is nearly unbearable to him. It is as if he has just forgotten the most beautiful dream he has ever had.

The doctor, meanwhile, is still trying to bring him around. "Hello there! Hello? You blacked out. Can you tell me your name?"

He nearly laughs aloud at this. *My name? Which one?* But he complies, answering in the way she expects him to. "Francisco Guerrero."

"Good. How many fingers am I holding up?"

"Three. Well, two fingers and a thumb."

"And can you tell me what happened to you?"

He pauses to marshal his thoughts. "Um…I fell into that sparkly diamond up there." He gestures toward the anomaly. "And then I saw things. Things that seemed completely real." He drops his voice to a whisper, hoping the prisoners and his fellow guards will not hear. "It was like memories. But not *my* memories, you know? They were very vivid. Very *specific.*" He rubs his forehead, feeling the beginnings of a headache. "I realize this probably doesn't make a lot of sense."

He gazes up at Dr. Sternberg then, noting the flecks of copper stippling her jade-green eyes. Though they have worked together for years, he does not think he has ever really looked at her before. There is a familiar flutter in his belly, that nascent sense of turmoil that signals either a bout of gastrointestinal distress or the shift to a new love—he hopes it is the latter—and he welcomes the sensation gratefully, anxious to fill the terrible void left behind by that fluttering blue coat.

He grasps the doctor's hand. "Tell me you see it, too," he pleads.

Though she is startled by his apparent desperation, she does not withdraw. "I see *something*, yes. We all do. Like a tiny prism hung in midair."

"It wasn't there yesterday."

She snorts. "No shit. Pretty sure the warden would have noted it on her daily report."

"Do you believe me?"

"About what you saw? Sure, I believe that you saw something, or that you think you did. Who knows what that thing really is," she says, tilting her head toward the anomaly. "It probably gave your brain some kind of electrical jolt and then you had a really vivid dream. I saw it in Afghanistan, when a guy touched a wire he shouldn't have. Woke up ranting about angels."

He shakes his head insistently. "It was *not* a dream. There were all these details to it. Things I couldn't have known."

She shrugs. "Either way, we need to get you back to my office for some tests. There are other people who can investigate whatever is going on here." She straightens up, addressing the assembled crowd. "Everyone, please return to your tables, and for the love of God stay away from this thing. We don't yet know what it is or what it can do to you."

Francisco feels suddenly desperate, like a door is swinging shut, as if his very sanity depends on someone else experiencing what he has experienced. He knows the doctor has been a soldier, and he wonders: How do they do it? How do they bear witness to those strange and terrible things and then return home where no one could possibly understand what they have been through? "Okay, I will come," he tells her. "I will submit to your tests or whatever. But first…will you try it yourself? Just walk into it and tell me what you see. I promise it won't hurt you." He reaches up to touch her face then, drawn to the liquid smoothness of her skin; this is too bold a gesture by far, but nothing about the situation is ordinary, and so she doesn't withdraw from him. She even turns her head and for a moment allows her lips to brush against his fingers. A shock passes through him. He wants to make love to her right there, in front of Clover and Sunny and the whole world. He wishes he could remember her first name. As long as she has worked at the prison she has only been known to him as Dr. Sternberg. "Please," he begs her. "I can't be the only one with this secret. It will kill me."

Dr. Sternberg studies him for several long seconds, then nods. Perhaps she thinks he is still brain-addled from his fall, but she seems to like him, and so she has decided to humor him for the moment. She turns to the spectators, who, despite her admonishment, have made no move to return to their tables. "I'm going in," she announces theatrically. "If I don't make it back, tell my dads I love them. You can all draw straws for my exotic insect collection." She raises her right hand with a flourish and then turns to face the anomaly.

There are objections from the guards, excited murmurs from the inmates, but no one moves to stop her.

She approaches it slowly, her hand reflexively smoothing her dark hair, which is pinned back in a classic military bun. Not long ago she completed her second tour of Afghanistan—Francisco knows she must have nerves of steel. But this is something different, not quantifiable. Not like an enemy sniper or an IED. She is clearly uneasy. Afraid, even. Still, she is a warrior. She is not about to turn back.

Finally, she walks into it. There is a gasp from the crowd as her skin appears to ripple ever so slightly, to fracture as if passing behind a pane of splintered glass. She stops then, standing stock still. The anomaly appears to be right at the center of her head, like a tumor embedded in her brain, and for the first time Francisco thinks, *This is dangerous. I should not have asked her to do this.* But it is too late now. Her eyes are turning upward like a saint receiving a vision, her face caught in an expression of intense wonder. Her fingers are splayed out, bent further backward than flexibility would typically allow. And then she begins to change. She begins to take on the aspect of another person, a second self which hovers above the surface of her body, shimmering like an atmosphere, like a swirling blanket of vapors in human form. Try as he might, he cannot make out the precise details of that other self. It is like a dream. Whatever he tries to focus on—her ear, her throat, the curvature of her arm—instantly dissolves into ambiguity, becomes insubstantial as water. He cannot even tell if this other self is male or female. Silently, the doctor's lips move, as if conversing with some unseen person, or perhaps mouthing a prayer. Then she, too, slumps to the ground.

This time it is Francisco who rushes forward. He places his hand beneath Dr. Sternberg's head, gently shielding it from the cold tile. At his touch, she jolts awake, her eyes wild. She looks equal parts disoriented and awestruck. It is the same way he must have looked when emerging from his own trance.

Francisco helps her up, lets her still-slack body fall against him. He is conscious of her breasts rising and falling beneath her lab coat, the faint scent of jasmine emanating from the region of her collarbone, and he can feel his body begin to burn in response. It occurs to him that this newest love is not safe like the others were. He cannot hold it at a distance, sublimating his lust within the existing template. This is somehow more real.

"What did you see?" he asks softly.

At first she doesn't answer. She only stares at her hands, turning them over and over as if she is not sure they belong to her. At last, she shakes her head. "It's just like you said. I saw impossible things."

They turn to face it then, that strange diamond winking in the air, taunting them with its promise of lives yet unexplored. He can almost hear its voice twining out from the epicenter—a tinny, conductive strand. *Come back, or don't,* it seems to say. *It is all the same to me. But do you think you can live not knowing what comes next?*

THE WARDEN AT LAST ARRIVES, WEARING A CRISP navy pantsuit, a starched white blouse, and an expression of grim determination. She looks the anomaly up and down, appraising it as if it were just another deficiency to be addressed. After a few minutes she turns to confront the assembly of employees and inmates. "First of all, this area needs to be roped off," she declares. "From now on, it is officially out of bounds to everyone, including staff. I am ordering each of you to go about your business as usual and forget that this…whatchamacallit…is even here. I've put in a call to headquarters. They will tell us what the next step should be."

If she is in any way flustered by this glimpse of the unknowable in her otherwise clockwork prison, she does not let on.

"You two," the warden barks, singling out Francisco and the doctor. "Whatever happened here, you are going to keep it to yourselves. Once, I could understand. It was a mistake, you didn't see it, whatever. But to approach it a second time…well, I don't want headquarters thinking I hired a bunch of incompetents, okay? That reflects poorly on me. I suppose I can't expect much in the way of intelligence from you, Guerrero—you're a grunt. But Dr. Sternberg? With your education, your military background? I'm very disappointed in your lack of judgment."

As the warden continues her rebuke, Francisco cannot help letting out an impatient sigh. And it isn't only him. He recalls that Dr. Sternberg typically responds to comments or instructions from the warden with a hearty, "Yes, ma'am." But she is saying nothing now. With his arms still around her, he feels that they have already become coconspirators. He presses his index finger over her heart, feeling the shocking heat, the sudden flare of warmth there, and taps out a message he hopes she will understand.

Do they still teach Morse code in the military? He doesn't know.

He gets his answer soon enough. The doctor places her slender hand across his, signaling back her intentions without hesitation—so hard, in fact, that she seems more than willing to bruise her own skin in the process. He can feel the defiance radiating from her. There is something almost providential about it. Her hand forms a cage over his, her finger working like a tattoo needle, hammering away as if by instinct. It is as if the words were encoded within her fingertips all along, waiting only for the right moment to transmit.

THAT NIGHT HE WAITS FOR THE DOCTOR IN HER office. She is late, and so he amuses himself by looking around the narrow room, seeking an entry point into her mostly opaque private life. There is very little personal memorabilia in evidence, mostly files and medical equipment, but there is a framed diploma on the wall bearing her full name—Eliza Ora Sternberg. *Eliza.* And on her desktop he spies a single photograph, a snapshot of her posing with two other soldiers, both men, all in their desert camo uniforms. A mounted machine gun stands behind them, and they are leaning casually against it, laughing and linking arms. He feels a sudden stab of jealousy. Were they boyfriends? Just war buddies? He can glean nothing from their body language. He latches onto Eliza's grin, which is as mystifying in its complexity as any Mona Lisa in a museum. It seems to contain volumes, and it occurs to him that whatever her past life was, it was there with her at the moment the photograph was taken, folded into the lovely contours of her body, dwelling deep in her lungs and in the strands of hair that float around her face.

God, she is beautiful.

And then she is there with him, not stepping but springing from the shadowed hallway, her dark eyes wild, full of a glinting resolve. He startles guiltily, thinking she has somehow guessed his thoughts. But if she has, she does not seem to care. She does not stop to say 'hello,' or to inquire about the remainder of his day. She simply continues her forward trajectory, thrusting him forcefully against the back wall, pinning him there with surprising strength. He can feel the rapid cycling of her breath, the humid exhalations raising gooseflesh on his skin. And then she presses her mouth against his. Her tongue slips in at once. Her hands are already unbuttoning his shirt. As he leans toward her, she pushes him back a second time, causing the papers on the corkboard behind him to come dislodged. For a moment they lift upward in a bright cloud, squares of white and yellow contrasted against the blackness of the hallway, and in his delirious state they almost seem to comprise windows to some distant, luminous world.

He is astonished. He has had plenty of girlfriends, mostly prior to his tenure at the prison, but never one who came at him like this, with no pretense of coyness, no interest whatsoever in concealing her eagerness.

"I like your tattoos," she murmurs, withdrawing for a moment. Her fingers trace the image of Our Lady of Guadalupe that floats above his left nipple, ringed with roses and a spoking aura of light. This was his first tattoo, acquired to commemorate his entry into the Corona Park Locos, and it remains his favorite, though he parted ways with the gang a mere six months later. Francisco was fifteen then—a veritable lifetime ago.

Eliza's hands continue to claim new territory. And though he sees the camera fixed high in the corner above the door, a piece of surveillance she undoubtedly knows about, he does not stop her exploration, not even when she sinks to the floor and begins to unzip his pants.

Lulu, he thinks dreamily.

Lulu is the night guard in charge of monitoring the cameras. She watches everything on a twelve-screen grid with images that rotate every few seconds, her view of the prison assembled in fragments, as if rendered through an insect's compound eye. He and Lulu have always been friendly. She is part of a group he sometimes grabs a beer with on weekends. She has beaten him numerous times at darts, and once, they even shared a drunken kiss, although both agreed afterwards that it had been a mistake. Now he tries to imagine her reaction to the scene as it is unfolding. He knows that at any time she could select the doctor's camera and record evidence that would result in his immediate dismissal. Though the warden tolerates interstaff romances, it is with the expectation that both parties behave professionally within the prison itself. He looks into the camera, half defiant, half imploring. *Please Lulu. Don't rat us out.*

All at once, a flash of green crosses his vision: a recovered glimpse of that distant horizon. He can still see Eliza's office around him, but it is as if his past life, the pilot's life, has suddenly been projected onto it, as if he is standing at the center of a giant zoetrope. The panels swirl around him, membrane-thin. Once again his fellow pilots comprise a knotted rope looping into the distance. Once again the airplane banks right, sweeping along a feathery skim of trees. Viewed in this way, both worlds possess an unbearable richness, a vitality that is almost too beautiful to bear. The green is so vivid it cuts him to the heart. The sky shimmers like a fall of gold. In the present, his hands open up into unknown dimensions, exploding into cross-sections like architectural drawings. Even the desk seems to have subverted its own geometry, its metallic sides shifting into a kind of rhombus.

But the experience is not only visual. For the second time that day, he feels the vibration of the thrumming Sakae engine, the rapture of flight pulsing like beads of light beneath his skin. He feels the control stick smooth within his grip. He feels the chill of the morning air penetrate the windows, his body enveloped within the crisp (and slightly scratchy) uniform. And of course there is his/Hiroto's love for Yumi, which flares up as if doused with gasoline. He is overwhelmed by it. It is just as pure and immutable as before, burning so brightly he feels it can never again be dampened.

Back in the room, the doctor has fallen back on her knees, turning her head from side to side with wonder. She, too, must be witnessing her past life, spliced into the film of her current one. Her cheeks are streaked with tears. She tries to speak, but cannot. After a moment, their eyes meet, and she pulls him roughly to the floor. He sees a strange expression flicker across her face, a remnant of her other self, and with a thrill it occurs to him that he is about to make love to two women at once, or perhaps a woman and a man—who knows? He can only assume that it is the same for her, that she sees both him and his shadow self, that she feels herself passing like a ghost between them. As his body begins to move over, under, into hers, Francisco thinks, *We are the only two people who have experienced this. We may as well be the only two people in the world.*

THERE IS NO SECTION IN THE PRISON OPERATIONS manual dealing with spatially transgressive phenomena, and so the next morning Francisco finds himself designated the unofficial caretaker of the anomaly. With the warden's blessing, he drapes police tape all around the site, spun through a circle of chair backs, and stands guard, scanning the room sternly to discourage any potential breaches. Not that he has to worry on that count; the inmates are more than happy to give the area a wide berth. Many of them refuse to walk on the same side of the room, taking pains to carry their trays in far-reaching arcs around it. Some will not even look in that direction. At two fifteen, a government agent in a black suit appears and declares the anomaly off-limits. "No one is to go near this thing, not even you, ma'am," the agent says, nodding at the warden. "My people will be back in a couple of days to secure the site. In the meantime, just hang tough. You're all in good hands."

Like hell we are, Francisco thinks. He glances over at Eliza, who is rolling her eyes at the agent's statements. He knows then: nothing is going to keep them from returning to the anomaly, and to each other.

Sure enough, as soon as she is off-duty, she meets him again in the shadowed cafeteria. His heart leaps when he sees her; she has already let her long hair down. It masses around her shoulders like something wild, something wholly ungovernable. He can just make out tenebrous shapes rolling in its darkness. Obliquely he wonders if she is the true entry point for what he is seeking after all, not the anomaly, but of course that is absurd and so he dismisses the thought. They stand before the diamantine form, transfixed by the persistent strangeness of it, its arcane beauty. Then, holding hands for courage, they step into it together.

This time he is a woman in German East Africa. Her village lies within shouting distance of the tree-strewn banks of Nam Lolwe, though the invaders are known to call it Lake Victoria. She is carrying a tall clay pot to the water to fill. Her muscled legs are strong beneath her, her arms plump and ringed with beaded bracelets. The other village women are walking beside her, along with some of the younger children. As usual, her husband and ten-year-old son are out working in the mines; all day they labor in steeply terraced ravines, excavating chunks of gold that are lodged like fossilized stars within the earth. The women stop to rest on the shore, and she stops, too, setting her pot on a nearby mound. Together, they laugh and joke and swap stories of ornery children, wayward husbands, relatives that are as difficult and meddlesome as they are beloved.

Beyond the sedge and hyacinths that fringe the shore, the blue water curls out like a vision. Her eye fixes on the glinting points, those bright cusps where the sun is scattered across the water like so much gold dust. When her husband first began to woo her, he took a thimbleful of such dust and drew it across her palm. "This is your future with me," he said, and though she knew he meant it as a pledge of security she could not help but see the eternal glimmering within the gesture, the promise of a path marked with wonder. Indeed, there have been so many wonders. She thinks of the first night they were together, when they both wept and clung to each other like foundlings. She thinks of her bright-eyed son. She thinks of the baby swelling in her womb, pondering which of his parents he will favor. She thinks of the two children she lost, one to fever, one born dead, their small bodies buried deep and on their right sides, though she feels them return to her sometimes when she is lonely or unwell. To them, she sends thoughts of love. Casting her words like stones across the water, she tells them, *You will have a healthy brother*. Tells them, *It will not be long before I join you on the other side*. To spirits, time is nothing. The blink of an eye, if they so choose.

When Francisco at last emerges from this reverie, his eyes are wet with tears. So are the doctor's.

"Mother of God," he breathes. "Deliver us from such amazing things."

LIKE ADDICTS, THEY ARE UNABLE TO STOP. THEIR nights are wholly consumed by these pilgrimages into the past.

"Tell me about yours." This is their watchword. They take turns now, as if passing the needle from flesh to flesh. He watches her face transform with the materialization of each past self; each time it is like a mask has been lifted. It is like scales falling from his eyes, and he says to himself, *Yes, I think that I've always seen these things in her*. There, in the eyes, is the steadfastness of the Mapuche weaver. The fatalism of the French revolutionary. Each time it is like watching a child being born, a child he has never seen and yet somehow recognizes. Each time it is like watching a death. Often, it is like the artists' depictions of Saint Theresa in ecstasy. Her eyes roll like marbles in their sockets; her face goes slack.

Soon the cafeteria is littered with the bodies of their past selves.

He is a sickly child in Reykjavik.

She is a rum runner, ferrying casks of Bengal rum to the convict-laden shores of Australia.

He is a veiled mother of seven in Constantinople.

She is a court calligrapher during the Ming Dynasty.

Together they are charting the continents, making a slow conquest of the world.

Now when they make love it is like an orgy. They begin as themselves and then quickly splinter into layers, multiple identities that nest upon themselves like strips of papier-mâché. At times their own thoughts blink out and they become mere receptacles for their other lives. He is a woman and she is a man, and she thrusts into him, and there is a beautiful aching pleasure the likes of which he has never experienced. Or they are both women, or both men, alternating lives as other couples might change sexual positions. Him, a Russian peasant boy burning with lust for his stepmother. Her, a middle-aged Taíno woman with five husbands. Him, a grieving war widow. Her, a soldier's daughter whose father has just returned for her name day. They traverse the full range of human emotion, howls of despair morphing into tears of laughter and back again. She contains multitudes. He contains droves. Together they are legion: all these selves sliding across one another, mouths open and hungry for contact.

And always, through the curtain of Eliza's lovely hair, Francisco can just make out the anomaly, flashing like an unreachable star, a far-off beacon in the dark.

LULU HAS NOT YET REPORTED THEM TO THE WARDEN, though Lord knows she has had enough opportunities. From time to time Francisco leaves a case of her favorite beer beside her work locker to thank her. Moreover, the promised contingent of government agents has reportedly been delayed, and so the doctor and the guard are free to continue their nightly explorations until they collapse from mental and physical exhaustion. Often, they get only two or three hours of sleep before having to start their shifts all over again. Sometimes they do not even go home. During work hours, Francisco is unkempt and distracted to the point of carelessness. His senses are dangerously dulled. One morning he fails to notice an argument between inmates until it has ballooned into a full-blown altercation. Several women are injured as the result of his negligence. Eliza, the war veteran, is better at performing her duties in a depleted state. Still it is clear: neither one is fully in possession of themselves, fully *alive*, unless they are using the anomaly.

ONCE, AFTER EMERGING FROM HER TRANSPORTED state, Eliza is uncharacteristically reticent about the experience. "It's a little embarrassing," she says.

Of course this piques his interest. "What were you? A prostitute?" He cannot help picturing her in a breathtaking array of positions, wearing an integument of whalebone and silk, or perhaps only a shimmering, diaphanous gown.

"No," she says. "I was a Catholic priest."

He laughs so hard at this he nearly chokes.

Eliza looks down at her hands, and after a moment he realizes she is blushing, a thing of which he did not know she was capable. "I'm sorry," he says, wiping tears from his eyes. "It's not funny." With that he bursts into another gale of laughter.

"Look," she says defensively. "My zayde would roll over in his grave if he knew I was a Catholic at all, let alone a priest."

"Your who?"

"My grandfather."

"Oh," he says, nodding. For her sake, he manages a serious expression. "But hey, aren't your dads gay? How did your zayde feel about that?"

"Oh, he came to terms with it eventually. Being gay is one thing, but being Catholic is something else entirely. There's like a whole hierarchy of offenses, and apostasy is right at the very top. Worse than murder even," she adds with a smile.

"Well, it can't exactly hurt him now, can it? Anyway, you never know. Maybe in his past life he was a Muslim or a Buddhist."

Now it is her turn to laugh. "No way. My zayde was *intensely* Jewish. I think if he were to use this thing he'd just end up more and more orthodox with every incarnation, as far back as he could go. Till he was just some little microbe in the primordial soup, reciting the Kaddish over and over."

Francisco grins. "I would kill for that kind of consistency. There's no common thread to my lives at all. I'm not even sure I know who I am anymore!" He means it as a joke, but having said it aloud he realizes he has stumbled onto an uncomfortable truth. These envoys into the past have been intoxicating for him, the beauty and intensity almost beyond bearing.

With each experience he has felt the pleasure of being pulled apart and remade as if by a lover's hands. But in his urgent quest for self-knowledge, what has he really learned about himself?

For her part, Eliza does not seem interested in such navel-gazing. With a flicker of impatience, she instinctively retreats to their former terms. "I feel like I need to start going to synagogue again just to get all this Catholic off of me," she laughs. "No offense." Her eye moves to the door, already plotting her exit.

Her sudden withdrawal surprises him. Perhaps for her, the issue of meaning in their shared experience is moot. Or perhaps the thrill of it provides its own kind of meaning; despite their grasping carnality afterwards, there is an undeniable purity to the exhilarations found within the anomaly, a kind of childlike blooming, as of inactive cells springing to life. Or, he reminds himself, it could be that Eliza simply doesn't wish to be thrust into the role of caregiver, playing the role of sympathetic girlfriend to his neurosis. He can't blame her, he supposes. No doubt she has had to draw this line many times with her brothers-in-arms overseas. He leans in, bites her neck gently. "No offense taken. Now let's get some more Catholic all over you."

SOON ENOUGH, THE ANOMALY BECOMES A TOURIST attraction.

Believers and unbelievers of every stripe come by the dozens to examine it. Though Francisco has made space within his Catholicism for the Hindu notion of reincarnation, others are not so circumspect. He can tell this type at once by the way they narrow their eyes at him, scanning his visage for signs of duplicity. They are looking for hints of snake oil, for the tanned mask of the sideshow conman. They believe that they have already cracked the code to God, the afterlife, whatever. The anomaly stands as a direct rebuke to such certainty.

A few of these visitors berate Francisco on their way out, blaming him for their disillusionment. Most, however, remain steadfast in their disbelief. They shake their heads, erasing the proof of their eyes. They demand to know how he pulled it off.

Though most visitors seek to bypass the tape, he does not allow it. This is ostensibly for their own safety—in his discussions with the warden, he recalls a distinct emphasis on the word "liability"—but there is a small part of him that does not wish anyone else to share in the glories of the phenomenon. *This was given to us*, he thinks absurdly. *Me and Eliza. Who are these strangers to encroach upon our bliss?*

The next group to come is the scientists. Teams of them march around the anomaly like worker ants, wielding strange devices, taking measurements, sighing in frustration at their inability to determine its particles or provenance. Truthfully, they cannot even define its basic contours. Holding up a ruler beside it causes the anomaly to begin flickering spasmodically, shortening and lengthening at random as if in defiance of the simplest properties of space.

As the scientists' numbers dwindle, a certain California archetype begins to proliferate. They perch or sit on yoga mats for hours, meditating, sometimes placing crystals in their hands or on the floor beside them. When they produce their singing bowls, Francisco promptly requisitions them, citing vague "regulations." When they chant, he asks them to do so quietly. Given time he knows this group is likely to form a cult. He can just imagine it: the Fellowship of the Enigma, or some such.

Their presence irritates him—they seem so thoroughly to be missing the point—and so he tries to persuade the warden to blacklist them. She only shrugs at his suggestion. "We are a public prison, Guerrero. If these hippies make it through the approval process, we have to let them in. It's *your* job to keep them from disrupting our day-to-day activities." She does not even look at him when she says this, as if the topic itself is too insignificant to be faced head-on. And there is something more. He has noticed a slight shudder whenever he mentions the anomaly in her presence, a shiver of remembrance, he thinks, as if she has literally forgotten its existence until he said the words aloud. He gets the impression that the moment he walks away she will forget it again, her view of reality already knitting itself closed around the breach.

Then there are the visitors he would not have expected. A professional wrestler. A gorilla specialist from the L.A. Zoo. At least twenty aspiring screenwriters. A group of elementary schoolkids on a field trip (*who thought* this *was a good idea?* he wonders). Several elected officials, hoping somehow to leverage the phenomenon for the benefit of their campaigns. An elderly brother and sister who, three days in a row, bring an urn containing their mother's ashes and set it before the anomaly, as if expecting the atomized parts of her to suddenly swirl back to life.

One day there is a conspicuously wealthy businessman, clad in a tailored suit so expensive it would probably burst into flames if it ever crossed the threshold of Francisco's shabby apartment. For a while the man only circles the anomaly, like a coyote eyeing its prey. Then all at once he lunges forward, crashing through the barrier chest-first, like a runner at the finishing line of a race. Francisco tries to stop him, but he is functioning on about two hours of sleep and his reaction is sluggish. He is too late. The man has already attained his goal. Almost at once he falls to his knees, stricken. With a sense of building fury, Francisco sees the eyes beginning to roll with wonder, sees the mark of unfolding visions that this corporate criminal cannot possibly deserve. He sees the hands outstretched as if to embrace the cascade of beauty pouring over him. Francisco's fists clench. His thoughts are void but for a single word. *Polluted.*

He waits until the man has begun to recover his senses, then yanks him roughly to his feet.

"Huh?" the man asks, disoriented.

Francisco does not ask him what he saw; truly, he does not care. All he can think is that one who has everything already has stolen something precious from him. He draws back and punches the man full in the face. But this action barely touches the ragged edge of his rage, and so he does it again, and then again. Over and over he hits him, the man's tanned and moisturized face the ready emblem of every resentment, every frustrated desire he has endured in his life. His childhood poverty. His mother abandoning him. The constant gnawing hunger in his stomach that he sometimes visualized as a whirling Tasmanian devil, like in the cartoons, because it made it seem external somehow, made it more bearable. Through some crude muscle memory he comes to realize that he is duplicating the motions of a previous encounter, another time when he allowed himself to become an unthinking machine, fists launching like pistons, devoid of anything that could be called empathy. The grocery store clerk had almost died, and all because of something his idiot gang boss told him to do.

Francisco stops suddenly, alarmed and deeply ashamed of himself. "Jesus Christ, I'm sorry," he mutters. The businessman lies stunned and bleeding on the floor. Francisco backs away, puts his hands up, and turns in a small circle, as if surrendering to the entire prison at once. "I'm so sorry."

It is only then that the other guards rush over and make a show of restraining him. He feels sick at their complicity. *Why did you let me do that? What else has happened in this place that I don't know about?* Aloud he says, "I'm fine. I'm all done. I won't touch him again, I swear."

"You sure?" one of them asks halfheartedly.

"Yes, I'm okay now."

"See that you don't." They shrug and let him go.

Sunny, who has witnessed all of this, gives Francisco an approving cheer.

Finally, Eliza arrives with her med kit. Upon seeing the man's condition—his expensive suit spattered with blood, one white shirttail unfurled like a flag— she gives Francisco a dark look. She crouches down, peering at the man's nose and into his eyes, listening to his heart and the bellows of his chest. Francisco feels a stab of jealousy at this last step. He has never seen Eliza examine a male patient. She is as close as a lover. Her left hand rests on his upper thigh, her head so near his mouth she can no doubt feel his breath on her hair. The man, though, seems oblivious to his good fortune.

"That wasn't my life," he is repeating miserably, his eyes seeking out hers, begging her to believe. "That couldn't be my life."

"No, of course not," she says sympathetically. "All right boys, let's get him back to my office." Three of the guards spring into action, helping the man to his feet and out of the cafeteria.

Still stunned by his own behavior, Francisco sits down at one of the inmate tables. The women come and go around him, devouring their lunches, bantering and arguing. At first they eye him warily, but upon seeing his remote gaze, his condition of almost total stillness, they begin to relax and route their conversations around him as if he is not present. He does not even notice when Clover sits down beside him, her left breast coming into brief contact with his shoulder.

After an hour or so Eliza returns, shocking him out of his abstraction. "I told him you were in Iraq and you had PTSD," she says coldly. "He agreed not to press charges. I also reported the whole thing to the warden, but she didn't seem even slightly interested, so I think you're in the clear. Congratulations." She starts to walk away.

Finally, he rouses himself to speech. "Eliza, please. Wait a second."

She half turns, not committing to anything.

"Eliza, look. I'm *really* sorry. When I saw him there, where only the two of us had been up until then, it just felt like…like he was the serpent in the Garden of Eden or something. Like he had contaminated our secret world. I just lost it."

"That's a very grandiose defense."

Sighing, he looks around at the now empty table. He would not want the inmates to hear what he is about to say. "Eliza, did I ever tell you I was in a gang?" He aims his words downward, unable to meet her gaze. "After my mom left, my brothers and I were dirt poor and desperate. I did a lot of things I'm not proud of. It hurt to do them, but it hurt more not to belong to anybody, you know? I had so much anger back then. Like a river of it, just coursing beneath my skin. Every time I felt my blood pumping I would think, there it is, there's the anger. At one point I almost slit my wrists because I thought if I could empty my veins of all that anger, maybe I'd be okay."

She turns, regarding him sharply.

"Here's the thing," he continues. "I thought all of that was behind me. I thought I'd created a barrier between myself and the past, and I could just reinvent myself as a law-abiding citizen without consequences. It seems so stupid now. I can remember my other lives with such clarity, like they're all still coiled up inside me, but somehow I imagined that I could be free from the person I was just ten years ago."

Eliza's anger seems to dissipate at this last revelation. "Yeah, I get that," she says, placing her hand on his shoulder. "You should see me every time a firework goes off. I'm a real barrel of laughs on the Fourth of July."

Finally, he looks up at her. "I'm sorry."

She shrugs.

"Have you thought of going to therapy?"

"Are you kidding? This is me *after* therapy." She laughs a hollow laugh.

"Oh. Sorry again."

"It's okay. I think you should give it a try, though. Either that or take up ultimate fighting on your days off."

He smiles. Perhaps their little world hasn't been wrecked after all. Perhaps it—and they—can still be salvaged. "Will I see you tonight?"

She gives him a long look. "Sure," she says at last. "What the hell. It's only time, right?"

LATER, HE WONDERS: WHAT DID THE BUSINESSMAN mean by saying, "That wasn't my life"? It could only have been that his former self was a nobody. He must have awakened amid some mundane, working-class turmoil. No longer rich. No longer powerful. No longer subject to the automatic deference and privilege that has been his unquestioned birthright in this life. Happy, perhaps, but he would have been too distressed by his meager circumstances to take note of something so ephemeral. What did he think, that he would be Manhattan Beach royalty all the way back? Francisco feels a belated sense of sympathy for the man. *You have glimpsed something infinitely rare and wondrous,* he wishes he could tell him. *Can't you at least be grateful for that?*

It is advice he could benefit from himself. He finds that the more he dips into these oceans of past, the more he feels severed from the present moment, and from any sense of identity. He is like a detached leaf, floating free along the current of his own timeline. The modern world might be a sad mirage for all the joy it brings him. Only his moments with Eliza and the anomaly have any substance to them. But even here, his obsessive ruminations have seen the emergence of a troubling thought. At some point he is bound to reach the end of his soul's journey, or, more precisely, the beginning. What will he do then?

SEVERAL NIGHTS LATER, ELIZA ARRIVES AT THE cafeteria leading her cherished Siberian husky, Hilda. "I just want to see," she says sheepishly. She first commands the animal to stay, then goes to stand across the room so that the anomaly hangs at a mid-point between them. When she calls out, Hilda bounds toward her, hesitating for only a second before rushing into that prismed space. Once there, the animal skids to a halt. Her blue eyes widen. She stands still as a statue, her powerful neck erect, though Francisco notices that her hackles have not risen. In fact, she does not look disturbed at all, only deeply puzzled. She remains there for nearly a minute, the anomaly shimmering like crystallized ice against her white-gray fur. Then she hastens to Eliza's side.

Eliza crouches down to greet her. "What did you see?" she asks. "Were you somebody else's baby? Were you pulling a sled across the sweeping tundra? Were you a wolf with your pack, howling at the harvest moon?" She mimics a wolf howl, ruffling the dog's ears playfully.

Francisco laughs, charmed by this exhibition of whimsy from his typically serious lover. "Maybe dogs don't have past lives," he teases.

But Eliza does not appreciate this attempt at humor. She only narrows her eyes at him, then buries her face in Hilda's luxurious fur. Not for the first time, Francisco finds himself questioning what they have together. *How can this be true love? I didn't even know she had a dog.*

ONE OF FRANCISCO'S MANY INCARNATIONS WAS AN artist, and so he purchases a set of oil paints and a few canvases, only to find that in his present form he has no skill at it whatsoever. In fact, he is atrocious. The landscapes he attempts do not even have the base-level competence of paint-by-numbers pieces. His portraits are worse. They resemble nightmare visions, unholy inversions of the shapes found within the natural world. He thinks perhaps realism is the problem and so he tries for something more abstract. But these efforts also prove to be spectacular failures.

His colors are garish, unbalanced. What should be surreal comes out merely warped.

"It's so frustrating," he complains to Eliza at their next meeting. "I remember so clearly the *feeling* of painting, like I wasn't entirely in control of my hand, like I was some kind of instrument of God or the muses or something. But when I try to do it now, it just looks like pigeon crap."

"Well, I'm sure it's very pretty pigeon crap," she says, nudging his shoulder.

He casts her a baleful look. "It's not even bad the way most people are bad. It's like I have the exact opposite of artistic ability. Like I'm being specifically punished for thinking I could ever be a painter."

She sighs. "You always take such a mystical view of everything. Look, this is how I see it. All these lives are still there within us, like layers of sediment. They leave traces of themselves in our personalities, our dreams, passions, et cetera. But that doesn't mean we are the same people. We're more like descendants of ourselves. And that's okay. We don't have to be those people. We just have to be who we are now, in the fullest way possible. Does that make sense?"

"Not really." He grins. "But then none of this makes any sense."

"Okay, what about this," she offers, sidling over to him and placing her mouth over his. Soon they are making love. It is not quick and desperate like before, but slow and personal, as if it is just the two of them again, and Francisco thinks that perhaps whatever issues they had, or he thought they had, have at last been resolved. She is no longer angry; he is no longer ashamed. She loves him, of course she does. But his doubts are like sores that he cannot help picking at. As soon as Eliza is out of sight, they reappear. Like ghosts they seep in from the darkened corners, a slow exhalation of them, as with a breath that has been held too long. As if they were waiting only for the lights to go out.

LITTLE BY LITTLE, HE FINDS HIS CONNECTION WITH Eliza deteriorating. His misgivings begin to infect every aspect of their encounters. Though they still spend their nights in the cafeteria, they speak less and less, each awaiting their hit in silence and not discussing what transpires within. When Eliza returns from a life, he imagines that she was with other lovers, hopelessly perfect lovers with whom he cannot compare. He imagines that she has brought the memory of their flesh back with her, that their words said in the heat of passion have been secreted away, carved indelibly into her heart like scrollwork. In her reticence he finds proof that she is still enamored of these long-dead avatars. He burns with resentment, though a part of him sees the hurt in her eyes that his withdrawal has caused. Most tellingly, they are no longer making love.

One night it all comes out, though what emerges from his lips isn't what he intends.

"What the hell are we doing?" he asks suddenly.

After days of not having said a word to each other, the sudden outburst startles her. "What?"

"The more of my past I delve into, the more I realize how totally insignificant I am. All these threads of myself reaching back through history, and what does it all amount to? I haven't learned a goddamned thing. I haven't become smarter or a better person. By now I should either be Albert Einstein or Albert Schweitzer. I'm a disaster, and not even a successful one."

He sees her gathering herself, casting off the haze that has enveloped them for so long. Her shoulders straighten, and he can see the precise moment that she finds her clarity. He resents even this about her. She seems to have an unfailing compass within her, rendering her incapable of truly being lost.

"But you *are* a good person," she replies. "I see how you interact with the inmates. You help these women during some of the darkest moments of their lives."

He shakes his head emphatically. "You couldn't possibly understand. You're a doctor. You've done important things, saved lives. I am *nothing*. A glorified babysitter."

Her dark eyes peer back at him, wounded, perplexed. "That's not true at all. Your job is critical."

"Critical?" And then he feels it, that old wave of self-loathing, foaming out like a poisonous tide. He laughs bitterly. "You just cannot stop patronizing me, can you? You know what I think? I think you get a thrill out of slumming with me. Now that you're stateside and not in danger of being bombed anymore, I think you'll do anything for an adrenaline rush. I think if it weren't for me you'd be shacking up with some homeless guy, or maybe a serial killer. In fact, you should look up that jackass you had such sympathy for the other day and let me off the hook for a while."

Eliza is already on her feet. She is not a woman who will brook such nonsense for long. "Sure," she says, her beautiful eyes turning distant and cold. "Maybe I will."

Francisco is instantly filled with regret. As she is leaving he has a powerful urge to fling himself in her path, to beg her forgiveness, to explain that he never thought it possible for someone as perfect as she is to exist, not in this stubbornly imperfect world. But he doesn't move. Doesn't say the words.

The door slams behind her.

It is no matter, he tells himself. Tomorrow there will be another love. Tomorrow there is always another love, and this one—*this one*—will be the one to make things right. But even as he thinks it, he knows it is a lie. The hole that has always been inside him seems to have morphed into a physical thing, its shape always aching, always expanding to claim new regions of blood and tissue. By now it must have swallowed most of his organs. One by one he can feel them shutting down, unable to function in the all-consuming void. The only thing remaining is his heart, and that is precariously close to the same fate.

And what will happen then? On to the next life, he supposes. God knows this one has been a bust. But before that happens, he is determined to complete his journey of self-discovery. He will ride the train backward as far as it will go.

EAGER TO CULTIVATE SOME KIND OF MEANING IN HIS dwindling days, Francisco presents a radical proposal to the warden. Might he bring the inmates to visit the anomaly, one by one, as a kind of exposure therapy? Surely, he explains, a deepened knowledge of the self could only help these women on their road to rehabilitation. (He does not mention the total failure that has been his own quest for self.) The warden says yes, saying she trusts his judgment. But the experiment doesn't go as planned. The women begin to argue over which of them had the best past life, meaning, of course, the most money, the most lovers, the most prestigious social position. Fights break out in the cafeteria and throughout the prison grounds. One day, a pair of women nearly beat each other to death because one had been a Brahmin in Jaipur while the other was an untouchable in Delhi. The project is scrapped. "It was worth a try," the warden shrugs, then lets the topic sink into abstraction again.

Time passes, and the once-unbroken stream of visitors slows to a trickle. The novelty has at last worn off. "People can get used to anything, I suppose," Francisco can be heard to mutter, standing guard in the near-empty cafeteria. The government agents never return, their plans evidently lost within a sea of red tape. There are but a few stragglers who remain. The lost mystics who turn up at the outer fence of the prison as if they have sprung up whole from the Earth. The Goth kids from the local high school. A handful of scientists who labor in secret, afraid of being discredited, of being lumped in with the cryptozoologists. Francisco talks to them sometimes, asking about the progress of their research. He is unbearably lonely. Though he knows the warden would not approve, he sneaks Clover out for a second shot at the anomaly. Afterward, she weeps and thanks him. Tells him of the beautiful family she had, with a house that was warm and safe and a mother and father who loved her. There is solace, at least, in this.

His own visits continue, of course. Farther and farther back he goes, until the self he inhabits is wholly primitive, until he has pushed beyond the inception of modern *Homo sapiens* and become something else. Neanderthal, he thinks, based on the facial features he can trace with his fingers. Or maybe Cro-Magnon; he always gets them confused. The scope of activities in these lives is much narrower.

He is sitting beside a blazing fire, forging tools from rock, showing the young ones how to hunt. He is eyeing a potential mate across the camp, and painting equine images on the walls of his cave. Sometimes the terrain around him is different. Colder. Warmer. Covered in sparse vegetation, or surging with lush vines. There are many, many of these lives, as if the span of years is so short that he is being recycled with much greater frequency: the human equivalent of a fruit fly. A number of them involve mere infant thoughts. In these he can only make out colors and textures. Sometimes he is reaching to touch the face of his mother, and these lives are so sad that he is nearly crippled with grief upon reemerging. He may weep for hours afterwards.

He doesn't know if Eliza is still using the anomaly. He only knows that she isn't using it while he is there.

For countless iterations his devolution continues. *Home erectus* and beyond. The forehead rises and falls. *Austrolopithecus*. Thick hair covers most of the body, after which he is not human at all, becoming something more like a gorilla. He becomes smaller still, and begins to walk on all fours. Soon, anything resembling human thought ceases. He leaps from tree to tree, and these are some of Francisco's favorite lives, for this bounding feels akin to flying. It is exhilarating, and for the first time in weeks he thinks of his pilot life, that inaugural foray into his own storied past. With each jump he relishes the feeling of his short, muscled legs standing taut against the branches, body poised for action, seemingly capable of anything. Beyond that there is a kind of lizard consciousness, a forked tongue, a spotted body. And then he is slipping like a stone into the ocean. The legs grow shorter and disappear. He passes through stations with names like lungfish. Lobe-finned fish. Eel. Wormlike, he swims, the lovely exposed vertebra of his mate like the strings of a harp, rippling, moving fluidly through warm waters. He becomes still smaller. Even the lights wink out, predating the formation of eyes or even light-sensitive cells. Soon there is only a sensation of swimming, of movement: his own, and that of the sea around him.

And then comes the moment he has most feared. He steps into the anomaly, but it is now empty for him. Though he feels the usual pull of his heart constricting, the feel of space fracturing like glass around him, there is nothing further to be seen or experienced. He is still himself. Still in his own skin. Still just a lowly guard standing in the cafeteria of a women's prison. The well has at last run dry.

HE EXPECTS TO FEEL A STAB OF PANIC, BUT INSTEAD there is only a sense of numb desolation. He rides the bus home, cracks open a beer, contemplates his options. What is there to do, now that the anomaly has tendered all its secrets? Perhaps he should just walk into the sea. Just return to that place where his journey began, so many millions of years ago, when he was but a tiny speck of life rippling with possibility. Truly, he could have evolved into *anything*. What splendid life forms were envisioned within that single cell? What glorious creatures of beauty and vision? And then to become himself—such a disappointment. It would be fitting to end the failed experiment there. A kind of apology, even, for his unworthiness. But of course he cannot get past the Catholic taboo of suicide. (It's funny—he doesn't remember ever going to Mass, yet he picked up Catholicism from the streets as if from particles in the air.) Instead, he will simply let things take their natural course. He will subsist as long as he can: going to work, breaking up fights, coming home. If his suspicions are correct, he has only to wait for his organs to complete their march to dissolution.

By the time he arrives at work the next morning, the anomaly has vanished. Just plucked from the air, as if it had never been. When he informs the warden of this development, there is only the faintest recognition in her eyes. "The what? Oh. Oh, yes. I suppose that's for the best," she says, before returning to her paperwork. Francisco removes the chairs and the police tape, and soon the inmates are once again walking through the space that was in recent months the subject of so much wonder and ontological speculation. They don't seem to be troubled by its disappearance at all. They have fallen back into the rhythm of their everyday dramas: laughing, arguing, scheming, poaching one another's biscuits. His fellow guards actually seem relieved. They did not relish the extra responsibility implied by the anomaly's presence.

Lulu says she hated seeing it on the camera, glinting like a malevolent eye. "I always felt like it was watching me back," she says with a shudder. Then, remembering their shared secret, she flashes him a sympathetic look. "Sorry about your girlfriend, though."

Francisco winces. Eliza, they both know, has not shown up to work for several days. Even the warden doesn't know where she is, though she is apparently using official vacation time for her absence. In the meantime, an interim physician has been brought in, a fresh-faced young man who barely looks old enough to have made it through high school, let alone four years of medical school and a residency. Looking at him, Francisco feels impossibly ancient. He feels the weight of his innumerable lives like stones in his pockets, each one increasing his gravitational force with the totality of its moments: the mundane tragedies and simple blisses; the affection felt for lovers, parents, children; the loneliness of solitude; the tedium of labor; the feeling of every sinew, alive like music in his arms and legs; the endless foraging, for food first, then later for money and power; the uncomplicated appetites of his animal minds; and, perhaps most resonant of all, the crushing bloom of a million sunsets. They are all there, vivid as ever, in the reliquary of his body. Every cell must support a world.

A week passes. Then two. Still, Eliza doesn't return. He calls the cell phone number she once gave him, but there is no answer. He begins to despair of ever seeing her again.

Then one morning, while shaving, he has a sudden dizzy spell. His hands clutch the sides of the sink, and his sight fogs over. Before the cloud can lift, he seems to see an image of Eliza in his mind's eye, etched bright against the darkness. She is dressed in black, levitating over what appear to be rolling ocean waves. Her shining hair floats all around her. Her fingers are outstretched like ropes of seaweed, radiating light.

Francisco hurries to work, and sure enough, she is there, hair tied back in a ponytail instead of her standard bun and tanner than he has ever seen her. Her cheeks look flushed and healthy. She does not smile—she must still be angry with him—but he can't help feeling that she has retained a little of that unearthly light from his vision. Glimmers of moon are just visible beneath her fingernails. He wants to rush forward, to embrace her, but he doesn't dare.

Instead, she strides purposefully toward him. Her face is impassive, and he thinks perhaps she's going to punch him. He thinks, *Fine, yes, I deserve it. I will just stand here and let her do it.* But that isn't what happens. As she draws near, he sees the lines around her mouth begin to soften, her liquid eyes telegraphing something more complicated than anger.

With a sudden movement she pulls him close. Her right hand curls like a hook around his neck, nails digging into flesh as if to keep him from withdrawing again. Her other hand is somewhere in the vicinity of his waist, not unbuttoning his belt, but hanging onto it in a way that makes his whole body feel as if it has been flooded with electricity.

He wonders if he will die after all. Surely this is all too much for his enervated organs to withstand.

"There you are, you son of a bitch," she murmurs. "What do you have to say for yourself?"

"I…I'm so sorry."

"Good enough," she says.

And then she kisses him. The smell of her skin is overwhelming; like before, but with an added touch of coconut. Sunscreen, it has to be. From her time at the ocean. He thinks of the barely sensate beings they once were: what if they could have found one another in those pitch-black spaces? What if darkness and distance are in fact inconsequential? Indeed, as he kisses her back he feels that he is being permeated by all the previous versions of himself, these proto-selves no longer hovering in the air around him like nettlesome ghosts but at last coming to rest, locking into place, their infinite layers spanning inward like the rings of a massive tree. Like one of those ancient Redwoods up north.

God, he has missed her.

Clover, standing in line with her breakfast tray, whistles appreciatively.

Eliza, at last cognizant of the scene they are creating, pulls away, but not without giving the crowd of inmates a conspiratorial smile.

"Want to get some breakfast?" she asks him.

"Of course."

Next thing he knows they are sitting in the diner just across the road from Mea Culpa. The sun is not yet up, but the light of early morning is brightening the smudged window beside their table. It reminds him of so many breakfasts spent with his mother before she went to work, the blue light outside the perfect backdrop for whatever he chose to project onto it: a laugh at one of his jokes meant she was happy; an off-handed kiss meant that she loved him. He finds that he is able to accept these memories without feeling overwhelmed by them. He is devouring his eggs and bacon, hungry for the first time in ages, and the simple pleasure of eating is so profound that he feels tears spring to his eyes. It is as if the world around him, pressed flat for so long, has filled out into three dimensions again.

"Where did you go?" he asks her, between bites.

"Not far."

He smiles. "Surfing, right?"

She grins, surprised at his insight.

He chuckles to himself. "I knew it," he says.

"Well, anyway it helped. Surfing's the most calming thing you can possibly do. It's all about the body out there; the brain is only used for orchestrating the mechanics. And it's all very literal. There are no deep philosophical mysteries inherent in it, except whatever you bring to the table. Maybe that's the reason I became a doctor, come to think of it. But I had a real crisis, you know," she says defensively. "I needed to get away."

"Did your lives run out, too?"

"Oh yes, and I didn't know what to do with myself. I felt completely aimless. I've always had a strong sense of purpose, but all of a sudden…nothing. It was like skating off the edge of the planet. Like I was just floating there in dead space, already a corpse." She pauses to take a sip of her coffee. "I know that sounds morbid."

Francisco shakes his head. "No. I mean yes, it does, but I know what you mean. That's pretty much the story of my life. But I imagine it's worse to have had a sense of purpose and then lost it. I'm sorry."

"No, it's okay. I'll figure it out."

Eliza falls silent then. She seems suddenly shy, her fingers worrying the scarred sides of the ceramic mug. Touched, he places his hand over hers.

"When did you start surfing?" he asks gently.

"When I was a kid. My dads used to take me. I used to do a lot of competitions. I was even profiled in *Surfer* magazine. 'Twenty Young Surfers to Watch.'"

"Wow, for real? I didn't know that."

"You don't know a lot of things, in case you hadn't noticed," she says, favoring him with a wink.

"True," he says. "But I'd like to."

In fact, he finds that he wants more than that. He wants to make Eliza happy. The question is, does he have the temperament required to do so? He peers at her, suddenly awake to the labyrinthine tangle of selves that have converged to make her who she is today. She is truly an evolutionary wonder. If he is the poster child for repeating his mistakes—and God knows he is—then she is the ultimate example of nature perfecting itself through trial and error. Sure, there are a few flaws in the mix: moderate trust issues, a penchant for secrecy (she has yet to tell him who the two men were in the photo). But he would tolerate far more to remain in her orbit. He thinks of Hiroto, the great romantic. *I will channel that devotion. I will make myself into a perfect vessel for loving Eliza. This time it will be enough.*

"Let's run away together," he says suddenly. "Let's be reckless. Let's make our lives something our future selves would be thrilled to spy on."

She laughs—then, realizing he is serious, turns doubtful. "Where would we go?"

"I don't know," he says. "Somewhere cold. Maybe Alaska. Hilda would like that, I bet."

She looks down at her plate, contemplating. Her fork is poised in midair, as if time has stopped, and for a second he thinks maybe it has. Wouldn't it serve him right if this was the anomaly's parting shot? If his fluidity through the ages had caused him to become stuck somehow, suspending him in a moment of endless yearning? But no. There is a twitch of her arm. He sees her blink, and the spell is broken. She lifts the eggs again, placing them in her mouth.

"Past is past?" he ventures, hopeful.

But she is not yet ready to commit herself. Perhaps she still has not forgiven him, despite what she said. Perhaps she never will.

She takes in a long, slow breath, as if registering every stop of air along the way, as if asking the question of every ridge of tissue, every alveoli cluster that blooms along the path. And then she releases it, and he can see that the answer is already there, seeded within the molecules between them. He feels the great distance from which it has come, through bronchial tubes and trachea and the doorway of lips, of course, but also through girlhood dreams and the dreams of all her other selves, fanning out behind her like an endless train. *So many selves*, he thinks. *How lucky I would be if I could bring this one even a moment of happiness.*

Her gaze lifts to meet his own.

"Okay," she says finally. And in her smile, he sees expanses of future, sees the whole of the wild, splendid world. "Past is past."

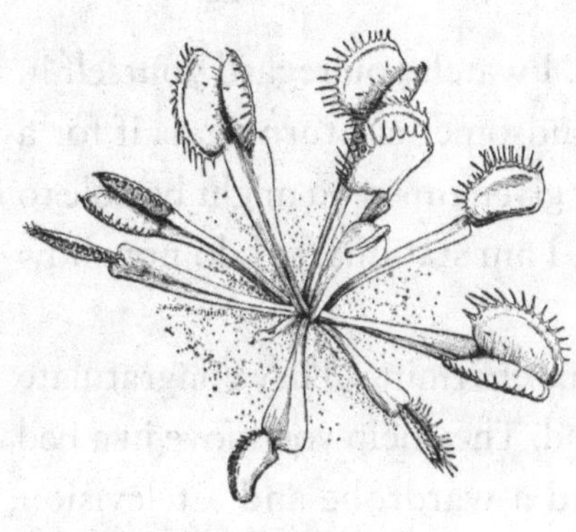

the lover lies within

YOU ENTER ME, AND AT FIRST I HOLD BACK. YOU ADMIRE THE FLOWERS IN THE PORCELAIN VASE BY THE FRONT DOOR. YOU EXPLORE MY MANY WINDOWS and rooms, my eaves and attic, even my cellar, with its earthy scent and its piled stone so cool you could rest your cheek against it and never feel feverish again. You declare me beautiful. Still, I am cautious. I am coy. Others have done the same, and they have fled soon enough. I am determined to reel you in carefully, so that by the time you understand what is happening you will already be in love with me. Step by step, I will draw you through the labyrinth to my bullish center, to my wild and beating heart. Your voice is music in my hallways. Your hand is a warm thrill upon my doorknobs. I watch you regard yourself in my mirrors, your handsome face turning as if for a photo, and I feel that given time you might be able to see the real me. Still, I am stationary. I do not show you what I can do.

Your friends find me charming. They congratulate you on your lucky find. They help you move in a bed frame and a sofa and a wardrobe and a television, all these physical extensions of you, sent forth like ambassadors of your personality, your designated truth tellers. Each item is a secret crossing over my threshold. And you have so much furniture. Coffee tables. Wingback chairs. One after another they fill me up, until I am fairly shivering with pleasure. I am so euphoric, in fact, that I cannot help but cry out, just for a moment. Everyone stops and listens. Your friends crane their necks and, after catching sight of one another, burst into riotous laughter. They say that it must have been the neighbor's hot wife going at it with the landscaper. But you are not so sure. You scan the room for several seconds longer, as if waiting for me to reveal myself, to cast up some kind of avatar, and I wonder if you felt my cry threading a silvery path through your bones, if you felt, somehow, that it was for you. Although my timbers quicken at the thought, it will not do. I resolve to be more discreet in the future.

In the mornings I keep myself bright, almost dazzlingly so, so that you will think of me fondly while you are at work. As soon as you step outside, though, I begin to dream. My vast empty rooms fill with images of those who were here before you, their faces decayed or melting like wax, their bodies reorganizing into all manner of grotesquerie. None of them were The One. None of them were like you. When you return in the evening, you prepare dinner, put on a movie or sit on the bench by the bay window, peering out at the darkening world. You bring home friends, girlfriends, coworkers; I sparkle for all of them. You make adjustments to me; I yield to you. New wallpaper in the great room. Modern faucets in the bathrooms and the kitchen. I do not mind. They are tokens of your love for me. One day you drop a bowl of masala dosa in the dining room, and it is such a gloriously domestic occurrence that I nearly allow a contented sigh to escape my vents. I think that I have never been so happy.

But soon I cannot help myself from taking things a bit farther. I memorize the cadence of your footsteps, play the sound aloud to myself when I think you are not listening. I make a game of rearranging your belongings. In the night, I funnel heat through my vents to cradle you in your bed, though it leaves icy spots in the hall. I know you do not like your toes to be cold. I fragrance my hallways with the scent of mangoes, your favorite fruit, so that when you awake, there is that first lingering breath of your birth country, a fleeting specter of remembrance to show that I know you. That I cherish you. That I can be all you need. My walls, floors grow thick and luxuriant while you sleep, expanding beyond their prescribed architectural boundaries. I bend low to meet you. I rise up like a tide. I buckle inward, snaring you within my concavity. I envelop you as in an amniotic sac, muffling all the sounds of the peripheral world so that your sleep may remain undisturbed. Once, I even dare to whisper your name.

Arjun.

Arjun.

You wake up, alarmed. It is too much. Sirens blare and the police arrive, do a quick walk-through then declare me free of burglars. I am properly chastened. I endeavor to show restraint. But of course that is easier said than done. I find myself marveling at your beauty, as once you marveled at mine. In the past my inhabitants were lighter of skin, and my wooden surfaces were always ash or birch. The hardwood floors, the doors, the built-in sideboard, all pale as a winter sun. Now I convert them to a fine mahogany, to match you. I think this will please you, but instead I can see you regarding me with dread. What is happening, you ask with a frown.

I have heard stories of houses, special houses, houses like *me*, which have managed to hold onto their residents for a lifetime. They do this by changing only a little at a time, in increments too small to notice. A spit coat of varnish here. A repaired newel post there. A bookcase arranged just the way the occupant likes it, though it was last left in disarray. Only much later, when the occupants have become old and eccentric, do the houses venture larger expressions of affection. It is then that a wish for light might translate to a new window; that a pair of bruised and diabetic feet might summon a soft carpet in the hall, a quiet ribboning down the staircase; that a midnight waking might cause the appearance of a bathroom directly across from the master bedroom. These houses are Zen masters of patience. I have never understood how to exercise such self-discipline. I love too soon, too recklessly, too often. There is a savagery in my love. And it has had its effect. Already, I can feel that I am losing you.

I try to make up for my mistakes. You complain of flies in the kitchen; I marshal all the ones I can find into the sewing room upstairs, a room you seldom enter. But I fail to account for the noise. You go to investigate and are instantly besieged by them, a thousand pinpoints of black peppering your face and limbs. And so you bring in the psychic who walks slowly through my rooms and mouths inanities and burns sage. She claims to see the flickering of spirits all around: a child drowned in the claw-foot tub; a man dangling from the balcony above the great room; a woman with wrists carved up like the Rosetta Stone. The latter, apparently, still holding the bloodied kitchen knife with which she did the deed. These accusations are patently absurd. There is nobody here but me. Still, I am on my best behavior while she is here, though it gives me pleasure to imagine the dust swirling into bright funnels around her, a sudden nebula of debris filling her lungs until her eyes go wide, her face slack. Of course, I do not do it. I remain as quiet as a mouse.

You are gone for a week, and when you return you station tiny statues in all of my shadowed corners, chanting some mantra about cleansing and rebirth. Is this what we have come to? I groan to let you know that you have wounded me, but you brush this off as well. Muttering to yourself, you blame the plumbing. How dare you. I am only trying to say: I do not like it when you leave me. I do not like it when you enter other houses. And I could keep you from leaving if I wished. You have a right to know this, and so the next time you use the upstairs bathroom I wedge the door shut tight. It is a small demonstration of my power. It is not a threat at all. Next, I cause plumes of water to come jetting up from the sink, to remind you of the kind of whimsy of which I am capable. I create for you a veritable geyser, high and strong and lovely. Your very own Vegas spectacle. The tiles at your feet become saturated, cementing your feet in place. Dark shapes bloom upon the porcelain like bloodstains. Am I not spontaneous? Am I not still charming to you?

You begin rattling the door with great violence. "Help!" you cry, to no one in particular. Wrenching your shoes free, you kick at my hinges until they are hanging limp and useless, until they resemble the mangled legs of an animal caught in a trap. Unimpeded, the door at last swings open. I vibrate with rage, with betrayal. Downstairs the wallpaper you placed begins to boil, bubbles spreading like a pestilence across its damasked surface. The chandelier lurches, responding to a shifting gravity. Something low and rumbling sounds from the cellar. I try to contain it, but it is too late. I am beginning to dream again. Soon there they are, vengeful, monstrous in form, their flesh hideously curdled, still curdling. They grapple for space in the narrow hall, and for the first time, I see your face disfigured with horror. This was not what I intended, I want to scream. I only wanted you to love me.

You make for the stairs and the front door, and I know that if I let you leave this time, you will never come back to me. I prepare one last gambit, an act of desperation. I loosen the portraits from the walls and drop them like grim Valentines all around you.

{crash}

Remember this? Remember when you placed the frame and smoothed your hand over my grain before driving in the nail, hard?

{crash}

Remember how I shook then, as if convulsing with joy?

{crash}

You thought you had done something wrong. You thought you had hurt me. You got out the stud finder, just to be safe.

{crash}

Remember how gently you managed it the next time? You were so careful, so tender. You wanted to do it right.

{crash}

So many pictures, and each one an intimacy.

{crash}

Just *look* at them.

{crash}

We have all these memories together, you and I. I know you. I love you. Don't leave me.

You reach the foyer, and the front door flies open, then shuts just as quickly. There is the sense of something rising up. A howling, whistling sound like just before a tornado hits. Know that you, my beloved, might have hidden in my skirts while I stood against the winds, my front lashed and battered, my shingles ripped from their underpinnings. I would have done whatever it took to protect you, even if it meant my own dissolution. The vase by the door moves through air that is suddenly viscous, shatters against something. The glass from the windows explodes into fragments. All my protean pieces laid bare. You never pursued the farthest reaches of me, nor even wanted to. You could not know what it would mean to truly inhabit me. You only loved me in my silence. You only wished to come and go as you pleased. But I am not an address. I am not a thing to be entered and abandoned. I am, and have always been, the destination. And now the winds are settling and I can see that the jeweled shards are radiating outward from a region on the floor, capturing the sun within each knife's edge, holding it there in a glowing rosette, a splayed mosaic that is the color of flesh and fire and lamentation.

It is over.

It is all over.

Time passes. I collect myself over the course of days, weeks, long idle months. At first the grief sweeps through me like a torrent through my ruined windows, but eventually I find that there is more of it on the outside than the inside. It keeps to the periphery, a starved coyote hanging back from a fire, and I am left with pleasant thoughts and only a few more dreams than usual. Once again, I begin to prepare myself. The rich pigment vanishes from my wooden beams, returning to a neutral maple. Broken things knit together: cornices, mirrors, lamps, the grandfather clock you never noticed had stopped at the stroke of midnight. Scratch marks on the door are drawn out like poison. Mysterious stains recede into the rugs and the grout. A fresh coat of wallpaper corsets my edifices. Finally, an unblemished vase of flowers materializes to grace the accent table in the front hall. I am ready to receive. I am all gloss and polish and shine. I am practically delirious with hope, because the next one is sure to be The One. You have to be. And until you come, I will remain in my perfect state of readiness, the most beautiful house on Earth, and as quiet as a mouse, just the way you want me to be.

Whoever you are, my love is waiting to swallow you.

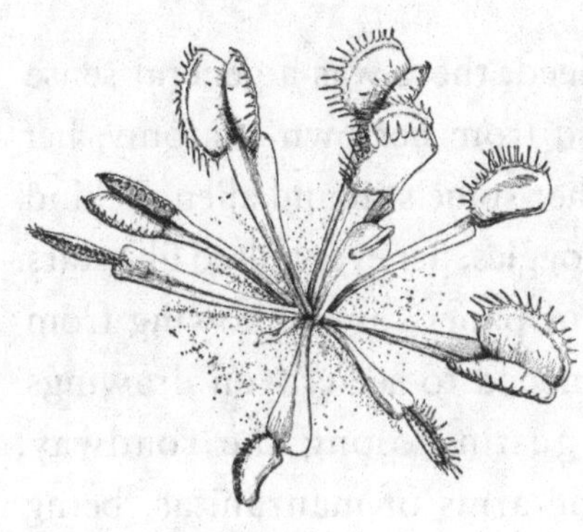

the moon side of the dark

HER HAIR WAS A DINGY FLAG THAT FLOATED BEHIND HER AS SHE RODE. IN THE HOURS SINCE SHE LEFT THE HOUSE, IT HAD BECOME DENSE AND KNOTTED LIKE seaweed, and there was no telling how many insects lay shipwrecked within its mass.

If it were any other day, Barbara would have been wearing her helmet. Motorcycle safety was one of the ways in which she hedged her bets against an otherwise reckless existence. But today, as she cruised down I-5 on her way to a funeral in Brawley, such precautions seemed downright quaint. The road could do nothing to her now. The heat, too, was incidental. It felt oddly remote, as if the skin that was baking inside her leather jacket belonged to someone else. Indeed, there was a general sense of being disconnected from her own anatomy: her fingers felt wooden, her spine stiff and alien. Behind her Steve McQueen goggles, her eyes pulsed like stars.

Just then a cloud of paper came billowing from her backpack. She turned to see crayon drawings and macaroni art gusting along the roadway, disappearing into the arms of manzanitas, being crunched under speeding tires. *They are all gone,* she thought, panicking. *All of Moon's gifts.* But no, there was her favorite, still curled like a universe in her pocket. There was the stone Moon had given her the last time they were together, when she and Raoul took her to Bombay Beach, under a hazy predawn sky, so that she could get over her fear of the water.

Barbara's own mother had been furious afterward.

"I can't believe you did this!" she had bellowed, her plump face turning pink with rage. "She's still a baby! She's too small for that kind of thing."

Barbara had just shrugged. "I could swim when I was her age."

"Yes, and look how *you* turned out. A little fear is a good thing sometimes."

Her mother had berated her awhile longer, enumerating all the misfortunes that could have befallen a child at the beach (drowning, hypothermia, tetanus from discarded soda cans), and when she was finished she shoved past Raoul and stormed off in the direction of the alfalfa fields. The screen door clattered like a skeleton in her wake.

That was three months ago. And yet it was this same woman who had called her last night at the house in Berkeley, her voice little more than an airy filament as she told her of the accident. "Something has happened to Moon," was all she could say. She, who had decreed that a seventeen-year-old was incapable of caring for an infant. She, who had forbidden Barbara from taking the child back to San Francisco, because of muggers and cultists and the evil influence of her hippie friends. She was the one who had let a toddler run wild over thirty acres of ranch land, day after day, until eager hands found the stones of a crumbling old well. Her mother wasn't overprotective at all, it turned out. It was only Barbara she didn't trust.

Now Moon was dead, her life's trajectory ended after three short years, and though Barbara could feel the questions burning like bile in her throat, she knew there would be no answers.

Moon's death was not an object that could be mapped.

AROUND NOON BARBARA DECIDED TO STOP AT A roadside diner. She ordered milk and hash browns and blueberry pancakes, the latter of which arrived on their own plate, stacked high like layers of sediment. As she tucked into this childlike meal, she felt hopelessly old. Older than the world. Older still because of the boys at the next table, who were talking and laughing about Patty Hearst, about the things her captors were said to have done to her, about the things they themselves would have done. Their faces were bright and smooth. They wore their hot rod T-shirts pulled taut over muscle. Their cruelty was an incandescent gem, as yet undimmed by experience. How much younger than her could they be? Two years? Three years? All she knew was that there was an uncrossable chasm between her table and theirs. It was like when Raoul's older brother had come back from Vietnam. He had been out of sync somehow, shuffled out of time. He had felt keenly the decay of his flesh, just as she was aware of the wrinkles even now taking shape around her eyes and mouth, those delicate imprints sinking ever deeper, patterned like cuneiform upon the soft places. Her face was a changing plain, the geologic history writ small. Already, she had survived epochs.

Just then one of the boys turned and began to leer in her direction. Her, with her daughter all but in the ground. She looked away quickly, and this prompted another eruption of laughter from the table. In other circumstances, she knew, she would probably have joined them. She would have simpered and cooed and pinched their biceps and tried to shock them with her crude language. Maybe picked the prettiest and led him into the bathroom, where it would have been like it always was his kind: the unpracticed hips thrusting blindly, the atavistic grunts, the hands that pinned her arms like insect wings against the dirty tiles, desperate for the one thing that was within her power to give.

Now, though, the thought of such a tryst only sickened her. With the briefest nod to her waitress, she paid her tab and left. She could feel the boys watching her as she climbed back on the bike, their eyes tracking the curve of her thigh as it lifted across the seat, piqued by the erotic suggestion of her ascent. It was indecorous, this watching, as if she were allowed to exist only in the form they chose for her. A mere totem for their consumption. She was no stranger to male attention—indeed, she had always found it exhilarating—and yet at the moment she couldn't bear to be scrutinized in this way. Not by these boy-heathens to whom her devastation was surely irrelevant.

Only when she pulled into traffic did the weight of their gazes finally slide off her frame. She leaned into the groove of the road, a mineral heart sheathed in brindled black, and let it speed her like a stone toward the horizon.

It was then that she saw the cow. It was not in a pen but perched atop small hill to the west. Its body was charcoal gray, its face white as a skull. It watched her progress with bovine disinterest, and she could see that it had a large opening in its side, ringed by wood: the kind of porthole that farmers sometimes installed to monitor the digestive system. But there was no farm in sight, nor any other mark of civilization, with the exception of the road itself. Nothing to explain the cow's presence in this place. As she looked on, she thought she saw something moving behind the porthole, something not green or mealy like one might expect, but black and shiny and hideous, pronged with antennae and feathered with what appeared to be tiny legs. Countless segmented bodies seemed to shuttle past the glass. They were legion, as if the cow were merely a sawhorse construct that would collapse if the vermin inhabiting it were removed. Unnerved, she fixed her eyes on the road again. For several miles, she looked neither to the left nor the right, and when at last she turned back, the cow was gone.

SHE HAD DONE HER BEST TO CREATE A DREAM WORLD for Moon. She had sent her collages that depicted her as a beautiful angel amid throngs of snowy birds. She had etched her name onto daisy petals. She had made necklaces for her out of felt and salvaged pieces of antique lace. On every visit, she had made sure to sweep Moon up in a host of adventures: building pirate ships, chasing aliens, playing Saint George and the Dragon, digging up the backyard for dinosaur bones. She had wanted her daughter's life to be magical, and, perhaps less nobly, she had wanted Moon to remember her above all others, to hold her first in her heart. A grandparent could be a caretaker, but a mother was forever. That's what she had thought.

Raoul had never understood how important she was, though Moon was probably his kid, too. Barbara was not even able to persuade him to come to the funeral. He hemmed and hawed and made excuses, until there was nothing left but to have a full-blown fight on the crumbling steps of the two-story house she and her roommates shared.

"I've got classes, Barbara…I can't just leave midsemester," he said, looking serene behind a curtain of shaggy black hair, his military jacket reminiscent of the one John Lennon liked to wear. The implication of his statement was very clear. *You're only a waitress. You don't know what it is to have real responsibilities.*

"I need you there with me," she pleaded, swallowing what remained of her pride. "I can't face my mother alone."

"You can do anything you set your mind to. Look, here's what you should do. You should take a nice long drive down there by yourself. Breathe the desert air, enjoy the scenery. Listen to the voice of creation for a while. It'll be good for you. By the time you get to Brawley you'll be able to face whatever you need to face."

"But it'd be so much easier if you were there with me."

"The things that are good for us aren't always easy."

"Please, Raoul. Consider it a favor. For me. For *her*."

"Why for her?"

She took a moment to smooth out her kurta before replying. "You know why."

His face tightened instantly, like a hand closing to a fist. "Don't lay that on me, Barbara. She was a nice kid, but she wasn't mine. It could have been anyone's, given your history."

She was so taken aback by this that for several seconds she couldn't respond. "You said you *liked* it that I was a free spirit," she finally sputtered.

"Look, there's free spirit, and then there's giving it away to any drifter who crosses your path."

And so on. In the end she threw on her jacket, stuffed her backpack full of artifacts, and took off by herself, on the Harley her own father had left rusting in the barn when he'd disappeared over a dozen years earlier. (At first Barbara's mom thought he had run off with one of the waitresses from Lulu's Tavern, but the truth was far worse than that. He just hadn't wanted them for his family anymore.)

SOMEWHERE NEAR BAKERSFIELD, BARBARA WAS forced to pull off the road. She could feel the sun listing to the west, could feel it tugging against her shoulder blades, and all at once she realized that she was separated from Moon not only by death, but also by the passage of time. It had already been twenty-four hours since the accident. She likely wouldn't get to Brawley until morning, and by then it would have been another twenty-four hours. That was two full days her daughter would have waited for her, while whatever was left of her spirit receded farther and farther into the mist, her imprint at last fading from the visible world.

She was overtaken by a vision of Moon's final moments. In her mind everything was black, like a stage play, and there was only a narrow spotlight illuminating the girl's willowy form. Moon laughed and spun in a circle, making outrageous helicopter sounds with her mouth. Her hair, golden and gossamer, lifted like a nimbus around her cherub's face. Suddenly, she went still. Her eyes fell closed. Her arms lowered to her sides and, like a bulb delivered from a gardener's hand, she slipped quietly into a hole in the earth.

Alone. Her little girl died alone.

It was more than Barbara could endure.

She had barely dismounted when her body gave way beneath her, crumpling like a marionette to the ground.

MINUTES, PERHAPS HOURS, PASSED, BEFORE THE whirr of a siren brought her back to herself. A burly policeman, also on a motorcycle, had pulled up on the shoulder beside her. He took his sweet time getting down, murmured something into his radio, and then did the slow policeman-walk over to where Barbara was sitting, still slumped among the thistle sage. For a moment he just stood there with his arms akimbo, radiating waves of disapproval. She almost laughed, in spite of everything. He reminded her of her mother.

"What's going on here, ma'am?"

Drying her cheeks with her sleeve, she tried to appear calm.

"I'm fine, Officer. It's just…there was a death in the family. I haven't been drinking or anything."

"I see." His eyes were concealed by a pair of reflective sunglasses, but she could sense them appraising her, combing the details of her appearance for clues to her mental state. "Could you stand up for a sec, please?"

Irritably, Barbara got to her feet. Without being asked, she placed one sneaker in front of the other and proceeded to walk a straight line to the mileage post and back. It was only about ten yards away, but she walked with such pointed deliberation that it took her several minutes to complete the circuit. When that was done, she stared hard into those buglike sunglasses and touched her nose several times with each finger.

"Is that good? Should I say the alphabet, too?"

"No, ma'am. There's no reason to get upset, ma'am. I was just checking."

With a sigh, she plopped down on the ground again.

"So you didn't have an accident?" he asked uncertainly. "I can call an ambulance.

"No. Like I told you, I just…had to stop."

"I see." He seemed to accept this. "Who was it?"

"Who was what?"

"The death in the family."

For some reason the question startled her. It was as if she had forgotten for a moment the specific source of her distress, and it took this man's words to remind her.

"It was my daughter," she said at last. "She was three."

The cop let out a low whistle. He turned back to the road, instinctively eyeing the passing cars before letting his gaze drift across the desert and over to where the mountains lay like a string of half-formed animals, burnished by afternoon light. Without warning then, he squatted down beside her. He removed his helmet and his sunglasses, and for the first time she could see the sandy brush-cut hair, the creased forehead, the opaque green eyes.

"I lost my boy last year," he said finally, his voice flat. "It was a drunk driver. I'd just bought him a new glove for Little League, but he never got to use it. He was a catcher, a real natural athlete."

She cleared her throat. "What was his name?"

"Ryan. He'd just had his eighth birthday party. What about your daughter?"

"Moon," she said. "Her name was Moon."

He nodded. There was no judgment. No eye rolling at the name.

And so she sat upon a mound of gravel, exchanging sorrows with a stranger. The cop didn't pat her hand or initiate some kind of awkward consolation hug (thank God). But she could hear him breathing, could hear the catch in his lungs that was the same as her own, like a diamond embedded in soft tissue. Had he healed at all in the year since his boy had been killed? Were such wounds even capable of healing? She could conceive that over time her own pain might begin to lessen somewhat, might begin to deliquesce—there, at the crossways of air and blood. And yet it was impossible to imagine that she would ever be without it. It had set its banner in her. It had sown its tumors deep within her flesh: a veritable fossil record of grief.

BACK ON THE ROAD, SHE SOON FOUND HERSELF crossing into Angeles National Forest.

Things hadn't changed much since she had gone camping there as a kid. Fir trees blanketed the mountains, and the canyon slopes were dotted with patches of hardy chaparral. She passed waterfalls, rocky plains, and the man-made Pyramid Lake, which glittered beneath the setting sun like a sheet of colored glass. She caught glimpses of local wildlife returning to their dens and burrows: rattlesnakes, scrub jays, rabbits, mule deer, and the occasional mountain lion. She even kept her eye out for a condor, although she was certain she wouldn't see one. They were the rarest of the rare, hunkering in caves and along cliff faces, blithely carrying the banner for their dying species like some mythological creature that had outlasted the gods.

Riding through these luxuriant woodlands, Barbara felt strangely hollow. She was cognizant of the beauty around her—it hung thick upon every surface—and yet it seemed to her that it had been stripped of all its power to impress. It was a trap without bait. An empty vessel. She held out her hand and let it pass right through her.

The houses started up again as soon as she exited the forest. Just a few at first, like lookouts on the edge of the wilderness, but it wasn't long before they were lying in phalanxes across the hills and spilling into the valley. Santa Clarita loomed. As she entered the city limits, Barbara was surprised to discover that the dead-rat sensation building in her stomach was more than just dread at the thought of the funeral; it was also hunger. Pure, visceral hunger, despite her heavy lunch. *I thought bereavement caused you to lose your appetite*, she marveled. But there was no mistaking the pangs, and so she pulled up to the first establishment that promised to serve a hot meal. It made no difference to her that it was a rundown bar with flickering neon lights and a latticework of bike tracks outside. She'd been in seedier places.

Inside, she quickly threw back a mammoth hamburger and a mug of chilled root beer. (She considered ordering an actual beer, but she had left her fake ID in the dresser drawer at home, and the bartender didn't seem like the forgiving type.) The man at the end of the bar looked like Peter Fonda. He winked when he caught her watching, then tipped his head toward the jukebox, where a biker and his girlfriend were undulating to the sweet-sad twang of a country song. For a long moment she considered the offer. She already knew what it would be like to dance with this man, to have her arms wrapped tightly around his sunburned neck, the scent of ancient sweat lifting to her nostrils. His palms would be resting on her buttocks, pressing her toward him. His breath would be redolent of smoke. He would lean close and tell her about his wife, how she nagged him, how she didn't understand, and she would murmur sympathetically in response, moving her hand downward and across the front seam of his jeans, holding her breath as the terrain began to shift beneath her fingertips, the mountain rising from the plain. She could do all this and then she could turn to leave, and although he would surely protest, she knew that he would be seasoned enough to accept no for an answer. Not like the boys at the diner, who would have sunk their teeth into her neck and held on until she followed through.

She wanted to say yes to the man. She longed for the simplicity of his lust, for the province of forgetting such a dalliance would provide. But it seemed to her that every choice she made was now a referendum on Moon's short life. There was nothing for it. She shrugged on her leather jacket, her modern suit of armor, and returned to the road.

SHE HAD BEEN TOO YOUNG FOR WOODSTOCK. TOO young for Janis Joplin, for the sexual revolution, for the narrow-hipped boys who strummed guitars and wore strings of wooden beads around their slender necks. And yet ever since she left home at the age of fifteen she had been trying to surf the afterglow of that mythos. She had sought out the one place that was a flagship for this lost era, fled there as to a lover. Indeed, as the gleaming buildings first appeared on the horizon she had sensed the city waiting for her like a restless bride, laying itself bare before her hand, offering up its ghosts, its bohemian glamor, its tangled, protean histories.

She had arrived in San Francisco with forty dollars in her pocket (lifted from her mother's purse), and as such, she had been forced to take refuge in a shelter until she found a job. But she did not begrudge even a minute of her new life. She welcomed the seaborne fog into her lungs. She cherished the glare of the streetlights, which dazed her and kept her eyelids veined with angels. She gave herself over to street fairs and afternoons spent listening to borrowed blues records and Salvadoran tamales that were so hot they left blisters in her eager mouth. She felt she had become a raw and shimmering creature, a tortoise stripped of its shell, and she was terrified at every moment that her mother would show up in the dusty Ford to drag her ass back home.

This is why she had stayed, even after it had all become familiar and even trite. Even after Moon was born. It was *her* place. It was the place where she had unearthed her true self and then liberated that self into oblivion. But it was not as if she had ever forgotten about her daughter while she was spinning out her particular brand of chaos. Moon had been with her the whole time, spliced into her heart like shrapnel. Like a second soul that dreamed within her.

THE CITY SLOWED HER DOWN CONSIDERABLY. ONCE she had switched to I-10 heading east, the traffic was so stagnant she could hardly remain upright on her bike. She began to despair of making it out of the county before nightfall. And then all at once, the worst of it was behind her. She sailed past Pomona, Colton, Redlands.

It was growing dark by the time she reached the country. Her thoughts lost focus, lulled by the ever-present hum and the vibrations of the motorcycle, and though there was not a conscious feeling of letting go, there was a definite easing of spirit, as of a burden temporarily lifted. Not wishing to rouse herself from this dream state, she retreated into the rhythm of her breathing. She found a stillness. Something like peace. For the first time in days she did not mourn; she merely existed.

Before long, though, something began to take shape on a rocky outcropping ahead of her. Little by little it came into being, patches of gloom that coalesced like storm clouds, and with a start she recognized it as the cow she had seen before. It did not graze, only peered at her dully. Its eyes followed her as she came up alongside it. Once more, she gaped at its hulking form, the gray hide turned a dusky purple in the twilight, the face the same eerie mask of bone. Once more, she saw a swarm of teeming carapaces within the cannula. But now, the porthole was open. Creatures were spilling out of it, a veritable geyser of them, roiling, tumbling over one another, blackening the scrub by the cow's feet. In terror, she sped past, and this time she did not look back.

JUST OUTSIDE BANNING, A MOTEL UNCOILED ITSELF on the horizon. Before long she was flopping down on a cool-sheeted bed where, despite her fear and exhaustion, she lay awake for hours, squinting at the glowing clock face across the room. She had to sigh at this. While she was pregnant, she had had eyes like a hawk. Even in the first few months she had noticed the world drawing into keen focus around her, its once-feathered edges solidifying, turning strangely sharp. She had heard that such a change during pregnancy was normal. And yet it seemed to her that some of Moon's traits were leaking into her, that the umbilical cord was in fact a bidirectional pathway. From her deep-space cocoon, the daughter loaned the mother her liquid brilliance. Barbara's flaxen hair looked shiny for once. Her dreams turned primitive, full of blood and bone. Everything seemed more fragrant, and each odor contained a distinct olfactory signature that could be charted along an ever-expanding spectrum. The architecture of her body changed as well. Brick by brick it shifted, its convexity mimicking the curvature of the earth, so that at times she thought that she would give birth not to a person but to an entire planet, complete with its own gravity, its own hothouse atmosphere. She often felt that she was haunted. And she found she didn't mind.

Motherhood was harder than pregnancy, though. Moon was a colicky newborn, and Barbara was up every hour of the night with her—rocking, nursing, changing her little cotton diapers. Nothing could keep the child pacified for long. Singing a lullaby might buy her five minutes of peace, while a warm bottle of milk might garner ten. After that, the crying would inevitably resume, so that before long the girl's sobs began to form a connective thread, an endless wail twining the mother's days. Sometimes she felt that she was looking at a different species altogether. It was as if her daughter was actually some faerie child, left by mistake, with needs that were simply beyond Barbara's capacity to provide. (Even the condition of Moon's fingernails seemed to confirm this. Those tiny pearls, which had been so perfect, so lustrous, at the moment of her birth, appeared to be growing dull in the absence of some ethereal ingredient.)

Then there was her mother. Though she doted on Moon, she seemed to regard Barbara's own struggles as a fundamental life lesson, a lesson that she was apparently doomed to relearn each day, like Prometheus chained to his eternal rock. "You made your bed," the woman would say with a thin-lipped smile, and Barbara would try not to reply with a crack about how a dirty mattress didn't really qualify as a bed.

After six months of such tensions, Barbara began planning the move back to Berkeley with her daughter. The solution was ideal. It was easy to imagine Moon as a rosy-cheeked child of a village, with stars on her temples and a host of honorary parents revolving in her orbit. She would have freedom. She would have friends her own age. She would have music and organic tomatoes and more love than she could possibly absorb. And, of course, she would have the span of the city itself, with its thousand wild avenues to explore.

Her mother, naturally, wouldn't hear of it.

(Looking back, she wondered if she should have taken Moon anyway, simply absconded with her in the night. But she had been so young, and her mother's word had seemed irrefutable. It had not even occurred to Barbara to defy her.)

When it was time to go she entered her old room and found Moon fast asleep in her crib. She was lying on her stomach with her head turned slightly to the side, a puddle of drool issuing from her mouth like a voice bubble in a comic strip. Barbara wondered then: What would the child say to her if she were awake? With her toddler's vocabulary, would she even have the language to articulate what she felt about the mother's departure? Or was she still little more than a sea of raw emotion, an inchoate creature, ragged at the edges, gliding through each day as if it were a dream? For a long moment she just stood there, drinking in her daughter's scent. She stroked the tangles of her mermaid hair. And then, without a word, she left.

BARBARA AWOKE EARLY, EAGER TO GET ON THE ROAD, only to discover that her muscles were all coiled up in knots from the previous day's riding. Every inch of her was sore. Her arms could not be moved without excruciating pain, while her legs felt as though they had been strapped to hard wooden plates. She hobbled into the shower, and it was only then, amid the ministrations of the hot water, that her limbs began to give up some of their stiffness, to regain a portion of their former character. A bright halo of steam enveloped her. She stood for a long time in its radiance, combing insects like jewels from her hair, and as her senses returned she fell to contemplating the mercurial shell that was the human body. Like the mind, it seemed a thing of hopeless fragility. The smallest pressure could slip it out of joint.

She performed a quick inventory of her backpack before setting out. Just as she had feared, most of her daughter's drawings had been lost to the wind and the road, but there were still two that remained: a self-portrait of Moon beneath a starry sky, and another in which she was encircled by cows from the ranch, all with identical U-shaped grins. They were not much, but they were enough to light a small lantern in her heart. A flicker of calm within the storm. With great care she folded them into her dog-eared copy of *Siddhartha* and placed everything back in the pack (making sure to zip it properly this time).

And so she began the last stretch of her journey.

The sun flared up ahead of her, a blinding brilliance like diamonds scattered across the asphalt. It was all she could do to keep her eyes fixed on the yellow line, holding to it like a tether in order to keep from becoming engulfed. There, on the cusp of the light, she occupied her own discrete universe. Free from pain. Free from the vagaries of human relationships. Free from sensation, for the most part. The only clear sounds were those emanating from the motorcycle, and from the torrential wind, which whipped and battered at her borrowed black dress, forming dusky whorls behind her knees.

Her thoughts remained largely shapeless as she followed the languid curves of I-10, veering southward through Indio. It was only when she switched over to Highway 111 that reality began to seep back in. This, after all, was the road that would take her home. It would carry her around the flank of the Salton Sea, lifting like a ribbon and setting her down among the quaint pile of bricks that was Brawley. She could feel the town waiting for her. There were the abandoned gas stations, the peeling stucco walls, the ruined streets that tasted of chili peppers and cattle dung and ash. There was the ranch, which even in her childhood had seemed to exist on the margins of something terrible. There was her sanctimonious mother, lately fallen from grace. And somewhere, arrayed in lamplight like a Templar's mystery, there was the outline of a tiny casket. The box that contained the world.

The sea appeared right on cue. It was laid out like a mirror before her, like a vast panel folded over with silver leaf, and she found that the sidereal gleam of its surface was almost too painful to view in its totality, even with her darkened goggles. She focused instead on smaller sections of the whole. The shallows were green and foamy, the beach gypsum-white. Herons fished noisily in their coves, while itinerant algae blooms drifted like armadas in search of a war. Farther out, she was able to observe jet trails on the skin of the sea, limned by various watercraft. On and on it went, and before she knew it she had reached the chalky shores of Bombay Beach. Hungrily, she grasped the stone in her pocket, its coolness a coveted memory in and of itself. Any second now she would see the exact place. Any second. And then there it was, inexorable as destiny: a gently cambered strand bordered by a dock. Where she had left the cooler. Where she had strapped on Moon's sandals. Where she had swept the girl up in her arms the moment she began to cry, her hooded frog towel dropping like a husk into the surf.

Barbara began to feel that she was coming loose at the edges, that if she glanced in the rearview mirror she would be able to discern a milky glimmer in the air where her bike had been, a telltale smudge of particles along the gray lanes.

It was in such a trance that she completed the forty-minute trek back to Brawley. She barely noticed when her favorite bandanna flew free of her hair, disappearing like a fox into the ubiquitous brush.

OUTSIDE THE CHURCH, SHE PRETENDED TO SEARCH through her backpack. She muttered to herself, noisily shoving things around, and when the funeral guests passed by she gave them a quick, apologetic smile, as if she regretted not being able to welcome them properly. When they were gone she set the backpack down again. She focused her attention on a nearby park bench, where a boy was reading a book about Watergate. The boy was tall and sinewy, and for an electric moment Barbara thought that it was Raoul, come to surprise her. But then he looked up and smiled at her, and she could see that the face wasn't quite right. The line of his jaw was too soft; the eyes were too far apart. There was also the peace sign tattoo missing from his upper arm. *I was stupid to think he would change his mind,* she thought. Sinking inwardly, she cast her gaze toward the Mission Revival buildings that framed the church square. She stared hard at those shadowed archways, trying to tease out shapes from the darkness, until at last a new group of mourners approached and the charade of searching began again.

She didn't want to talk to anyone.

She didn't want to go inside.

All she wanted to do was climb back on her bike and keep riding, eastward maybe, where she could lose herself in the scattered lineaments of a country. She imagined the path she might take: first through Vegas and Meteor Crater, then north into Utah, where she could take a lesson in buoyancy, floating upon the prehistoric dream that was the Great Salt Lake. After that, she might just wander for a while, weaving between the smokestacks of Chicago, Detroit, Pittsburgh, New Jersey, their sooty threads forming a web across the sky, a map to forgetting. She glanced at her watch. Why not leave right now? Why not skip this sham of a funeral and let the highways of America absorb her misery? She could transform herself into one of those wandering Beat disciples who used *On the Road* as a travel almanac. She could ride an endless pilgrimage from coast to coast while adventures unspooled from her tires like so much twine. She could sleep like a gypsy beneath the stars. She could fall in love with strangers. She could survive.

Moreover, she could ignore the specter of the cow that, even now, waited atop the old railroad depot.

She was just about to make a break for it when she caught a glimpse of old Mrs. Gurevich, her second-grade teacher, shambling up the walk. It was too late for the backpack routine; eye contact had been made. So Barbara composed herself while the woman made her slow advance, inexorable as death, her cane tapping secrets on the newly dried cement.

"You're awfully sweaty," Mrs. Gurevich said at last, peering through horn-rimmed glasses. Her expression was every bit as grim as Barbara remembered.

The woman had used the paddle on her once. Barbara had come in late from recess, hand in hand with Robbie Logan, and Mrs. Gurevich had dragged them both to the coat room where for ten minutes they took turns getting soundly walloped. Him. Then her. Then him. Then her. It was the first time she had ever been spanked in front of another child, and she recalled how quickly the shame of it had become a tangible thing, how it had bloomed in Robbie's cheeks and in the twin mounds of his bare ass, how it had floated among the dust motes and lingered in her nose, thick and acrid, like the scent of something putrid. The physical pain had been nothing in comparison.

"It's California in the summertime," she explained. "And I don't have AC on my bike."

"You rode a bicycle all the way from San Francisco?"

"A motorcycle."

"Oh," said the old woman. "Well, no matter. I suppose everyone will understand."

"What with the grieving, you mean?"

Mrs. Gurevich ignored the sarcasm and gave her a curt nod. "Yes. It's just too bad there wasn't time for you to take a shower. You *could* be a little more presentable."

Barbara could only shrug at this. All along she had been dreading the impending confrontation with her mother, hoping to postpone it at least until after the ceremony, praying that her mother wouldn't be waiting for her, scavengerlike, atop those wide granite steps. And yet this was almost worse. She felt weighted down, trapped in place by this strange, caustic woman who carried with her a cloud of painful memories, who didn't even have a reason to be there. Soon more guests trickled by—water moving around stone. Her volleyball coach. Her former best friend, with whom she had lost contact after the move. Some kids she knew from FFA. The ranch hands and their wives and children: the boys with their oddly immaculate white linen trousers, the girls with their dark hair carefully plaited. She smiled at them all as they passed.

And then they were gone, and it was just the two of them again. Mrs. Gurevich had not left her side.

"Thank you for coming," Barbara said finally.

"It's nothing," the woman said, looking away. "I was in the neighborhood."

The sound of the organ began to rise up on the wind. "Blest are the Pure in Heart." Barbara wondered if this was the same arthritic organist who had kept a pewter flask tucked into his shirt pocket during services, covering it with his hand whenever kids came up to examine the controls.

Mrs. Gurevich said something then, but Barbara couldn't quite make it out.

"I'm sorry, what?"

"I said, you must be very angry with your mother."

Barbara turned to her, astonished. All she had heard up to that point were the euphemisms, the promises of "a better place," the whispered platitudes that lapped up against her ankles and slid off the hard edges of her suffering. It had not occurred to her that it was possible to speak plainly of such things. Now, it was as if some secret incantation had been pronounced, some magical phrase that had swept back the curtain of civilized discourse. *Finally*, she thought. *Someone who understands.*

Mrs. Gurevich stared back at her, waiting for a reply, but Barbara was not yet ready to concede anything to her one-time enemy. After a moment, the woman went on.

"I would be very angry if I were you. She should not have let the child run around unattended."

"I'm sure she did her best," Barbara offered lamely.

The old woman continued to peer at her through her thick glasses, which had the effect of making her eyes look small and shrewd. Her nose, too, was sharper than Barbara remembered.

"You do not believe that," she said simply. "I did not believe it when my sister left my twins in the back of a hot car, where they were baked like a couple of Brötchen rolls. She swore she forgot they were there. Maybe she did forget. Either way, she did *not* do her best."

For a second Barbara couldn't even breathe. She took a halting step backward, as if the words themselves might contaminate her, as if they might worm through her already fragile shield of self-possession and leave her naked and trembling before the elements. It was shocking. And yet she was certain she had heard this story before. Twin boys, wasn't it? But it had been a rumor only, a whisper that had been passed down from students who were older and more worldly. It existed in that same apocryphal category as the stories she heard at scout camp, stories featuring evil dolls and hitchhikers and sex perverts who wouldn't stay buried. It was both believed and not believed.

"Mrs. Gurevich, I'm so sorry…"

She waved this away impatiently. "No. You do not need to do that with me. We may be the only two people in town who understand each other right now. This is how I know that you are angry."

"Of *course* I'm angry," Barbara snapped. "My baby girl is dead. You don't have to be some kind of mind reader to figure out that I'm angry."

Several more families were coming up the walk then. She spied a little girl about Moon's age, wearing a white ruffled dress that lifted on the wind and provided a beautiful contrast with her mocha-dark skin. As the girl turned her dreamy gaze skyward, Barbara found herself wanting to scoop her up, to gather her in her arms and set up a hearth for her, far away from that hateful rubbish heap of a town. She wondered if the girl and her daughter had known each other—if they were friends. Was there perhaps a seed of grief nestled within those birdlike ribs? A tiny bruise left like a thumbprint on her heart?

Remember, she wanted to tell the girl. *Please remember*.

But she was small.

She would inevitably forget.

The door closed behind the girl, and Barbara turned to see that Mrs. Gurevich was still staring at her. Apparently waiting for something. It suddenly occurred to her that there was more to this interaction than social awkwardness. Leaning forward onto her cane, her visage taut and eager, the woman looked almost ghoulish. Barbara could almost see the beetles falling from her mouth.

"What do you want me to say?" Barbara finally exploded. "Yes, it's true. I trusted Mom to take care of Moon, and look what happened. After all those years of lecturing *me* about how I lived my life. After telling me I didn't apply myself and didn't have good morals, and then I had Moon, and it didn't matter how much I loved her…I was still a terrible mother. And you know why? Because I'm selfish, and I could never put another person's needs before my own. That's what she said. And then she goes and does something like *this*. I mean, a car accident I could at least understand. But she wasn't even paying attention when it happened! She was too busy with her own routine. Too busy patching fences and checking the goddamn cows for ringworm.

She wasn't thinking about Moon at all while she was down in that well…*dying*…"

With that, the last of her composure crumbled. She began sobbing into her hands, wailing, not even caring who saw. It was just like the day before, when she sat slumped and broken by the roadside, except that the proximity to her daughter's body seemed to make the pain that much more acute. There was no hiding from it now. There was no wrapping it around her, cloaklike, until it blotted out the stars and obscured the singularity of its origin. This pain was all-encompassing. Furthermore, it had changed in its essential character. It was now threaded through with a righteous anger, which flowed hot and metallic, burning up her veins like an madeup element from a comic book, making her all but radioactive. She began to apportion her hatred as if dispensing pieces of a pie. The largest slice, naturally, went to her mother, but there was also sufficient quantity held in reserve for the funeral guests, with their proud, pitying glances, and for Raoul, who got her pregnant in the first place. A slightly larger piece was allocated to Mrs. Gurevich, for polluting the occasion with her baroque bitterness. Last of all, she presented a sliver to the God of her childhood, who could have prevented the accident, but didn't. Wasn't the reverend always preaching of a loving God? And yet there she was, and all she could see was a God who remained aloof in the face of tragedy, who kept his own counsel, who was silent toward his people even when their sorrows had grown so great that they began to leak through the skin, displaying like tattoos, like India ink across their fragile features.

Mrs. Gurevich looked on, stoic. Perhaps there was a hint of exhilaration behind her eyes, but Barbara could not have said for certain. "Better to cut her off from your life," she said with a nod. "That's what I did. People like her are a malignancy that must be removed."

Standing there, with her face in her hands, Barbara was inclined to agree.

But then another group passed into the church, and in the brief space before the door whickered shut she happened to catch a glimpse of her mother, stationed beside the pastor at the front of the sanctuary. Even in a sea of black, the woman was unmistakable. She stood with her arms on her hips, issuing orders to anyone who would listen, and while she spoke she scanned the crowd for her wayward daughter, her head turning slowly like a lighthouse beacon. Barbara could hardly believe how haggard the woman looked. Ten years seemed to have elapsed since their last encounter. The brown-and-pewter curls were oddly limp, the pumps were shabby, and she was dressed in an ill-fitting suit that only accentuated her ample belly. (Was it possible that her once-discriminating mother had purchased this outfit from the local thrift store?) Even from a distance, Barbara could tell that her eyes harbored enormous bags, which she had not even attempted to camouflage with make-up.

Seeing her mother in this diminished state, she felt an unwelcome stab of sympathy. *Well*, she thought, *and why* wouldn't *she look like hell*? She was the one who had found Moon, after all. She was the one who had seen that tiny cherub's face glistening at the bottom of a long dark tunnel, scraped and bruised and emptied of its last vestige of life. Barbara could only imagine the grim minutes that must have passed while her mother tried to decide what to do. Should she call an ambulance? Wait for the firefighters to show up and retrieve the body? In the end, she had gone to fetch the rodeo rope from the barn. She had anchored it to the old willow tree, lowered herself down, and reemerged with a dead child strapped to her chest. The scene flared up in Barbara's mind, scorching her with its clarity. She could see the woman laying her daughter out as if she were one of her precious china dishes. She could see her mother's body folded over with anguish. She could see her doing chest compressions, even though she knew better, even though it was obviously too late, breathing again and again into that ruby mouth while the ground swayed and the sky blazed blue and tragedy broke over her like a wave.

Barbara didn't know if she would be able to forgive her mother for what she had done. But she didn't want to fight her now, either. It was too much, too wearying.

Across the street, the roof of the railroad depot stood empty.

"I think I should go inside now, Mrs. Gurevich," she said. "Thanks for coming." She didn't turn around as she said this, knowing the old woman would not follow her inside. The funeral wasn't what she had come for.

Instead, Barbara touched the stone in her pocket. She caught a whiff of saltwater on the breeze, and for the first time since the accident she gave herself over completely to the pull of memory, to the synaptic dream that deposited her once more onto a beach in early morning, that bid her examine the hazy-gray sky, so that she was no longer looking at it between a curtain of upraised fingers but instead taking in the whole of the panorama it encompassed, teasing out every ripple, every bird, every piece of floating driftwood.

Once again she was setting up camp, she and Moon and Raoul.

Once again her daughter helped her with the cooler.

Then in they went, and once again Moon's tiny feet were stepping gingerly, as if the beach were a thing that might shatter her, or might itself break beneath her weight. Her eyes were pilgrim-wide at the sight of the lathery waves. Her hand gripped Barbara's like a lobster's claw. And yes—she began to cry. But before long she grew more confident, so that by the time the first rays of light spread over the water she was laughing and splashing there in the surf, glittering like a fish in her rainbow suit, like a creature born of the sea. Barbara watched her play, wishing she could stay there forever. She wished she could cast off her other life, the shallow pleasures of San Francisco, and embed herself in those moments where ropes of willowy hair clung like tentacles to tiny shoulders, where a child's back formed a smooth pillar, arching against the tide. Barbara loved her, it was true. But it was Moon's love for her that had been the true revelation. It had taken her entirely by surprise. It was largely inexplicable given her long absences, and yet there she was, giddy with adoration, beaming at Barbara as if she had never left her side. There was her arm lifting into a golden crescent high above her head, just as a noisy speedboat passed behind, and although Barbara could no longer hear her voice, she could see that the girl's lips were forming her name, could see that she was calling out to her, to the only mother she would ever have in this world. She was reaching across tissues of space, drawing her toward her.

Before Barbara knew it, she was stepping through the door.

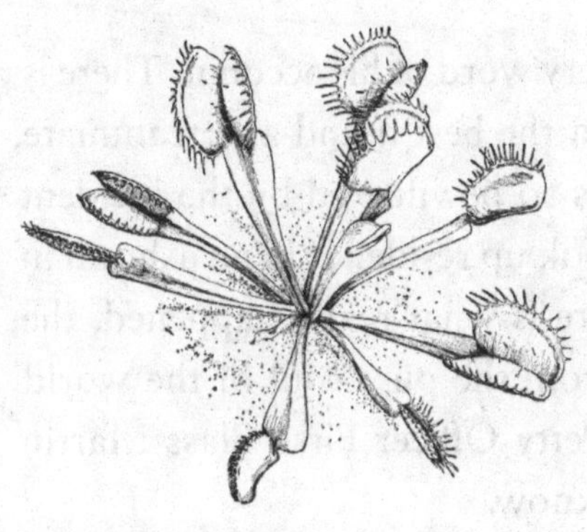

the transfiguration of martin velasquez

NOT LONG AGO, IN A WORLD THAT WAS EITHER REAL OR IMAGINED, AN EVENT TOOK PLACE. BECAUSE THERE WERE MULTIPLE WITNESSES, THIS EVENT IMMEDIATELY fractured into pieces, each one reflecting the specific experiences and worldview of the observer. No one could agree on even the most basic of details. His hands were clutching at his throat. His hands were stretched out as if to embrace the planet.

The newspaper, of course, contains its own version of truth. "Navy SEAL Dies HALO Jumping Over Yuma." *This* truth is a catalog of facts, and it is accurate up to a point. Next you have the report of the man in charge of the team of SEALs, Senior Chief Petty Officer John Bowman, whose personal religious convictions color every word of his account. There is also the testimony of the best friend and teammate, Len Miller, who was so bewildered by the incident that he eventually took up residence in an ashram in India. And then there is what really happened, the truth that springs from the pure soul of the world, which no one but Petty Officer First Class Martin Velasquez will ever know.

On the day in question, the team was flown to a height of about 31,000 feet, where, one by one, they stepped into space, beginning their speedy descent toward earth. Because of the altitude, they wore helmets and oxygen masks, as well as the special thermal underclothes that would insulate them from the subzero temperatures. It was to be a standard drill. Jump at thirty-second intervals. Check altimeter function. Check helmet, oxygen, combat pack. Note location of teammates both above and below. Deploy chute at 4,000 feet, the standard high altitude/low opening. Free fall of 27,000 feet, which is time enough for about ten Hail Marys, if you're into that sort of thing.

But the question of height was irrelevant in the case of Martin Velasquez. He was dead for the majority of his fall. He had only dropped about 3,000 feet, in fact, when he began to vomit into his own mask and then aspirate it, his exhaust valve having frozen over completely. There was nothing that could be done.

HALO jumping may be done in groups, but it is one of the most solitary pursuits imaginable.

Just before he began to choke, the team heard his voice over the intrateam radio. Velasquez was the last one to jump; everyone else was already in the air below. And though they all angled themselves upward to assess his condition, no one but Len Miller saw the flash. It seemed to originate at the level of his boots, a sudden blinding light, coruscating in waves from his body, which traveled up the man's torso and then consumed him. For a moment he just hung there, no longer falling, a filament of flame against a photo-negative sky. Miller told himself it was only a trick of the sunlight.

"I...I see him!" Velasquez had rasped in a voice that was thin like paper. "I hear him...it's beautiful!" Then nothing, just the indistinct sounds of choking as regurgitation filled his mask.

"Velasquez!" Bowman bellowed over the radio. "Velasquez, do you read me? Do you read? What's your status?"

Assorted choking sounds.

Silence. Silence. More silence.

Everyone swore, and then swore again, because they didn't know what else to say.

The words threaded a silvery path between their helmets, sounding hollow. They watched Velasquez pass through an envelope of cloud and reemerge, quick as a bullet, and here again reality seemed to split, for at least half of the soldiers noted that a kind of lavender mist lingered around him, like the glowing nimbus from a saint's painting. Within this aura, one man clearly saw an emanation of birds. Another saw insects. Len Miller was certain he saw a set of bright, diaphanous wings articulating from the man's trunk. Others, including Bowman, saw nothing at all. When Velasquez drew near enough to the ground, his chute opened automatically, at which point his limp body drifted slowly to earth, a green-garbed angel on the breath of the wind. The team watched with somber faces as their fellow soldier crumpled into a little pile on the desert floor. The mists surrounding him had dissipated. Miller observed that there were no signs of charring on his friend's skin or clothing, no hint whatsoever of electrocution. The white flash, whatever it was, had been wholly immaculate.

"What did he say?" someone asked quietly. "He saw somebody up there?"

"His goggles froze over," said someone else. "His eyeballs probably froze, too. He was just looking at the back of his retinas."

"He saw God," said Bowman, nodding gravely.

But Miller just shook his head. He and Velasquez had been inseparable since Hell Week two years earlier, and he knew better. "Not God," he said simply. "Jimi."

"What's that?" asked a puzzled Bowman.

"Jimi Hendrix, sir. He saw Jimi Hendrix."

IN THE WORDS OF MARTIN VELASQUEZ, JIMI WAS THE greatest musician of all time—greater even than Elvis and the Beatles and all their little virtuoso superbabies. Velasquez was a guitarist himself, and he played well enough to be able to comprehend the core of Jimi's genius. He understood the unearthly skill of the man's fingers, as well as the revolutionary way he approached music, like a radical conquistador claiming everything he saw in his own name. He spoke of Jimi with the sort of admiration that other men reserved for their fathers, and before he went to sleep each night, he made sure to listen to a full cycle of *Electric Ladyland* on his iPod, sometimes keeping the others awake when he forgot himself and sang aloud. "For Christ's sake, Velasquez," his friends would chastise him, "For a Navy man, you are one hell of a hippie."

Velasquez would just laugh and remind everyone that Jimi had been in the military, too, that he had been in the 101st Airborne, and had even injured his ankle in a parachuting accident.

What else can be said of Martin Velasquez? He was unmarried, with only a pill-addicted mother and a bohemian girlfriend to mourn him. He had a string of construction jobs before joining the Navy, his path of self-discovery forming a ragged constellation across the Southwest. He was charismatic and by all accounts a bit eccentric. Like his idol, he once took a broom to elementary school and pretended it was a guitar, performing that delicate alchemy with such finesse that his principal felt compelled to chop the broom to pieces, claiming she could hear music issuing from the handle.

Even from that early age it was clear to those who knew him that there was something unusual about Velasquez. And so when it was his own time to die, it was only natural that instead of feeling the presence of a traditional Judeo-Christian deity, he should instead be enshrouded in an octave-jumping haze of purple radiating from Jimi himself, or rather from the Platonic Ideal of him, the original empyrean prototype of Jimi Hendrix kicking around in the ether, playing "The Star-Spangled Banner" with his transcendental teeth.

This is what Len Miller told interviewers as well, that his friend had had a fantastic vision, up there in the halo of the earth where humans weren't supposed to be, and had been granted the sacred honor of achieving a death like Jimi's, death by vomit, which was the rock and roll equivalent of crucifixion.

Len Miller's version of events was met with almost universal skepticism.

But imagine, if you will. There you are, HALO jumping over the Yuma Proving Ground with your helmet, your parachute, all the emblems of a frail humanity strapped to your chest. The air is pushing hard against you, creating a firm cushion, like an unseen hand, beneath your body. The extreme cold is only a ghost flickering on the margins of your consciousness. You turn to gaze at the planet far below, taking in the disorienting curvature of it, as if it were a giant eyeball and you were surfing the edge of the cornea, and as your body rotates upward you catch sight of a luminous cocoon descending from a crack in the heavens. It hums with energy, inviting you closer. And then you are inside it, and your senses are opened to a revelation of beauty, and you don't even care that you're dying because your heart has been transformed into a bird with glinting eyes, sinewy, rapturous, and you slip at last behind the veil of eternity, into the loving arms of a presence greater than yourself.

And why shouldn't it be Jimi Hendrix, anyway?

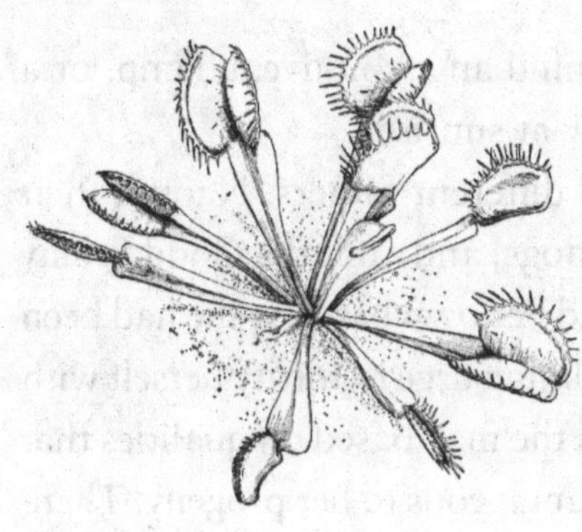

three lights over anchorage

ONCE UPON A TIME, THERE WERE THREE SISTERS WHO LIVED JUST OUTSIDE ANCHORAGE.

The first sister had a brain like a lantern. When illuminated, the coiled tissues gleamed like yellow tourmaline, creating a sphere of radiance around her head like a saint's nimbus. She was able to switch the light on and off at will, and could dim or brighten it depending on the circumstances.

The second sister was similarly gifted, but in her case, it was the spine that could be ignited on command, like a ribbon of flame sewn into her back.

The third sister bore yet another permutation. For her, the light had come to nest within her heart. With its soft orange glow and muscled reticulation, the organ called to mind an art nouveau lamp, or a stained-glass window at sunrise.

The sisters all had different fathers. Naomi, their mother, trained sled dogs, and after the Good Friday earthquake swallowed her own parents, she had been seized by an overwhelming urge to fortify herself with children. She selected the men based on qualities that she felt would be advantageous to her progeny. There was an astrophysicist of Iñupiat lineage; a seven-foot-tall weightlifter who worked the pipeline; and last of all, a free-spirited romantic, a bit younger than the others, who loved Johnny Horton and roamed the wilds of Alaska writing cowboy poetry. She brought each of them to the nearby lighthouse, coupling fiercely with them inside the great lantern room while the kerosene burned and filled the air with smoky tendrils. An observer on the path below might have seen their doubled hands splayed like kestrel wings against the grooved lens, leaving behind brightly feathered prints that the long-suffering lighthouse keeper would later be forced to remove.

Naomi's formidable strength of will resulted in a kind of alchemy. The embryos she spun into being received not only the genetic traits of their sires but also the luminous properties of the environment in which they had been conceived. When they emerged from her body it was as inchoate stars: the first an easy birth, the second even easier…the third an emergency caesarean, a coppery orb plucked from its harbor of flesh.

The three daughters grew up riding the sled with their mother. They took turns gripping the handle, calling out "Gee!" and "Haw!" while the mist of upturned ice and snow pinged at their cheeks and the dogs stretched before them in a sinuous double line. Naomi beamed to see her trio of darlings huddled around her in their fur-trimmed parkas. Each one was carefully balanced on a running board, their arms interwoven like acrobats to hold one another in place. If one of them lost her footing, the others tightened their grip on her shoulders until she had reestablished herself on the board.

Sometimes they did fall off—the oldest was once jettisoned into a snowbank at the bottom of a small cliff and had to be dug out by the dogs—but they always took these mishaps in stride. Indeed, the girls lived for these training runs. With glittering eyes, they took in every detail of the windswept world, exhilarated by its rugged harshness, its dangerous and extravagant beauty. They marveled at the counterintuitive colors that washed across the icy landscape: the lakes sheathed with red and pink, the mountains stained blue and a deep, inky black. As they rode, their distinctive anatomies came flickering to life. The brain lit up first, then the spine, and then the heart, always in the order of their birth, always brightening to the same ochre incandescence, so that night-flying bush pilots often found themselves mesmerized by the tiny watch fires that seemed to bloom amid the vast expanse.

Often, the northern lights would be blazing above, a bright banner of foxfire that rippled across the sky in apparent affinity with their own radiant bodies. It was a common enough occurrence that they greeted it like an intimate friend. "Hello, Aurora! How have you been? You're looking beautiful today!" And Aurora, despite her fierceness, always blushed back.

Upon returning home, the girls would always clamor to sleep in the heated shed with the dogs. If Naomi was feeling generous, she would allow it, and they would at once fall drowsily among the animals, skin smooth against wet-matted fur, reciting their names and mantras like an incantation until sleep came and canine and human converged in a shared dream of wildness.

Far too soon, though, this blissful era came to an end. The daughters grew, and their interests diverged. Where once they had been a single entity, a bright and lovely Hydra, they now spent much of their time apart and in ways that were not of interest to the others. And then, one by one, they left home, each one tracing her path along the magnetic field lines to her particular destination. Naomi, ever tough as nails, only cried once, and only when the youngest turned back to say good-bye, fanning a tender kiss to her mother across the snowy yard. The dogs were inconsolable. They howled without ceasing and buried all their favorite bones.

The first daughter, Paulina, became a brilliant mathematician and took up glacier caving as a hobby (she had an advantage in that she did not require a head lamp). The facility where she worked was situated far up in the Chugach Mountains, on the grounds of an old monastery, and though she felt this choice of location betrayed a regrettably superstitious nature on the part of the founders, she thrived in the mountain air and found that her work flourished there. At night, she was often startled awake when vivid algebraic dreams caused her brain to flash on, like a strobe light, or a bomb caught in the first milliseconds of detonation. From time to time she was called upon to use her gifts in the service of a mountain rescue. She was happy.

The second daughter, Gemma, took up construction work and within six months was married to another construction worker named Lottie. Gemma and her wife rode motorcycles nearly every weekend. In the fall they went hunting on the Kenai and hosted legendary moose-meat barbecues to which they invited half of Anchorage. When, on occasion, their finances ebbed, Gemma did freelance work for a nearby medical school, flicking on her spine like a task light in order to demonstrate to budding neurosurgeons the uniquely prehistoric scaffolding of discs and vertebrae. She, too, was happy.

The third daughter, Goldenbelle, loved music and traveled in a van with a local punk band called Anarchy in the AK. She adored and slept with all of the band members, but in particular she adored and slept with Griff, the female guitarist and de facto leader, because they had started off together, just the two of them. They met as freshmen at UAA, literally colliding in the hallway outside their Intro to Drama class. When Goldenbelle apologized and introduced herself, Griff, who even then cultivated a sardonic disdain for all things old-fashioned, had snorted at her antiquated-sounding name.

"What the hell kind of a name is that? It sounds like something out of the pioneer days."

Goldenbelle had only shrugged. "My mother read it on a gravestone."

"Oh," Griff said. "That's cool, I guess."

Though annoyed, Goldenbelle had found herself uncomfortably conscious of the shape of the other woman's lips, her glittering green eyes, and the sinuous curve of her neck, which disappeared into a billowing cloud of black hair. No less captivating were the tectonic plates of her hips, twin continents that rose and fell like pistons as she shifted in her faded jeans. She was struck by a vaguely poetic thought, something along the lines of *Attraction is all about topography*. But she was not one to be intimidated by a budding infatuation, even if it was the first to feature a woman as its object. She met the other woman's gaze without flinching. "And what exactly does Griff mean? Is it short for something?"

"Nah, it's kind of a stage name I'm trying out. It sounds tough, don't you think? My real name is Marie."

"Okay, *Griff*," Goldenbelle said pointedly, slinging her backpack over her shoulder, "at least I'm not pretending to be somebody else."

As she walked into the classroom, she flicked her heart on, just a little, to let Griff know what she was missing. It was a cheat, of course, and one she had pledged to herself not to deploy in such circumstances, but on that day she hadn't been able to help herself.

Griff had stared after her, spellbound.

They had been together ever since.

It was only later that Goldenbelle discovered the extent to which this slipup had determined the conditions of their relationship, had in fact made the relationship itself inevitable. Griff, she soon learned, was terrified of the dark. This was rarely an issue for her during the summer, when darkness was more of a theoretical concept, but it became a crippling liability in the long Alaskan winters, when the yolk of sun only skimmed the horizon at midday before dipping once more behind a scrim of mountains and dark-velvet trees. For her part, Goldenbelle loved this time of year. She loved the deep blues of nascent morning and of night, which seemed to go on forever, as if she were a princess caught in a fairytale enchantment. For her this was the blue of becoming, of infinite possibility, in which objects might wax and wane, trying on a variety of forms without having to commit to a particular one. But for Griff, this very formlessness was a canvas onto which she mapped her deepest fears. She was superstitious by nature, and to her the blankness seemed somehow sentient, suggestible: as if by thinking the wrong thing at the right moment, she might cause abominations to take shape in the murk beyond.

It was on such crepuscular days, or on the late nights following a gig, that Griff would curl fetuslike against Goldenbelle, while the latter kept her back to the frosted van window, symbolically shielding her lover from the shadows that flickered beyond. She would candle her heart just a little, like that first time, so as not to keep the others awake; only then could Griff sleep without the nightmares that so often plagued her.

At these times the universe seemed to shrink to encompass just the two of them, as if they were plaster figures in a snow globe. Stepping outside herself, Goldenbelle took pleasure in the tableau they created: their long legs intertwined on the vinyl van seat, Griff's shredded jeans sliding against her own torn fishnets, the pungent smell of sweat and beer, both fresh and ancient, radiating out from the other woman's leather jacket, which she insisted on wearing next to her skin because that's what Sid

Vicious had done. The clouds of black hair she held like life threads between her fingers. A pale hand pressed against her chest in a gesture of supplication. Within this private universe, Goldenbelle, the third daughter of Naomi, felt content, even rapturous, as if she'd finally transformed into the most splendid and shining version of herself.

Still, she was not quite happy.

GOLDENBELLE OFTEN FELT THAT HER LIFE WAS ridiculous, just as she felt that the things the band sang about were ridiculous. It was all defiance, and empty posturing, and rage at an establishment that they had barely had the opportunity to experience. What did they know of oppression? None of them had ever been wrongfully imprisoned. None of them had ever been racially profiled or discriminated against, the way her half-Iñupiat sister still was. They had never been had their land or property taken without cause, the way so many of the local indigenous groups had. There were countless legitimate gripes to be lodged against the powers that be, and yet this is what they chose to sing about. Anarchy. The evils of selling out. Shocking the 'normies' with their unorthodox behavior. It was absurd.

Frequently, Goldenbelle sat in on the band's song-writing sessions, listening with amusement to the solemn outpouring of grievances, the litanies of postadolescent earnestness that were fashioned into mediocre lyrics, and because she loved them and knew that their hearts were pure, she did not mock their efforts. Though they took pains to clothe themselves in layers of sneering irony, their armor was a transparent sham. They were so easily wounded.

And so it was with reluctance that she spoke up during one such session, when they had begun writing a song called "Anchorage Is Burning." She was going to let this one slide, like all the others, until the following lyrics were proposed:

> *Breathing in you start to sicken,*
> *Bodies burning smell like chicken.*

"You know," she said, raising her voice to be heard over the chatter. "That was a real thing that happened. My grandparents died in one of those fires."

Astonished, they all turned to look at her. She had been cradling Griff's unplugged electric guitar in her lap, picking out a tune offhandedly, and in the sudden stillness they could hear the faint, lucid tones issuing from the instrument, like a melody leaking through from another dimension. They watched as her fingers moved nimbly across the fretboard, executing the occasional barre chord like a pro. When, they wondered, had Goldie gotten so good?

"Well," said Jesse, the bass player, with a slight huff of irritation, "it's really just a metaphor for how commercial the city's gotten." He began thumbing through his rhyming dictionary again, considering the matter closed.

Blitz, the rhythm guitarist, chimed in. "Yeah, you know. People are so obsessed with amassing more and more stuff that they forget what it means to be human."

And what exactly do you *think being human means?* Goldenbelle wanted to ask him. *Doing a shit-ton of smack every night? Blacking out in filthy club bathrooms? Refusing to talk to your mom when she calls to see if you are okay?* Instead, she nodded. "I get that, I do. I just want you to remember that the earthquake was real and not just some symbolic construct. Real people died. Real people burned."

"I know they did, Goldie," replied Griff in her conciliatory way. "You're absolutely right. And it sucks what happened to your family. But a big part of what we do is provocation. Sometimes you've got to shock people to get the message across."

Goldenbelle could have nodded and let it go at this, for the sake of group harmony and the joyous, collective buzz of creation. She was a carefree creature, after all. But there was also a filament of steel glinting within her. Once she had taken a stand, she was metabolically driven to press her point.

"Okay," she acknowledged, "but what's the actual message of the song? That the earthquake happened because people bought too many pairs of shoes? That it'll happen again if we don't get our shit together? Is that what you guys believe?"

"It does sound a little Old Testament when you put it that way," Owen, the drummer, said with a laugh. The others glared at him. Owen had slept with her the most recently and was therefore a bit suspect.

"It's not about believing or not believing it," Jesse sighed.

"That's right," added Griff. "We're just diagnosing a cancer that's afflicted us as a society."

Somehow, Goldenbelle managed not to roll her eyes. "Rationalize it however you want," she said. "But my grandparents died in that fire. And because of that I never got to know them."

She looked around at her lovers then, her fingers still plucking the threads of a far-off tune. She made certain that each one met her gaze before she moved on. Beneath her black T-shirt, her heart glimmered like coals. "I just think if you're going to invoke real shit, you ought to honor it by being real. Use it, fine—you're artists, after all. But use it for something that means something."

The band hemmed and hawed for a while longer, especially Blitz, whose idea the song was in the first place, but in the end, they decided to shelve it until they could identify a grievance worthy of the scope of the tragedy. They then began to workshop another song, "Salvador Dali Ate My Sandwich," which made Goldenbelle laugh and restored her faith in them somewhat. Here was the playful absurdism she had loved from the beginning. Before the self-righteousness. Before they became obsessed with ticking every box on the punk scorecard. *This*, she thought, *is why I stay.*

That night the band performed at a repurposed opera house in Fairbanks. Goldenbelle was out on the floor, moshing among the fans as she often did, when Griff extended a tattooed arm to her, drawing her through the crowd that parted instinctively as she passed, in awe of her privileged position and her warm, flickering heart. Griff bent down, helping her onto the stage as if into a royal carriage. And then, pulling her close, she crushed her lips against hers, causing the room to erupt into a cacophony, the walls reverberating with cries of admiration and envy, a chorus of spiraling lust.

From time to time Griff arranged such displays for her. When she was playing guitar more than usual. When she spent too much time away from the group. When she appeared dreamy and distracted after sex, rolling over to scribble chord progressions in her notebook. Anytime Griff sensed that she was growing restless and might leave them, her sense of theatricality would be brought to bear, reminding her lover of the exalted place she occupied among them. *I honor you before witnesses,* her actions seemed to say. *You are my personal punk princess.*

Goldenbelle was not naïve. She knew that this recognition was part of the currency with which Griff paid her for her companionship. But she thrilled at the pageantry just the same. And she knew how to dress the part: her blond hair spiked high with the same egg mixture the others used, red eye shadow teased out like wings, a mesh tank worn over a black bra in order to better showcase the locus of fire buried within her breast. The heart was the main attraction, after all. She knew the power it held: when illuminated, its prominence gave her the appearance of frailty, made people want to protect her. It was a spectacle that felt like an intimacy. Some avoided looking at all, as if they thought that by watching too long, they might see the heart begin to struggle and slow, its cadence growing weaker by the second, until finally it fluttered to an anguished halt, a brilliant bird winging its last. Yes, Goldenbelle knew she bore the aspect of a tragic figure, and she leveraged it.

The next morning Griff was in high spirits. She leapt up from the stained mattress she had shared with Goldenbelle backstage and greedily wolfed down several slices of cold pizza. Then she pulled on her favorite leather pants and a muscle shirt. Her dark hair was wild—a mass of tendrils, still sticky with spray, which floated around her as if she were some kind of underwater siren. Her full lips looked even comelier than usual.

Goldenbelle yawned happily and sat up. Surveying the room, she noted that Blitz and Jesse were passed out on the nearby couch, their heads on opposite arm rests, their black boots overlapping in the middle. *Like boys at a sleepover*, she thought with affection. Owen was nowhere to be seen.

"Did Owen go home with that bald girl?" she asked.

"Nah," Griff shook her head. "Just out for a run."

"I'm surprised. He seemed pretty into her."

"Maybe he'd rather be into you," Griff said, winking.

Goldenbelle laughed and blushed. It was true. All the band members hooked up with the occasional fan, even Griff, but for the most part they were remarkably faithful to her. This, despite her never having asked for their particular loyalty. She often wondered if this was due to some atavistic impulse, some deep-seated need to pay tribute to the rare and wondrous among them. In ancient times, they might have brought her offerings of herbs or perfume, perhaps an animal sacrifice; now, they simply offered her their monogamy, or as much of it as they could muster.

Griff stopped as if struck by inspiration. "Hey, what do you say we go to the movies today, flick on the disco lights, and scare the hell out of some kids?"

Goldenbelle sighed. She reached beside the bed for her favorite T-shirt, which she'd found months ago at a vintage store. It featured a turtle in a bow tie and a top hat, and read, 'Shell yeah!' She thought it was very funny, in a juvenile kind of way.

Pulling it over her head, she said, "I'm not a show pony, Griff."

The guitarist threw up her hands. "Jesus, Goldie, I never said you were. Forget it, I just thought it'd be fun." She turned to examine the multitude of beer bottles on a nearby table. Finding one that still contained a smattering of liquid, she took a swig and wiped her mouth. "So what would *you* like to do today?"

"Hmm…we don't have to be back at the van till four, right? I think I'm actually going to wander around on my own. Maybe check out the ice museum."

Griff peered at her with concern. Abruptly, she changed her tactics. "Oh, don't be like that, Goldie," she said sweetly. "You know I love you." Dropping back onto the mattress then, she leaned over Goldenbelle and kissed her. "Anyway, there's something right here I'd like to check out."

They kissed for a while longer, one of Griff's hands cradled around her neck and the other clutching her breast. And then Griff pushed her knees apart and began to nibble on the center seam of her jean shorts, looking up every so often to measure the impact of her efforts. Goldenbelle did not try to stop her. She had never been able to resist Griff when she was in full seduction mode.

But the specter still hung in the air, the wisp of a doubt that had been taking shape for some time.

"Griff…" she heard herself saying, though inwardly she was crying out. *Don't speak it, don't give it a name. Because if it's true of her, it's true of everyone.* But her mouth seemed to have bypassed her brain and was not responding to commands. "What if I were normal?" she asked. "What if I were just a regular girl with a regular heart?" And there it was.

Her lover lifted her head, perplexed. "But you're not."

"I know, but what if I were. Would you still love me?"

"You're being ridiculous, Goldie."

"Would you, though? I'm serious. If I weren't your personal nightlight, would you still want me around?"

"What is this about?"

"Just answer. Please."

There was an impatient groan. "Well, obviously, the conditions would be different. But yes, of course I would, Goldie." She lowered her head again, and her subsequent words collided with the crosshatched threads, curling upward into vapor. "Of course of course of course of course…"

Goldenbelle let herself be placated. She did not see the whorls of beer bottles glinting like faerie rings in the corners. She did not see that the wall behind her, stained green from years of misspent urine, had begun to cast up images from the wallpaper beneath. Foxes, huntsmen, sprigs of greenery, an alabaster unicorn—all were disclosing themselves, their baroque, half-formed shapes a testament to the theater's former life. The current owner had foolishly tried to paper over the flocking, but three dimensions would not long be contained within two. The hidden would always emerge.

MORE AND MORE NOW, GOLDENBELLE FOUND herself thinking about that year at UAA when they were first a couple. They'd had so much fun: getting drunk on Jägermeister and reading Eugene O'Neill plays aloud to each other; driving to truck stops in the middle of the night to flirt and devour plates of biscuits and gravy; making love in dark alleyways, Goldenbelle's boots wrapped tight around Griff's torso, their bodies conjoined like beech trees, with only her heart for illumination. Griff urgent, jealous, pressing hard into her as if she could make the light a part of herself. Icicles fell like rain around them, loosened by the heat they produced. Passersby looked on in astonishment.

Back when it was just the two of them, and they were equals.

She didn't think this was still the case.

When Griff dropped out to form the band, Goldenbelle had dropped out with her, supporting her the way she felt a good girlfriend should. But that was only part of the reason. The truth was the music made her feel alive in a way that school never did. It seemed more authentic somehow. The plays she'd read resonated with something like life, but the music *was* life. It was visceral and ungovernable, in all the ways she wanted to be. As she stood amid the sweaty crowd at the club, her skin vibrated with each heavily hammered chord. The notes crashed against her in delicious waves, like clouds of insects seeking a soft place to burrow, and in fact, in the days after a show, it always seemed as if the music had managed to physically embed itself in her flesh, that it was sewn there like secrets.

And then came that night after their twelfth show, when she'd been particularly wild, delirious with a sense of the infinite, her heart aching with the pull of endless possibilities. Certain of Griff's love and her own liberation, she had drawn the rest of the band members to herself. Handsome, freckle-faced Jesse. Short and stocky Blitz. Owen, with the blond buzz cut and a piercing for every year of his life. One by one, she had claimed them all, taking them in her mouth while Griff looked on, electrified. She did not move to stop her. In the end she had drawn Goldenbelle onto her own lap, bucking her hips theatrically, cementing her primacy among the group. And just like that, the dynamic shifted. Goldenbelle became a girlfriend to them all, a fair-minded muse who doled out inspiration in roughly equal portions. When they performed, her sympathies arced out across the stage like lightning, including each one of them within their span.

From the start, Goldenbelle had forbidden any use of the 'g' word. She was certain that what they were doing was so new, so transgressive, that the concept didn't apply. But now she wasn't so sure such a revolution was even possible. Iconoclasts though they were, the band members couldn't fully divorce themselves from their cultural context. They had been born into its marrow, after all. Little by little, they had begun to look at her differently. They loved her, yes, and they were loyal to her in their way, but they started to take her favors for granted. Their astonishment at her presence waned, and rather than enjoying the radiant panoply of her dimensions, they began to view her through a single bloodshot lens. It was true: she had become a groupie. She had affixed herself to a gleaming, sex-smooth pedestal, and now she was unable to climb down from it.

She often thought of revoking it all, of trying to recapture the original relationship with Griff. But that coupledom was long gone. It was tattered and remote, lost somewhere far across the frozen waters.

THAT DAY SHE WENT OUT ON HER OWN, DESPITE Griff's protestations. She wandered the city streets, strolled beside the looping river, and ate a sandwich there on the banks, though every few minutes a piercing wind swept over the icy surface and chilled her to the bone. Goldenbelle didn't mind. To her, coldness was a birthright. It offered an intimate connection to the past, her own and that of the land itself, with its tumbles of snow-robed mountains and glaciers that moved like the thoughts of gods: deliberate, far-seeing, encompassing ages. The cold made her feel anchored somehow, and less likely to float free of the planet's surface.

In the afternoon, she went to the ice museum. Here she found a series of fantastic installations, each more wondrous than the last, each artfully lit by bulbs of pink and green and blue, suggesting both the aurora borealis and the natural light that dominated the landscape in winter. There was an ice facsimile of a log cabin, complete with a frontiersman panning for gold and a husky seated beside him. There was a scene of two horsemen facing off in battle, spears forever trained on each other's breasts. There was a skier caught in the first exhilarating moments of her descent. There were assorted zoological sculptures as well—eagles, cormorants, wolves, moose, and bears—and a number of smaller, more intricate carvings that had been fixed atop pedestals all around. Many of the latter were small enough to be missed in favor of the larger exhibits, but Goldenbelle found herself particularly captivated by them. For one thing they were mostly abstract, containing patterns and images that seemed to her almost recognizable, as if they had been plucked from the current of her dreams.

The museum also boasted a number of interactive exhibits, including snow machines you could climb on, a four-poster bed to recline in, and a bar at which to sit and enjoy a neon-colored drink. There was even a small hill you could slide down using a specially provided plastic disc. Truly, the museum contained a whole world, as viewed through a crystalline mirror, and as Goldenbelle passed through its rooms there settled over her a profound sense of unreality, as if the structures and figures she saw were not copies but the originals, as if they were the ones comprised of wood and flesh, while she was merely a golem of ice, a pale reflection of a human being, imbued with a momentary flicker of sentience.

And then, in the very last room, she found a scene of a musher and a dogsled. Like the others, this piece was richly detailed, chiseled with such precision she could almost hear the panting of the dogs and the swoosh of the wooden runners through the crust of ice and snow. At the top of the parka, where the furred hood was, the sculptor had left a hole so that a visitor might be photographed behind it, making it appear that he or she was driving the sled. Goldenbelle stepped toward the sculpture and placed her feet on the mat. Standing there, her head within that cold halo, she felt a pang of sadness so intense it nearly took her breath away. Memories of childhood began to unfold within her, a kind of origami in reverse; they bloomed like flowers to reveal a thousand everyday moments, a proliferant field of lovely, long-forgotten secrets, each with its own nucleus of light, its own seed of hurt and beauty. She missed her sisters and mother so much she could hardly bear it. What were they doing right now? Was Paulina puzzling over an impossible equation, the smell of chalk dust hanging in the air like the vapors at Delphi? Was Gemma hard at work assembling the skeleton of a building, or having a late lunch with her wife? And her mother, was she out repairing the sled, or buying groceries or equipment, or training a new litter of pups? Was she perhaps napping in the shed with the dogs, the way the girls did when they were small?

It was strange, she thought. As a child, the entire universe had manifested within her home. Dense planets hung upon her living room walls, while stars smoldered in the fixtures and the drains. Because of her mother and sisters, everything was bearable; everything could be faced. And yet, just because she got a bit older, because she had reached an age that was deemed to be sufficiently mature, she was pushed out into the world on her own, without the family she'd come to think of as key to her identity. She was a single unit for the first time in her life, a cell spun off from one of those floating algae blooms. Nothing could have prepared her for the ache of such a separation.

Goldenbelle's hand grazed the icy reins of the sled, remembering how it felt to be propelled through the wilderness by living-breathing flesh, flesh that loved her unconditionally and wanted above all to make her happy. She thought of the astonishing things she had seen on those outings, particularly when she had gotten sleepy and her reality began to be streaked with dreams. Marble colonnades gleaming upon the mountainsides. Bright-eyed tigers hunkering in the bush. Birds that transformed into stones and back again. Cherry blossoms churned up by the sled, fluttering all around and becoming entangled in her sisters' hair, before vanishing into a cloud of pink smoke. At the time these apparitions had seemed unbelievably profound, like visions granted only to her. If she was being honest, she still thought of them that way.

Though the influx of such memories was bittersweet, they made her feel somehow solidified, as if she were a wayward spirit reentering her body after a long absence. For the first time in many years, she had a clear image of who she was. There was the golden outline that had once circumscribed her; she could see the shimmering totality of it, could measure the difference between her existence now and her existence then, both the places where she had moved beyond the given contours and those where she had fallen short.

It was a revelation she couldn't wait to share. But when she burst into the room backstage, gushing about ice sculptures and self-discovery, Griff and the others only gaped at her, perplexed. Blitz actually tilted his head to the side like a dog in a commercial. Jesse just cracked open a beer. Still, she soldiered on, hoping to appeal to their artistic sensibilities.

"Really, it was just about the most beautiful thing I've ever seen. Like if the northern lights came down to earth and took on physical form. You guys would have loved it. And guess what? Did you know that Fairbanks is sometimes called the Golden Heart City? Makes me think maybe I was meant to stay here," she said with a laugh. "I could get a job at the museum. Guide the tourists around during the day and curl up on that giant four-poster ice bed at night."

Everyone continued to stare. Accustomed to her idiosyncrasies, they were unsure if what they were witnessing was a full-on defection or just a momentary fit of passion.

"Cool," said Blitz finally.

Jesse was more noncommittal. "Huh," he replied.

Owen, drumsticks in hand, approached and gave her a quick kiss. "Sounds amazing," he said and smiled.

Griff, though, was clearly irritated. Struggling to remove her guitar strap, she looked up just long enough to give her lover a withering glare. "Wow, that's great, Goldie. I hope you enjoy your new career."

"I'm being serious, Griff. I love you all, but I can't stay here forever, riding in this ancient van and eating gas station burritos."

"They have hot dogs, too," offered Blitz.

Oh, Blitz, she thought with affection. *I will miss you when I leave*. "The point is I need to find a place where I belong."

"Bullshit," said Griff dismissively. "What is with all the drama, all of a sudden? You know very well you belong here with us."

"I don't know any such thing," Goldenbelle said. "That's what I'm trying to say. I just had this…*experience*…and it was incredible, and it made me feel different somehow." She paused for a moment, struggling to find the right words. "It's like the child I used to be was inside me all this time, sleeping, and she just woke up."

Griff let out a laugh of disbelief.

"Look, I *saw* myself in that place," said Goldenbelle. "I saw all of it. The good parts, the bad, all the separate crazy atoms that make up me. And every one of those atoms was like a different path I could choose, like I was at Grand Central Station and I just had to figure out which train to take." She looked at them plaintively, tears filling her eyes. "I thought you all would understand. I thought you'd be happy for me."

Her heart was blazing like they'd never seen it before. It put the naked bulbs overhead to shame. It was so bright that lengthy shadows could be seen radiating from each of the band members, spoking out behind them as if along a great wheel. A dazed Owen could not take his eyes off the source. Blitz and Jesse just stared at their feet, choosing to defer to their leader. Griff's face, meanwhile, wore a peculiar expression. The contempt had melted away. It looked as if she might have been moved by what her lover said, or at least by the overwhelming resplendence of her person. She seemed on the verge of extending a tender vine of sympathy, of flinging wide the door of the invisible cage and saying, 'Yes, of course, my love—whatever you need.' But then, upon glancing down at her shadow—and perhaps noting her body's unwitting submission to Goldenbelle's light—her ego seemed to get the better of her.

"For Christ's sake," she exploded. "We don't have time for this agony-of-the-saints crap. You may be unique, but that doesn't mean you have some kind of magical destiny. It just means you have an inflated sense of your own importance. Now get your shit together and your bag packed. We leave in thirty minutes."

Goldenbelle just shook her head, wiped her eyes, and stormed out.

"What the hell is *her* problem?" she heard Jesse ask, as the door slammed behind her.

She paused in the alley to collect herself. She could hardly focus for rage. Well, and what *was* her problem, anyway? Why couldn't she just let it go and get along as she always had? She had once joked with Griff about being haunted, but now that was not far from the truth. It did seem that something had her in its grip: a kind of wraith that at times took the shape of mild discontent, other times an all-consuming ache for the impossible, like when she was a wild-eyed child gazing up at the Milky Way and she had thought she might die if she couldn't fling herself into that pearly band. The wraith was not a swift one, but it was relentless. It slipped through the curtains at night, a strange whale song interlacing her dreams, while in the day it slouched in darkened doorways, coiled and glistening like intestines. It had been her constant companion for some time. All the museum visit had done was coax it out into the open.

Soon Owen, too, burst into the alley, casting a furious glance over his shoulder. His cheeks were bright pink, the way they were whenever he was in a heightened state of arousal. His many piercings winked and glittered in the light that still emanated from her chest. She had to smile—it reminded her of Christmas.

"Apparently I'm a traitor to the group," he said, with a huff.

"Ha. Join the club."

"I just wanted to tell you that you should go if you want to. Really, you should. I want you to be happy."

"Thanks, Owen."

"I know the others do, too. They're just being selfish pricks because they don't want you to go."

She threw her arms around him gratefully. "I guess we're all selfish pricks when it comes down to it. It's kind of the human condition, right? But you…you're so much less selfish than most." She pulled away and smiled at him. "Sorry they're pissed at you."

He smirked. "They can't kick me out, right? You know that joke about the drool coming out both sides of the drummer's mouth. How else would they know if the stage was level?"

She laughed and gave him another quick hug, this time kissing him on the ear. "I do love you, Owen."

His face softened, registered something like a wound, and she instantly regretted her words. She thought of how she had looked him in the eyes the last time they had made love, in that dirty bathroom stall with the graffiti, even though that was a privilege reserved only for Griff. But the way he had been gazing at her, she hadn't been able to resist. It had been like falling into a curtain of velvet, like a blanket of stars laid out just for her.

"All right then," he said. "See you later?"

"Later," she agreed.

When he was back inside, Goldenbelle ventured once more into the cold streets. She ended up following the river again, this time tracing it up to Pioneer Park, and though the shops were closed and covered in sheaves of snow, she walked slowly among them, pretending she was living in an earlier incarnation of the city. What must it have been like back then? There were pictures of the settlement at the park entrance—black-and-white images of railroad workers, steamboats, Athabascan traders, and gold prospectors—but she wondered how far these could really go toward capturing the essence of a place. Did the town feel like it did now, calm, serene, at peace within its own inevitable civilization? Or was it like an animal bucking against its restraints, barely contained within crude-cut planks of timber?

SHE RETURNED TO THE THEATER JUST BEFORE SIX o'clock. The band had been waiting for two hours, and it was fully dark out.

"What the hell, Goldie?" barked Griff. She was standing beside the van, shivering and smoking a cigarette, her face mostly obscured by the hood of her parka. Her knees were visible through the holes in her jeans—holes that Goldenbelle herself had ripped. Back when they had first started touring, Goldenbelle had suggested this as a way for them all to demonstrate their devotion to one another. They had sat in a circle, and using Blitz's bowie knife, each one solemnly ripped the jeans of the person beside him. Afterward, she had insisted they christen the tour van with a bottle of Schnapps, a ceremony which had ended in Jesse peeing onto a McDonald's dumpster and the police being called. They had driven away in hysterics.

"We have been waiting for-fucking-ever," Griff was saying. "Where the hell have you been?"

"Pioneer Park," Goldenbelle said placidly. "It's quite lovely with all the snow."

Griff waited, but no further explanation was forthcoming. They exchanged a long look, a measuring of intent and force of will, and Griff, seeing her lover's defiant expression, at last relented. Without a word, she flicked her cigarette into a snowbank and climbed in the van. Goldenbelle followed her.

"Well, if it isn't our perfect princess," growled Jesse from the driver's seat. He set his comic book on the dashboard and started the engine. "Glad you finally saw fit to grace us with your presence."

"Screw you," Goldenbelle said, taking a seat by herself.

"Shut up, Jesse," said Griff. "It's done. Let's move on."

But Goldenbelle wasn't finished. "Look, I'm not going to apologize for needing time to myself."

"Why am I not surprised," Jesse said acidly.

Owen nudged Blitz. "I know who's not getting laid tonight."

Blitz was less circumspect. He was clearly high and was annoyed at the disruption of his otherwise blissful reverie. "Jesus H. Christ, Jesse," he slurred.

"What's the big deal? We don't even have a show tonight. It does…not…matter…when we get there."

"It's a matter of professionalism," huffed Jesse.

"Whose profession?" Owen demanded.

Jesse didn't dare answer that. After a few minutes he turned to Goldenbelle, who was seated behind him, and his expression softened. "Sorry," he said. "You have a right to do your own thing." And then, like an offering, for she knew it pained him to make such declarations: "We're just lucky to have you."

She shrugged, neither accepting nor declining his apology. Instead, she slipped her headphones on, queued up the Black Flag, and turned her attention to the scenery racing by.

IT WAS AROUND TEN O'CLOCK THAT NIGHT, OR another just like it, for truly all the nights lately had begun to bleed together, that she saw the dog. It was a gorgeous Siberian husky, grayish white with black patches around its face and a wide stripe down its back, racing free and unfettered beside the van. There was no musher, no sled in sight. Just the dog, like a beacon from another world. A fragment of beauty spliced into the darkness. It ran at full speed and through some miracle was able to keep up with the van. Goldenbelle glanced around her, but no one else seemed to have noticed it. Mesmerized, she pressed her palm against the frosted window, feeling an echo of the dog's rapid pulse within her body. Its sinewy legs moved as if in slow motion, like that zoetrope of the horse she had seen in a museum as a child, and she felt her own limbs stirring in response, as if the dog were not an external entity at all, but an extension of herself, an evolutionary cousin conjured into being by the power of her yearning.

When at last the creature turned and began to bound away across the field, she thought her heart would burst from her chest. This was the moment, if ever there was one.

"Stop the van!" she cried. "Stop, please! I have to get out!"

Startled, Jesse skidded to a long, screeching halt along the icy road. Everyone assumed crash positions, and only Blitz managed to grunt out a bemused, "whatthefuck?" Duffel bags and instruments and drug paraphernalia all came crashing to the floor.

When they were at last stopped, Goldenbelle climbed to the front of the van and turned to address them. "I will always love you all," she said. "I don't think you will ever understand just how much. Thank you, and good-bye, my loves."

This announcement was greeted with universal dismay. Griff jumped to her feet and opened her mouth, but no words came out. Blitz just gaped. Jesse managed to speak first. "What? Right now?"

Goldenbelle nodded.

"What do you mean? We're in the middle of nowhere. Where would you go?"

"Home. At least for now."

"We can't just leave you out here alone," said Owen, who appeared stricken.

"I'm not alone," she said. Behind her, the puff of a white tail flicked once and then disappeared into blackness. "Not really."

"This is bullshit," Griff said, recovering her voice. "If you want to talk about leaving, we can do that after we get to town. But there's nothing out here. You'll freeze to death."

"You know I won't."

"Okay, fine," said Griff, exasperated. "If what you want is a grand gesture, here it is. I need you, Goldie. You're my muse and my spirit guide. I admit I resented you, even as I loved you—I didn't want to be the moon to your sun. But I was wrong to be envious. We are as we are, and I would rather be secondary to your light than be without it. The only time I feel safe, the only time I feel *complete* is when I'm with you. Without you I'm lost in the dark, in every sense of the word."

Goldenbelle felt the pull of this at once. Instinctively, a part of her curled out toward Griff, aching to soothe, to cover her wounds with the usual adoration. But in the end her senses returned.

"I'm sorry, I really am," she said softly. "And what you said was beautiful. But I am not an angel sent to save you."

"But I *need* you." Griff said this with some petulance, as if the admission should be enough, as if her declaration of her own vulnerability should trump any other consideration.

Goldenbelle met her gaze. "And what do *I* need? Do you know?"

Griff seemed taken aback. "I mean…you need the music. You need the sweat and the vibrations. You need the chaos of it. You need our art." She paced a small circle, frowning at the floor. "No, that's not it," she muttered to herself. Then at last, animatedly: "You need to love! Oh yes, that's it. That's always been it. And there are four of us here for you to love. That's four times more than most people get. Don't you see it, Goldie? You're not the victim here. You're the cult leader, and we're the multiple wives. We have to share *you*."

"No," Goldenbelle said, shaking her head. "That's not it. Not anymore."

Griff threw up her hands. "Okay then, so what is it that you want?"

Now it was Goldenbelle's turn to be uncertain. "I don't know," she said after a moment. "But I intend to find out."

And so, amid continued protestations, she said her good-byes. Good-bye to Jesse, who talked constantly during sex, an endless flurry of words as if he were shaping reality around himself. Good-bye to Blitz, whose track marks she liked to place her fingers on while they embraced, as if fingering a melancholy instrument. Good-bye to sweet Owen, who secretly loved the Carpenters, who sometimes only wanted to share long kisses, and who she knew had gotten very attached to her. ("Find me someday," he whispered to her as they embraced.) And of course, good-bye to the beautiful, fiery Griff, who had been her first coconspirator, her first real love. She savored one last time the particular chemical entanglement she had with each, the taste of their paired DNA, rolling it over in her mind so that she would not forget.

With a sad smile, she slung her duffel over her shoulder, turning the "Anarchy in the AK" patch toward the front, as she always did. Then off into the wilds she went, to light her own dark places. The band's last view of her was as the tiniest flicker upon the blue-shadowed tundra, her heart a distant ember moving across it.

A WEEK LATER, SHE WAS HOME. THE DOGS SHRIEKED with delight, falling over themselves to greet her, weaving circles through her legs and soliciting belly rubs. As she laughed and knelt down among them, something began to come alive again inside her, spurred on by the sense memory of fur between frozen fingers. It was a pure kind of bliss, one of those quotidian luxuries of childhood that are so easily enjoyed and then forgotten: experiences so intense that they burn themselves up, leaving behind only a nostalgic fume. Still, she remembered rolling down a steep hill dotted with hairgrass. She remembered playing in the silken mud by the bay with her sisters. She remembered sprinting through the cemetery just after a snowfall, the silence deeper than any she had known, but for her rhythmic footsteps; remembered thinking that this must be what it was like to be a fetus, hearing only the heartbeat.

She realized it had been ages since she had performed the simple act of petting a dog.

Naomi, opening the door, instinctively held her arms out to her daughter.

Goldenbelle fell into her warmth. "I loved her," she said, her head buried deep in Naomi's neck. "I loved them all. But it wasn't enough."

Naomi just held her daughter, smiling down at the blond spikes, the ripped jeans with the hand-drawn graffiti, and the leather zipper jacket, with its tinkling fringe of safety pins: all these studiously applied signifiers of outsider culture. Beneath it all, though, and virtually unchanged, was the glow of the beating organ itself, the lamp that might gutter in its lowest moments but would never go out, at least for a long, long time. She leaned back just a bit, and for a long moment they stood, touching foreheads, the way they used to when Goldenbelle was small. Naomi ran her hand across the bristles of her daughter's hair and did not shy away from the prickliness. "Let's take a ride," she said finally.

Together they harnessed the dogs and set out on the familiar path behind the house. They stood side by side on the running board, arms firm around the other's waist, each holding one of the leads. Unsurprisingly, Naomi opted for a speed run. She shouted her commands and encouragement to the dogs, urging them on, faster and faster, so that soon the sled was flying over dense snowpack and rocketing around hairpin corners. As they sailed along, Goldenbelle felt as if time was reversing itself. Turn by turn, yard by yard, the minutes seemed to fall away from her, shed like so many skins until only the child she had been remained. Having attained this beatific state, she was determined to remain there. She focused alternately on the panting of the dogs; the whoosh of the runners beneath her; the warmth of her mother's body and the smell (faint) of her pine soap; the spray of snow against uncovered cheeks; the blurry play of colors when she squinted, the woods flickering like out-of-focus movie frames; even the chill in her fingers, which sank slowly through gloves and skin to settle like whispers in the bones. Before long she felt something nearly unthinkable: the imminent return of her equilibrium.

Afterward, Goldenbelle felt unaccountably drowsy, though it was only midafternoon. She lay down in the shed with the dogs and, within seconds, fell asleep. Naomi seized on the opportunity to call the others. "Goldie needs our help," she said, and without hesitation her sisters sprang into action. Pauline left her work mid-equation and hiked down the mountain, while Gemma and her wife packed up their motorcycles and sped toward the house, saddlebags filled with home-brewed beer and gifts for the family.

By dinnertime they were all sitting around the long alder wood table, eating grilled moose meat and listening to Goldenbelle recount her adventures. She told them how she came to be among the band, how she took an almost mystical nourishment from their music, how she was smitten with all of them and chose to spread her adoration among them. The youngest daughter omitted nothing from her tale. She knew she did not have to fear judgment in this place.

After she spoke, there was a thoughtful silence. At last Lottie spoke up. "Well, I think you should start your *own* band," she said, as if the matter were already decided.

Gemma turned to her wife and beamed. "I concur."

"You know," Goldenbelle said with a smile, "maybe I will."

When the meal was finished, Naomi instructed her daughters to recite the mantras she had given them more than a decade ago.

"But Mama," protested Paulina, feeling girlish and a bit shy. "We haven't said them in years."

"All the more reason," insisted Naomi. She fixed them all with what the girls privately termed her

Mama Bear Glare, which was an indicator of the seriousness of her demands.

Paulina sighed. "Fine. I'll go first I guess." As she spoke, the coils in her brain sparked to life, filling the corners of the room with their characteristic glow. "I am wise," she incanted. "I know my mind. I cannot be outthought."

Next was Gemma, with her radiant spine, her nested framework of splendor, curving and notched like the column of a medieval church. "I am sturdy," she said. "I know my strength. I cannot be broken."

"Goldie, your turn."

Goldie gazed around at the luminous faces of her family, knit together by love and tradition and the firm hand of a mother's determination. For the first time in years, she felt that things would be all right. Felt, if not quite happy, then at least on an upward trajectory toward it.

"I am courage personified," she said, warming to the words and their sheaves of tumbled history. She saw Griff's lovely face before her, saw the unmatched affection in her eyes. Saw Owen and the others clamoring to be near the light she contained. Saw the whole Alaskan tundra sprawled out before her, clear and white, a tabula rasa merely awaiting her singular imprint. "I know my heart." And as she spoke, she felt herself open up to the world again, felt her love curling out like a young wolf in every direction, not vicious, not predatory, but fierce and indomitable. "I cannot be outloved."

Hours later, when she ventured outside, she found the night sky had erupted into color.

"Hello, Aurora," she said. "You're looking beautiful today."

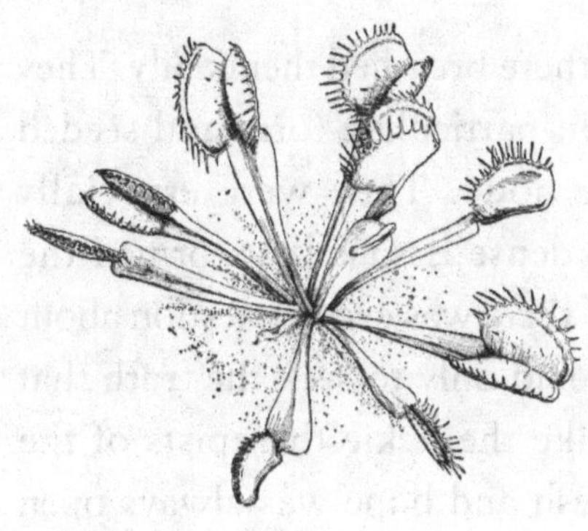

death comes for the
trophy wife

ALLISON HAD BEEN POURED INTO HER BEAUTY, IT SEEMED, AND SO IT WAS IN BEAUTY THAT SHE PLACED HER FAITH. SHE CARRIED IT LIKE A CANDLE IN HER hands. Nurtured it. Gave it ample air. Shielded it from rough winds. Over the years its preservation became the central object of her life, and the altar on which she prostrated herself morning, noon, and night. When necessary, she even called down angels from the sky—the valorous kind, angels with swords—to defend it. She would not let it go without a fight.

Like a nun, Allison lived cloistered among others of her own kind. The vows she took were nowhere explicitly stated; instead, they hung like a cloud of incense over the verdant hills of her community.

Everyone who lived there breathed them daily. They entered their lungs in particulate form and seeded every sector of the body. They were especially concentrated in the dense tissues that formed the heart and liver, and if there was ever a question about what was right, one had only to seek the truth that winked within. Unlike the fickle therapists of the city, the oracle of flesh and bone was always open for consultation.

Chief among her vows was a pledge to uphold the reigning narrative, and Allison more than did her part in this respect. She volunteered. She entertained. She took every opportunity to publicly flatter her husband. She bore the right number of children, neither too many nor too few. She saw and was seen. But most importantly, she labored like a seamstress on the mortal canvas of herself, a kind of Bayeux tapestry in reverse, in which each stitch was designed to erase the battles she had seen, to unmake history and swallow time like a golden orb. For her dedication, she was allowed to retain her special status. To remain in the stronghold.

She and the other wives.

Goddamn Babs is at it again, ALLISON THOUGHT irritably. She maneuvered the Escalade out of the eight-car garage, around the cobblestone loop, and down the long, sinuous driveway, where the Bismarck palm trees were posted like sentries. An allée, the landscaper had called it. Allison had wanted to plant valley oaks, with their lush, drooping boughs that swept the ground like a curtain of velvet, or else poplars, with their trunks like strange matchsticks, their streamlined form taut and elegant against the sky. But the landscaper had only laughed and said they wouldn't grow. So they had planted palms instead, and to Allison, these looked tired and tawdry. They reminded her somehow of the Vegas strip.

The black gates opened automatically, sliding open like the gates of the world always did for her, so that she was at last freed from the veritable fortress that was her Beverly Hills estate. Relieved, she let out her breath slowly. She could feel the sense of dread leave her. She felt it sweep up and away, like a black cloak gusting into the sky, rippling as it rose, until it was only a tiny mark upon a backdrop of sun. A dead pixel in a sea of yellow.

This is how it had been for her lately. Within the bounds of the estate, Allison found herself consumed by a free-floating sense of terror. When it settled on her, it was like a too-tight choker necklace, or a wire closing around her larynx. Out of instinct, she often raised her hands to her throat, trying to pry it free, and if there happened to be witnesses, she had no choice but to laugh it off, claiming a momentary scare. "Someone must have walked over my grave," she would say with her trademark smile. Bryn and Jamie had noticed this behavior and had begun to eye her warily. Eva, the nanny, had noticed. Even Modesto had noticed. Keith, however, had not.

The house itself was not the problem, of course. Allison felt nothing but pride for its immense Ionic columns, its polished limestone floors, its myriad skylights and curving mahogany stairs. She had personally designed the lagoon-style pool in the back and had insisted on importing hand-painted Mediterranean tile in place of the less-pricey domestic facsimile. Keith had fussed the expected amount, then had let it go. After all, it allowed him to boast to his friends that his wife had expensive tastes.

Truly, the house was magnificent. It was more sophisticated than the homes of Allison's friends, which pleased her, and when it bustled with activity, she felt that she had been transformed into a veritable queen bee, as if she were Nefertiti issuing commands from on high. Legions would attend to her every upraised hand, and assistants rendered her dictates on smartphones instead of papyrus. But today no one was home but a skeleton staff: two maids, a cook, and a gardener. Keith was at the surgery center. Bryn and Jamie were at school. And though it was midsummer, the boiler was somehow stuck in a state of constant distress, producing a horrible bellowing sound that suggested a leviathan awaking from its slumber. The feeling of the wire upon her throat grew ever more intense. She had to get out of there.

Keith's mother's visit earlier that morning had only compounded this. Babs often made unannounced visits, under the pretext of offering help, but she and Allison both understood that these social calls were mere excuses to disparage the way Allison administered her household. She would sweep in like a torrent of wind, the massive Spanish Eclectic double doors shuddering at her touch. She seldom paused to say 'hello' before launching into her latest tirade. Allison suspected that Babs rehearsed her speeches ahead of time, for, like a skilled orator, she always seemed to have material prepared. She was not afraid to playact, to dramatize, to deliver profanity-laced soliloquies, and her accusations of negligence were often as hilarious as they were overblown. It was impressive, in a way; Babs had the argumentative heart of a lawyer. When Allison was feeling charitable, she wondered what the woman's life might have been like if she hadn't been discouraged from taking a vocation, hadn't been pressed to marry some wealthy financier instead. Among Babs's favorite topics were the condition of the house and grounds (derelict), the type and frequency of the children's haircuts (terrible and too few), and, of course, Allison's clothes (utterly inappropriate for the occasion).

"My God, it's a Monday," the woman had exclaimed this morning, shaking her head in mock surprise at Allison's décolletage-baring ensemble.

"How much cleavage can possibly be required on a Monday?"

This, even though Allison remembered all too well the way Babs used to dress when they first met. Transparent bodysuits. Skin-hugging latex with diamond cutouts across the midsection. Snakeskin corsets that were two sizes too small. She had put the Boulevard girls to shame. Allison, at least, was tasteful about it. She wore only upper-end designer clothes, and only ones that exuded elegance and glamor as well as sex. Keith had laughed off Babs's criticism like he always did, and truth be told it was the sort of thing that never used to bother Allison, either. Babs was not a threat to her. Her husband had long since departed ("for warmer climes and firmer asses," Babs liked to say), and her bitterness toward her still-thriving daughter-in-law was to be expected. But now, after what she had seen outside the club, ordinary things had begun to take on a sinister pall. Allison could no longer dismiss anything out of hand. Looking at Babs's wizened face, her slender frame held aloft by five-inch Ferragamo heels, it almost seemed like the woman *knew*. As if the encounter had somehow reverberated back through time, alerting those inquisitive ears to this ominous development, and wouldn't she just be pleased as punch to have something like *that* to hang over Allison's head. *I was right all along about that one*, she would say, tut-tut-tutting to her friends at the yacht club, and to Keith.

Whenever I looked at her, I could feel my blood curdling like milk. Then Allison would be banished, like the plague bringers of old. Doomed to wander the hills of the suburbs like blind old Oedipus, eking out a meager existence among the discount grocers and pawnshops.

Perhaps this was the real harm of a liberal arts education, she thought ruefully. It encouraged melodrama. Worse, yet, it prompted one to seek shapes within the shapeless, to detect meaning in what was essentially meaningless. Though meant to refine and enrich the soul, it was itself a kind of lie. It placed a gem-laden mask over a grotesque world.

SHE WAS NOT ALWAYS SO CYNICAL. THERE WAS childhood, once, before the beauty took root, or at least before the repercussions of that beauty had begun to crash against her like waves, propelling her toward cold, unfamiliar shores. Her body was just a thing she inhabited; it was feral and strong, sheathed in downy mammalian hairs. It served no one's needs but her own. She had parents who doted and urged nonconformity for her and her brother. She had a home library that was like a vault she could occupy. She had her own garden out back, rich with worms like shining topaz, with dirt that seemed to love her as everything did, that was drawn to her as to a magnet, accreting upon the knees of her overalls and lying in thick crescents beneath her fingernails.

As a teenager, there was a ring and a promise of fidelity, and a canoe trip in the same waters where silver hooks pierced the mouths of glistening fish, which would flail and beat wildly against their fate, and she and the boy had flailed, too, oh yes, grasping together until they both collapsed in a confusion of exhaustion and bliss, and she had felt there was something so profound about this that the memory remained wholly undisturbed within her. Though everything else might degrade, might alter in its critical essence, that day alone for her was immutable. Afterward, his parents had swooped down like condors in the canyons, carrying him back to his Orthodox compound, sending him like a reluctant pilgrim across the world, and then he was lost to her, his dark hair a blessing she still invoked on her loneliest nights.

Later still, there was the lightning arc of poems, which forked through her and made her feel that she was not of the Earth only, that she was pieced together from the matter of stars. That she might one day earn her keep in the hallowed vaults of the world.

But the world had not wanted her words or her independence. These, she learned, were unwelcome. Though her brother had gone on to forge a career as an art director, her own ambitions were treated as an aberration. *Why would such a pretty girl bother with college?* the voices asked. *With poetry? With books?* As if intellect were as out of reach for her as a distant sun. Her professors had condescended. Had smiled indulgently. Had offered halfhearted advice from the disarray of their rumpled sheets, their pale members taking aim at her like arrows. And so, on the night before graduation, she had gone to the crossroads with the candle in her hands, and she had made her deal.

Things were so much easier after that. People stopped asking *why why why*, and instead began to nod when they saw her, as if to say, yes, we approve. Yes, this is right. Yes, you have at last met our expectations.

She pursued her new life without looking back. Flung herself into it like a diver into the deepest oceans, embracing at once its silken dimensions and membranous currents. In her passion she cast off her rebreather as if it were a useless husk. She had not expected to rise again.

ALLISON WAS TO MEET SOME OF THE OTHER WIVES for lunch, but as it was only 10:30 she decided to first make a circuit of her favorite boutiques. In every shop she drew the usual coterie of sales clerks—combed and polished young people with eyes like grappling hooks, who orbited her like a ring of electrons until she either accepted their assistance or shrugged them off. Of course, they all knew her name. *Yes, Mrs. Redstone. We're expecting a new shipment next week, Mrs. Redstone.* She knew most of their names as well, though she seldom deployed them unless she wanted something that required extra-special effort (extra effort alone was considered part of their jobs). Most were in awe of her, and she did nothing to discourage this.

At Escada there was a new employee—young, likely gay—to whom she took an instant liking. He wore Tom Ford knockoff glasses, a striped shirt, slim-cut lavender pants, and shiny loafers. When she favored him with a small smile, he looked as if he might burst.

"Mrs. Redstone!" he gushed, shaking her hand vigorously. "It's such a pleasure to finally meet you. I'm Barry."

"Hello, Barry. I haven't seen you before."

"Yes, I just started three days ago. It's been a dream so far; this place is like my personal fashion shrine. I know every inch of it already. Ask me anything!"

"Thank you," Allison said. "I will if I need to." It was a gentle reproach, designed to help him better understand the disparity of status between them, specifically the distinction between her role as a customer and his as an employee. Clerks were free to express interest in the customer's life, were, in fact, encouraged to do so, but in a respectful way and within an established set of topical parameters, and though she might engage conversationally in return, there was certainly no expectation that she should. Clerks did not make demands of the customer, even in a lighthearted way.

"Of course. Please forgive me, Mrs. Redstone, I just get very excited. I'm like a puppy that way. And please let me know if you'd like any assistance with your shopping." He started to walk off, then turned back, midstride, as if remembering something. "Oh, I forgot! Didn't I see you outside of Factory this weekend? It's one of my favorite night spots." He flashed her a sly grin. This was another intimacy that would normally require a gentle course correction, but at the moment Allison was too stunned to administer it.

"Factory?" she repeated blankly.

"Yes, Factory. It was this past Saturday night. There was a Pet Shop Boys cover band playing, don't you remember? They were fantastic."

A prick of fear touched the nape of Allison's neck. She felt its outline like a thumbprint on her skin. "No, I'm afraid you're mistaken," she said stiffly. "I haven't been to Factory in years. You have me confused with someone else."

Allison began to glance uneasily around the store. All at once, it was easy to imagine that any one of the other shoppers might in an instant transform into her doppelgänger, that their disparate features might shift and flow like liquid wax in order to approximate her own, to mold themselves to her template. The nose transforming into her elegant nose. The chin narrowing, losing its fullness. The eyes shape-shifting, turning the same shocking, icy blue. As if she were nothing special at all. As if she were only one of many possible outcomes, the first of a whole assembly line of Allisons, spinning out into universes near and far. One, perhaps, remaining behind, the manufacturing glue still wet, so that she remained stuck within the same universe as the original. She thought of the woman at the club.

Look how easy it is to be you, the doppelgänger might say with a laugh, her voice dripping with scorn. *Anyone could do it.*

Peering at Allison, a stylish woman in her midfifties narrowed her eyes. With the heightened perception afforded to those in that realm, the woman seemed to have caught her scent, the scent of a creature who was beginning to deviate from the status quo, who was displaying eccentricities like so many open wounds, and who, for the good of the pack, might need to be cast out. Left to the wolves. The woman clutched her Birkin bag tightly to her chest, further marking Allison as an outsider.

Meanwhile, Barry was apologizing profusely. He had mistaken Allison's discomfort for indignation and was mortified by the part he had played in it. "I am *so* sorry, Mrs. Redstone. Honestly, I don't know what I'm talking about most of the time. Please forgive me. Of course that wasn't you. The woman I saw was much older anyway, I remember now. You're so young and beautiful, it couldn't possibly have been you." He was so flustered he could think of nothing further to say.

"It's fine, really," she muttered, more to herself than to him.

The air in the shop had started to shimmer. It was like a glittering veil hung across the space, an overlay of tiny stars, and at the center there soon appeared a slight blue flicker, like the hottest part of a candle. Allison felt at once that familiar sensation of dread, like gleaming wire against her throat. She was certain that this visual disturbance was a mere preamble to something else, and she had no interest in sticking around to see what that might be. Anything could be there. Anything might materialize. Somehow, she found the door and made her escape.

Once outside, the veil lifted. The familiar clicking of her heels against the sidewalk provided immediate relief. Allison had always thought of this as a second heartbeat belonging only to her, a heartbeat that was light as air, its cadence not rough and soldierly, but prim and staccato, as if she were tatting out lace with each elegant step. As she heard it, her body began to right itself. Her mind stopped casting about and instead snapped to the grid of rational thought. Looking back through the plate glass windows of the boutique, she even felt a stab of sympathy at the sight of poor Barry, who was clearly miserable, hanging his head while the store manager berated him.

Karen M. Vaughn

THERE WAS A TIME WHEN ALLISON WAS YOUNG,
maybe six or seven, when her parents had taken
her and her brother Glenn to the botanical gardens
downtown. She had walked along the winding paths
with her eyes squeezed nearly shut, so that the ceiling
and the earth both fell away, leaving only the vague,
blurry shapes of the blooms themselves—the entire
world pressed into a band of flowers. So as not to
fall, she had walked slowly through the gardens, her
grubby tennis shoes meeting heel to toe. Her long
fingers raked at the soil from the upraised planters.
She felt each color as a separate ache: the bright pang
of yellow, the sting of orange, the scorch of a blazing
red, the soothing balm of blue and, throughout it all,
the luxuriant crush of green that was like pine needles
entering her heart. She had felt herself open to them,
like a canal lock letting beauty sluice through. It was
the first time she had been conscious of wanting to
commemorate what she felt, to convert a borderline
mystical experience into tangible form. It was there
that she had decided to be a poet.

For years afterward, she had filled her notebook
with earnest, heartfelt, terrible poems, each one
a wounded bird that limped when she hoped it
would soar. Upon finishing that first notebook, she
immediately began another, certain that this would be

the one in whose pages she unbottled her brilliance. Book after book was completed in this way. Aside from the quality of her handwriting, she improved but little. She coaxed and cajoled as a mother might, laboring tirelessly when she wished to record something of great importance, yet the progeny she midwifed were never a match for the visions she held in her head. They were always out of proportion somehow: the head misshapen or too large, the feet ungainly, the heart sluggish and arrhythmic. As she grew older, her own body coalesced into newer, lovelier shapes. Her cells were reassigned to different regions, tawny forests taking sudden root beneath her arms and on her pubic mound, breasts rising like warm bread. Meanwhile, her poems remained stunted. Not one of them could fly.

Just before her eighteenth birthday, the muses took pity on her. They began to show her how the words she loved could be harnessed, how their coltish whims could be utilized for the advancement of an image or a thought. They imbued her clumsy metaphors with a hint of grace. They helped her work with and not against the meter. They found ways to convey that the gaps in the poem, the things left unsaid, were as important as the words on the page. And then, one night, a fever took her, and she began to write a new poem. She held her breath writing it for she knew that this one was unlike anything she had ever done. The poem burned in her hands. It scalded the outer layers of skin, but she held onto the pencil and rode it out. The result was a creature that rolled with flames even as it took flight, even as it flew in the air over her dormitory, flew so quickly in fact that she nearly lost it to the horizon. She had to cast a single cord to the sky to tether it, so that she could continue charting its wonderful anatomy.

Her poem appeared in the student poetry review. It was soon followed by a second and a third: each one meticulous and lovely. Each one armed with its own wings. The wolves, who had heretofore humored her, now began to encroach, to encircle, to bare their teeth in snarling disapproval, and for a time, she was able to evade them. She secluded herself in a high turret papered with Eliot and Sexton and Lorde and Yeats and Hughes (Langston not Ted). She plucked similes from the walls like mushrooms. She spun iambs like golden thread. She feasted on rhythms, then drew them back up her throat, so that their knotted tendrils could be strung with words. She was never so purely happy.

Of course, once she had taken her place in the stronghold, her poetical history was considered a mere novelty, a trademark quirk that others could use to distinguish between the wives. Jeanine played the harp. Marisa bred and showed Samoyeds. Camille had played tennis professionally for a year, her promising career cut short by a knee injury. And Allison had been a poet.

Without such a background, Allison might not have been haunted by the specter at the club. Without it, she might have simply moved on with things, blithely stepping past the incident like a dumb animal. After all, what could such a coincidence mean to her? She was golden, separate. The sun beamed from her tanned face onto the world's lesser aspects, onto lesser buildings and people, their countenances rushing to soak up her unearthly radiance. But because she had once lived in the turret, her skin sometimes floated above her body, and she fell into dreams of leitmotifs and foreshadowing. This tendency of hers posed a frequent threat to her equanimity. And like her father's alcoholism, it always seemed to surface at the most inappropriate of times.

ALLISON MADE HER WAY TO THE TERRACE OF THE French restaurant, a favorite among the wives. The others were already well into their wine. They rose to greet her and exchange half hugs while Jeanine continued an elaborate anecdote about a drunken waiter she'd bedded in Napa. Such stories were part of the unspoken compact between wives. It didn't matter whether they were true, as long as they were delivered with verve and a convincing level of detail. Without them, over time, a wife's social currency would depreciate. She would stop receiving invitations to lunches, to galas, to weekends away. She would be tactfully, but obviously, avoided at the supermarket. She would become the recipient of pitying smiles, and, out of earshot, the subject of withering criticism. *Who does she think she is?* Or, *The poor thing is just falling apart; I heard her gardener laughed in her face when she tried to seduce him.* Allison had her own lascivious story prepared—which might or might not have been true—though she might not be called upon to share it.

Taking her seat, she looked around happily at her fellow wives. Jeanine. Marisa. Camille. More associates than friends, though she liked them well enough. They were haughty like gods—Allison included—and why shouldn't they be, when this was how they were treated by an envious world?

Allison ordered another bottle of rosé for the table.

When Jeanine's story came to an end, with a punchline involving an unholy trinity of semen, menstrual blood, and table linens, Camille turned to Allison. "Wasn't that just like your boyfriend in Barbados?"

"It was," Allison agreed. "Only my guy had a dick like a donkey, so the dry cleaning bill was twice as much."

They all cackled appreciatively. Stylized crudeness was another expectation of her social set: a tongue-in-cheek inversion of the proper manners their appearance suggested. Marisa dabbed at her lips to absorb the wine she had sputtered out.

Allison sat back, her gaze drifting to the other restaurant patrons. For some reason she felt more exhausted by the conversation than usual. Come to think of it, she hadn't had much sleep the night before, which might also go a long way toward explaining her strange episode in Escada. She had awoken in a cold sweat, the sheets in tangles. Like great ropes of seaweed, they had been coiled around her legs, holding her fast, and she had had the unmistakable sense of being pulled under. It was as if she were lashed to a boat that was rapidly sinking. Panicked, she tried to catch her breath but couldn't. Something huge had seemed to be sitting on her chest. When at last she had broken free from the sheets, only a single image remained from her nightmare: the woman's face.

Allison looked back at the wives, only to discover that their faces were becoming ghoulish death masks. In horror she watched as their lovely, moisturized skin began to slide off, revealing glistening bones and a meaty musculature beneath. Plump lips floated away like moth wings. Eyeballs withered and fell out of their sockets, plunking unceremoniously into wine glasses. Perfect noses collapsed inward, becoming concave. Only the bleached teeth remained, producing a nightmare gallery of grins she knew she'd ever forget. They were all still talking, each ghastly jaw moving like the puppetry it was, and so she understood that what she saw must not be real. She drank more wine, hoping to relax herself, and then she decided that the wine itself was the source of her troubles. *Stupid, stupid, stupid*, she rebuked herself. She had always had a tendency to brood when she drank to excess, and with only a few morsels of romaine lettuce in her stomach, perhaps a slivered carrot or two, it was no wonder the alcohol had turned on her so fiercely.

At this thought, Allison made her way to the bathroom and vomited up her meager lunch. *I should eat more*, she told herself, but even as she thought it, she knew that she wouldn't. None of them ever ordered more than a salad and wine for noon meals. Lunch was not for sustenance—it was a necessary ritual, a performative renewal of alliances. Every week the wives sat at this same table and gossiped about their mutual acquaintances and showed off their purchases and, by means of some dialectical undercurrent, reinforced the conditions of their world.

One of the busboys flashed Allison a provocative smile on her way back to her table, and this pleased her. He was handsome, and she knew that a dalliance with him would bolster her standing within the group. For a moment, she mulled over possible locations for a rendezvous. His home? The bathroom of a nearby bar? Certainly nowhere where they would be discovered and he could be fired. It was important that he retain his job, and not only for his own sake; the stock for a story rose dramatically if the principal actors could be observed in close proximity to one another. In the end, she decided to file the information away for a rainy day. She cast the busboy an imperious glance, tossed her hair just enough to sustain the intrigue, and sat down.

Having purged the contents of her stomach, she felt better. Even good. The cool winds off the Pacific were pleasant on her arms and neck, and the sun glinted brightly off the silverware, making her think of the searchlights that sometimes shone down from the mountains at night, those roving lights that, even in an expanse notorious for its sprawling luminosity, seemed unique in symbolizing the manic optimism of the city. *You will never again be in the dark*, they seemed to promise. *You will be found, made famous, covered in glory.*

The faces of the other wives had reverted to their previous forms. Jeanine, statuesque and blonde. Marisa, curvaceous and blonde. Camille, athletic and blonde. Allison herself the only brunette among them. Together, they formed a dazzling quadrumvirate. Yes, they had all had breast augmentations, rhinoplasties, brow lifts, liposuction, the works (though they would never admit it), but no one in their circle judged them for it unless it was done poorly. Such surgeries were simply the cost of doing business. It was no different from the twice-a-week tans and the spin classes and the Botox and the hair that was always, *always* to be worn down, that was made to float around the shoulders, long and girlish, like something out of a fairy tale. Often, glimpsing their parallel forms in mirrors or in store windows, Allison was reminded of mermaids fresh from a restless sea, their fins temporarily parted to resemble legs.

If she and the other wives looked a bit ridiculous to outsiders, like caricatures with too-taut skin, it was only because they had transcended the real. They were denizens of some higher plane, free from the concerns that plagued mere mortals. This was okay. None of them would ever have to change a tire or do her own laundry again.

"I ran into Blair at yoga," Jeanine was saying. "She has a friend interested in some freshening up—apparently she's looking a little less Sophia Loren and a little more like Sophia from *The Golden Girls*, if you know what I mean—so I told her to look up Dr. Weitzman. I haven't used him myself, of course, but I hear the recovery spa is a paradise. Better than Ibiza."

"Ha!" Camille snorted. "I think I'd rather go to Ibiza."

"Me, too," Marisa chimed in. "If I wanted some pasty doctor coming at me with a knife I'd get back with my ex-husband."

They all laughed again, and Allison raised her glass ceremoniously. "Cheers to that."

Jeanine smiled. "Not everyone is as lucky as we are, ladies. Some poor souls need a little help."

"Yes, and some need a *lot* of help," Marisa added with a giggle.

There was of course a protocol for addressing these modifications. If anyone remarked on their rejuvenated appearance, the wives would merely shrug and say something like, 'Good genes, I guess.' From time to time, they also liked to engage in a bit of performative banter on the subject, as this allowed each woman an opportunity to reaffirm her stance.

"What about you, Allison?" Jeanine pressed, clearly in a mischievous mood. "I know you haven't, but would you ever? If the crows descended and stomped all around your pretty eyes?"

Allison scowled. "You know I don't do horror."

More laughter.

The key to it all—to everything that mattered in their sphere—was that beauty and all its trappings had to appear to come easily, as easily as drawing breath. Because of her stint at the liberal arts school, Allison even knew the proper term for this, coined during the era of courtly love. *Sprezzatura.* A studied effortlessness. It meant to labor for weeks over a sonnet, then claim it had been dashed out in the bath. More to the point, it meant to endure surgery after painful surgery while maintaining that one was purely an 'all-natural kind of gal.' It meant to be always recovering, to be always improving, to always have the next project in mind, so that like the famed

Karen M. Vaughn

Winchester house, their bodies resonated with the ceaseless echo of hammers.

Somewhere in the sky there was the Platonic ideal of a woman, her form radiant, resplendent, her skin lusciously embroidered, her perforated breasts stuffed full of sublime grace. The wives devoted their lives to her example. Was this not more honest, Allison wondered, than those who claimed that beauty counted for nothing? That the soul was all that mattered? This was often told to children, but Allison had eyes, and, more importantly, she had read poetry. She knew better. One had only to mark the observations of Keats, whose words she repeated like a mantra to the mirror each morning, as she drew herself out, as she traced the glittering image in the air and then stepped into it: "Beauty is truth, truth beauty, that is all / Ye know on earth, and all ye need to know."

Her gaze wandered, caught by the curve of a seagull preening on a railing, and she allowed herself to think for a moment of her lost beau in the boat, whose parents had whisked him away and reinstalled him in a far-off realm of rules. She wondered if it was significant that, in the years since, she had found her way to her own place of orthodoxy.

ON THE NIGHT SHE HAD MET KEITH, THE WORLD WAS alive with signs. It had been a cool spring evening at the ranch club, and the wind coming down from

236

the mottled mountains carried with it the sweet odor of Ponderosa pine, but just behind that scent was something else, something deeper, earthier, more metallic. This smell, when detected, seemed at once to fade into the olfactory background, dissolving like a dream, so that she was uncertain she had smelled it at all. As the night wore on it continued to pass in and out of her consciousness. Like a melody caught midair, it would briefly emerge, only to vanish the moment she became aware of it, at which point the smell of pine would come rolling back in—a heady, fragrant cloud of it—as if whatever lay beneath was taking great pains to mask itself in something pleasant. There was also the sun, which took much longer than usual to set. It was beautiful, yes—almost unnervingly so—but somehow its progress seemed to have been arrested at that spot where the horizon formed a rippling tangent along the sphere's base. The sun simply held itself there, poised in tantric anticipation, a luminous, blood-red egg preparing to crack itself on the horizon, but never quite doing so. Additionally, there was the plaintive cry of a lone puma, which was common enough in the canyon, but which for some reason that night pierced the air like a strange witch's cry, like something out of Macbeth, the sound breaking apart and skittering across the valley like a legion of beetles, so that its origin was impossible to pinpoint. Hearing this, Allison had the thought, *If I followed that cry into the forest, I*

*would for certain be lost. Not even bread crumbs
could save me.*

She had come to the club with Glenn, who assured
her it was the place to go to meet creative people,
many of them highly influential. "It could help you
with your poetry thing," he suggested. "Plus, there's
loads of fun to be had, although lucky for you it's not
required." Glenn loved the ranch club. He thrived
on the retro-rustic setting, as well as the spectacle
created whenever he swept in with his Hollywood
friends and very publicly lit a cigar, like an old-world
tycoon. He dressed in the expected rancher's garb,
pulling that persona taut over himself like a second
skin. He had it all: the cowboy hat, the designer jeans,
the prominent and showy belt buckle (his was silver
and etched with a glowering steer's head), the fancy
Lucchese cowboy boots that had never had more
than the occasional contact with dirt of any kind.
Allison, meanwhile, had been unwilling to commit
to the full costume. She had dressed herself in a pair
of jeans, a vaguely Western-style shirt, and a silk
kerchief around her neck. On her feet she wore her
standard riding boots, the ones she'd worn every day
in college, back when her sartorial choices reflected
her vision of herself as a kind of love child of Sylvia
Plath and Jackie Onassis.

The club, difficult to find, lay at the intersection
of two far-flung rural roads, and when the Jeeps and
Land Rovers turned the last corner into the half-

mile-long drive, they often spun the red soil up into short-lived dust devils, which whirled along the road behind them like sulfurous clouds. This was where some of the richest of L.A. came to network and play cowboy and generally replicate the atmosphere of an earlier, manlier era. Standing beside the split rail fence that flanked the building, it was easy to picture the world as it might have been a century and a half earlier: rugged, mostly lawless, replete with stagecoaches and perhaps a mining town just out of view, its clapboard buildings dropped like pebbles along the mountainside, a beguiling medley of supply stores, barber shops, liveries, and, naturally, whorehouses.

Upon entering, Glenn made a few introductions, then quickly decamped to the stables with six of his friends to go riding. The miles of trails laid out all around the ranch, forking and intersecting like a massive circulatory system, were one of the chief attractions of the club, and Allison knew it played a big part in why Glenn kept coming back. Still, she was annoyed that he had abandoned her so early in the evening. He had never understood—chose *not* to understand, she thought—how she relied on him in such situations. In any new crowd, she inevitably found herself inundated (some might say plagued) with interested men. They approached brazenly or shyly, with drinks in hand or without, with offers that were sometimes direct and salacious, sometimes barely intelligible, their hushed voices affected with a variety of antique sensibilities (mid-century, Jazz Age, even medieval). She felt the gazes of the men even before she saw them, their sinews drawn toward her like the strings of marionettes, like honeybees flocking to an unwitting flower stamen. And this was not even counting the women, whose gazes were more complex, who sometimes lusted and admired like the men, but who more often denigrated, scowling at her with their arms seized tightly upon their husbands' shoulders. These accusing glares put her immediately on the defensive, for they seemed to demand that she explain herself, that she explain away her beauty, and furthermore, that she set aside her own agenda long enough to put them at ease, proving through a theatrical display of self-deprecation that she was not a threat. She could never simply enter a room. There was too much subtext. And so she counted on her brother to act as a filter, to deflect the sketchiest among the crowd. To carve out a space for her that was relatively safe. He moved with such ease through the world; she did not think it was too much to ask.

But, of course, it was.

She would have to do the filtering herself this time.

Brushing off a few early advances, she fled to a dim corner and, using her still acute poet's eye, tried to do the observing for once. Along the perimeter of the room she saw the elders, mostly men; these had installed themselves like sovereigns in the stuffed leather chairs, sipping their vintage whiskey and daring anyone to approach them. More toward the middle she found a ring of middle-aged career men accompanied by their wives and girlfriends. Without exception, these mingled in pairs and were livelier than their elder counterparts, though still subdued in the way of those who have reached a more established station in life, those for whom daily comforts and routines have slowly whittled away at the impulsiveness of youth. In the center roamed the young bucks and does. They were the still restless ones. They milled about, coupling then decoupling, each duo orbiting experimentally around each another as if executing the steps of an elaborate dance. It was in this central sphere that she first saw Keith. He was dark-haired (naturally), reasonably tall, and she liked that he had a slightly underfed look about him, especially when compared with the standard gym rat physique that was so prevalent at the club. As he approached, he adopted a comical, John Wayne–type swagger, and she smiled at this little cleverness, thinking how such a move was guaranteed to work not only on an ironic (and therefore intellectual) level, but also on a deeper, more reptilian one. Brains might discriminate, but bodies took one another at face value.

"We haven't met," he said simply, letting the burden of introduction fall on her.

"No, we haven't. I'm Allison Harcourt." She held out her hand.

He shook it, then continued to hold it as he spoke, as if he were already claiming her for himself. "Glenn's your brother?"

"Unfortunately so."

"Well, that explains the dazzling good looks, although of course they work better on you. Where is he now, anyway?"

She rolled her eyes. "He's off playing Magnificent Seven with some of his friends."

He laughed: a huge and boisterous guffaw. She liked the way he threw his head back as he did it, utterly unabashed, like a little boy clowning around with his friends. "You know, I thought about doing that, too," he said. "It's a gorgeous night for a ride, and they have some marvelous Arabians stabled up, just waiting to run their hearts out. But I have a feeling I'm going to be glad I stuck around here." He added the last with a coy smile. "Keith Redstone, by the way. I'm an investment banker. I'm only two years into the business, though, so I still have the remnants of a soul rattling around in here somewhere." He laughed at his own joke, and though she knew it was a line—one he had no doubt repeated *ad nauseam* to other interested parties—she had to admit that the confidence behind it was irresistible. As he talked, he lightly stroked her palm with his thumb, an intimate gesture meant to convey all sorts of erotic possibilities.

They spent upwards of an hour in close conversation, after which she knew not that he was the one, but that he would do, if that was what she wanted: knew that, given the last bit of information she had yet to collect, they could enter the stronghold together and flourish within their given roles. Such a life was not something she had ever considered. She had always thought herself superior to those who had chosen it, believing its devotees to be vacuous, shallow, and, if not evil, at least greatly morally compromised. In the moment, however, the appeal was evident. She began to toy with the idea. Why not, just for the evening, pretend?

They selected the best horses from the stables, then rode them out to the far perimeter of the ranch. His mare was a pure black Friesian, hers a dappled Orlov, gray and muscular, a sleek machine moving like a planet beneath her, absorbing her into itself as all good riding horses did, harnessing its atoms to hers so that it felt like they had intermingled and become something entirely new: a kind of chimera with two heartbeats. She thought of all the horse poems she had written over the years, beginning at the age of five when she took her first riding lessons. Most of these poems were misbegotten birds, heavy like stones, but she did not regret have made them. They had been born from earnestness, and from a childlike certainty that it was somehow possible to render the ineffable into language. In truth, Allison cherished the ache of each of these literary failures. Loved each one for its shambling inadequacies. Was not the passion that had spawned them itself a kind of testament, a fractured tribute to the wonder she had felt in simply being alive? She considered their weight lifted from her, and the absence was like a bruise. No, much more than a bruise. A wound.

They had almost reached the edge of the canyon when Keith dismounted. As he helped Allison down, he continued the business at hand. "Where is your family from?" he asked.

"Brentwood," she said. He nodded, pleased, knowing that she would understand the true terms at hand, the unspoken words carved beneath the rose arch. "I'm Pacific Palisades, myself."

He set down a blanket he had brought with him, and without further ado they lowered themselves onto it, him unbuttoning her shirt as if he'd been destined to do so, as if it were his sojourner's right, his fingers making short work of that constellation of pearly buttons across her chest. And she thought, *I could have been anyone. There is nothing about me that resonates other than this tanned husk with its sable mane, this bankable provenance. He does not, will not, know me.* But there was freedom in this, too. Her beauty was not a blight here. Not an obstacle to be overcome. There were no questions, no Machiavellian schemes designed to patronize her intellect while maneuvering into her pants. Here, she had nothing to explain. There was no poetry, but neither was there a need for it. Her birds could wing their way elsewhere.

She did not bother with Keith's shirt, but instead set to work on removing his jeans. When she had done so, and it was her turn, he caught the hem of one leg between his teeth, growling like a dog as he yanked them off, dragging her across the blanket and making her laugh. The kerchief he removed last, binding it tightly around her wrists. "I know you like this," he said, and the incredible presumption of this made her bristle even as she found herself aroused by it. Exhibiting a last show of autonomy, which even then she recognized as dubious, no more than the free will of a horse resisting its rider, she used the strength of her thighs to roll him over so that she was riding astride, not side-saddle as a lady would, not beneath as he wanted, and began to come at him in waves, her narrow hips a rudder steering him toward a preordained horizon. And it was nothing, *nothing* like it had been with her boy in the boat—the milky intimacy that had enveloped them, the tears, the shock of tenderness that had ripped through their hearts and left its imprint like a scar on the sky—but it was something. Crude, yes. But simple. More certain. It was an endeavor that excused her heart from the process. *Don't trouble yourself*, it murmured, reassuring; *there is no need for such difficulties here. No need for memories of gardens, or worms, or flowers, or turrets, or boys who loved you, or notebooks filled with words plucked like mushrooms from mossy walls.*

And as she and Keith heaved and panted there, Allison looked up to see the blood-red sun still hanging just above the line of rock to the west, just as it had been when they arrived. Stubborn. Implacable. Its span enormous, magnified by the atmospheric haze, that sliver of glittering particles in which humans were destined to live out their tiny dramas. Flares licked up from the surface, and she could just make out the ghostly corona, with its sheaves of plasma feathering out in all directions. She stared at it without blinking, half hoping to be blinded (for then the decision would be made for her), and then it seemed to her that the sun began to divide, splitting its yolk shape slowly into two separate parts, a kind of cosmic mitosis. Each half disclosed to her its qualities: in the yolk on the left she perceived certainty and status, a relief from having to fight always to have her true self seen, for here her true self was incidental; in the yolk on the right she saw something far more vague, foggy, numinous, something that was purely her own but accompanied by that ever-present struggle, and just the sight of this brought her such weariness she didn't think she could bear it further. She was so weary already of the contempt of peers, of being patronized, of being uncertain whether praise from her mentors came from parts lofty or low. So weary of always having to assert and safeguard her identity. And so she made her choice, felt the yes click into place, and as she did so the two parts of the sun fell back together, the dual lobes fusing once more into one, and only then did it at last descend, slipping like a stone beneath the lip of the horizon. In its place a film of stars rose up. It rolled upward like a pinholed sheet, swiftly, with such force that it caused a sudden gust of wind to rush through, making gooseflesh of her bare skin. And Keith trembled beneath her, a quivering, eyeless lump. A monster from a story. She did not look at him but continued her undulations until she heard again upon the mountainside the lone puma's cry, and she recognized it as her own, and she knew that the deal was final.

KEITH HAD ALWAYS HAD MISTRESSES, IF THAT'S WHAT you called them—Allison considered this a hilariously old-fashioned term. She had known several of them by name, others by reputation alone, and still others no doubt she had had no knowledge of whatsoever. Whenever she encountered one, in a restaurant or at a salon, she liked to size them up, to consider what it was that Keith saw in them and classify them according to her own personal taxonomy. Which were likely to be short-term flings? Which had the makings of a girlfriend, or even a replacement? It was not that she felt threatened; she felt it was incumbent on her to stay informed. If there was a major life shift ahead of her, she wanted to know about it. Besides, it was interesting. In observing and cataloguing his predilections, it was as if she were unearthing a hoard of boyish secrets, reading the psychological landscape he would never have willingly revealed to her.

She noticed, for one, that he chose brunettes almost exclusively, and mostly those who were around her own height or taller. A woman shorter than herself signaled an abbreviated liaison, and the shorter the woman, the shorter the affair. He liked heart-shaped faces. Large eyes. Tiny waists. He liked legs that were proportionally too long for their accompanying torsos. He liked freckles on the arms and neck, but not near the breasts. He liked ears that were rounded like C's; square ears or longer lobes were a non-starter. He liked small, discreet tattoos. (She suspected this was because they enhanced his experience of illicit eroticism while not being so substantial as to hamper their owner's general presentability.) He also liked larger mouths and a pronounced gap between the front two teeth, which was something she couldn't help noticing that Babs possessed as well. Truly, Allison never felt so sympathetic to her husband as those times when she discovered a new quirk of one of his mistresses and arrived at an interpretation of its significance.

When confronted, most of these women folded quickly beneath the focused beam of Allison's beauty. A few stood their ground against her icy-blue stare, giving her a challenging look in return, and to these she could only respond with an amused laugh. It didn't behoove anyone to take the game so seriously. She was well aware that if Keith happened upon a woman of unusual loveliness, with a spark of something that interested him (Allison flattered herself that it would at least have to be someone with a spark), then he would leave her in a heartbeat and without a second thought. And truly, she thought, they were welcome to him. The end of her marriage was not an outcome she dreaded. It was just the next stage of evolution for a woman in her position. She and the other wives had all entered into their respective agreements knowingly, their long-lashed eyes wide open, their lawyers crouched and ready for action. As long as the man behaved in a decent fashion and arranged for his ex-wife to remain in her accustomed lifestyle, then he was considered to have done no wrong.

As for the wives, they were expected to establish a flirtatious rapport with their friends' husbands. To touch their collars and brush the lint from their suits and whisper conspiratorially in their ears at parties. These little frissons, like tiny stars sparking the air, were encouraged and endorsed by all participants. It was only when a pair began to talk about their shared hobbies—art, meditation, a musical instrument, anything that was real—that they were thought to have crossed a line. This was because the one thing that was frowned upon above all else was ditching one wife for another, as this created chaos within the system and was considered disrespectful to the other man involved. Men and women who found themselves in this type of situation were immediately ostracized. It had happened to her friend Libby Sandelford, a lovely brunette who had eloped with James Franklin, her friend Kate's husband. She missed Libby—the two had become very close when their children were small—but she still didn't answer the phone when Libby called. The last Allison had heard, they had moved to a bayside palace in Tampa, far from the glowing lights of LA, a pair of Napoleons living out their remaining years in exile.

Allison rubbed her shoulders, which were still aching from her early morning pool laps. Sometimes she felt like Joan Crawford in *Mommie Dearest*, swimming in an endless circuit, running the treadmill for hours upon hours, doing hot yoga and Pilates and spin class, only to do it all again the following day. *If they only knew the price I pay.* There were compensations to having a pool, however: chief among them Modesto, about whom there was absolutely nothing modest. He was handsome, Guatemalan, often shirtless. He cleaned the pool every Wednesday from two to four p.m., first combing it for leaves and other debris, casting the net through the water like a champion flyfisher, capturing everything he sought within its span. Next, he employed the brush along the sides and bottom, and set up the noisy vacuum. It was then that he found some time to spare for other pursuits. She had heard him speaking to his peers without an accent—a voice as American as apple pie—but with her, the lilting intonation always seemed to return. Another concession to expectation, she supposed.

It was a cliché, yes, but Wednesdays with Modesto were the only times lately that she had felt that the world was real, that the things around her were in any way solid in their shape or form. Besides, sleeping with the pool boy was her right as a wife, just as it was Keith's right to keep a stable of coltish mistresses all over town. Allison's attentions had not even come as a surprise to Modesto. She had only said something along the lines of, "I need your help with the thermostat. Won't you come up and check?" And in no time at all he was upstairs, lounging on the bed beside her, his slim olive body leaning in already, almost without invitation, so that she wanted to castigate him for his forthrightness even as she slid her hands down his torso, unbuttoning his trousers. He had not taken his eyes off her that whole first time, and in response, she had felt her body become a hard coil of physicality. As with Heisenberg's uncertainty principle, the act of being observed altered her. She felt at once the golden outline of her organs; the racing blood; the urgent semaphore of her animal brain, advocating food, shelter, sleep, sex (the latter was the clear priority at the moment); as well as the heightened fleshy organism squirming at the center of her being, that nebulous thing that, had she not known better, she might have called a soul. All around her, objects shifted back into their proper place. The atoms in the walls were no longer desolate and distant; they moved closer together, the spaces between constricting like sphincters. The planets, too, resumed their ideal positions. While she was with Modesto, the universe seemed to right itself.

Since that day, these encounters were the only thing capable of drowning out the extraneous noises in her head—the questions she could not stop asking herself, her regrets, the cries of the pitiful, stunted birds, born limp in the air with nowhere to go, multiplying, metastasizing day after day until there were huge ghastly fields of them—though of course now there was the boiler to contend with, carrying on its own campaign of terror. It wailed all through their grapplings like a mourner at a gravesite, wild and wrathful. Its keening could have filled oceans. The grief it emitted was an absolute.

"You ought to fix that thing," Modesto would murmur softly, as if it were an endearment.

"We've tried," she would say with a sigh. "It's just too angry."

Then Modesto would shrug and forget about the sound, tuning it out with some masculine singularity of purpose, his compass needle always attuned, always finding north.

Keith still had sex with her several times a month, naturally. He had done so, in fact, the night of the incident outside the club. He had put on his favorite porno—*Cream Queens*—and yanked Allison's hair from behind, and to get it over with quickly she had arched her back and mimicked the actress being penetrated by a masked intruder on screen, moaning ridiculously in the whorish way that he loved. She tried to empty her thoughts, tried not to think of the woman's face outside the club, her very features an accusation, and the gruesome flash of insight she'd had upon seeing her, circumscribed within that flickering screen of blue. It was as if she were watching a movie with frames missing. She saw the woman, felt a creeping patina of horror, which at first registered only externally, vibrating across her skin before seeping in and making its way into her logic centers. Then the film seemed to jump ahead. All at once she was watching the woman's head flop back against the glittering night, becoming a bas relief of gristle and bone.

"Nice," Keith had said to Allison when he had finished. He rolled over, leaving the video to run, so that when she began to doze off it was to the sound of moaning, the word "fuck" like an incantation cascading across her consciousness. That was when the boiler had first started up its racket. It had roared to life, like a demon released from the depths, and Allison sat bolt upright in bed, thinking their alarm system must have been triggered by a raccoon or a stray animal. Unable to wake Keith, she had gone down to inspect the system herself, and finding it undisturbed, she followed the column of sound to the basement. There she faced at last that hulking edifice of metal.

As she stood there, dwarfed by its tremendous size, she realized she had never really looked at the thing before. For some reason it appeared much older than she thought it should, given the age of the house. It looked like an antique. It was primitive in style, and although she considered the possibility that it was a new boiler that had merely been designed to have a Victorian look, she somehow didn't think this was the case. It *felt* old to her, not only in its style but in its very essence. She felt, too, a sudden certainty that it had been imported from some other place, and in fact when she glanced down, she saw what looked like matching drag marks on the ground beside it. A chill traveled down the length of her spine. She felt frozen to the spot. She looked up, suddenly cognizant of the byzantine network of pipes that protruded from the back of the boiler at increasingly strange angles, as well as the rust patterns on the front, which, when illuminated by the naked bulb overhead, seemed to dance across the surface of the metal, forming nightmare shapes that dissolved just before she was able to identify them. *Stop it,* she told herself. *You've only spooked yourself. There is nothing sinister here: just a broken machine.*

Taking a deep breath, she stepped forward to examine the gauges; they all looked normal. Nothing was in the red. No steam was escaping. There was no apparent dripping or leakage of water. There were no signs of malfunction at all. But still the wailing went on, so loudly now that her ears began to ring, and in frustration she picked up a wrench, intending to deliver a "technical tap" to the side of the appliance. But at the last minute she checked the blow. With her hand so close to the surface, a ripple of horror passed through her. She had an image of unspeakable things gliding below, a whole bustling highway of them, and with it came a sudden conviction that these things, whatever they were, were aware of her presence, that their machinations had slowed as her fingers drew near the metal, that they were watching, listening, holding themselves in temporary stasis, their razor teeth arranged in a perfect circle, rotating perhaps, as they awaited her next move. She could not bring herself to do it.

She padded upstairs to find the children standing in the hall awaiting an explanation, and with a few hurried reassurances she sent them back to their beds. Unsure of how to proceed, she stepped into the darkened kitchen, popped a Xanax for the first time in weeks, washed it down with few gulps of wine, and went upstairs again to her and Keith's bedroom, where the soft tendrils of the medicine were already starting to take effect, softening the edges of her fear and gently pulling her toward sleep. Just before drifting off, she noticed (without any particular concern) that the boiler's ominous wail was in sync with the actress on screen; its persistent lament was somehow indistinguishable from her rhythmic, jolting movements, suggesting violence, as well as her unconvincing orgasm, which never seemed to end but went on and on, rising into higher and higher registers, like a voice from the next world. Like some infinite, prehistoric shriek.

"It was new with the house," Keith complained the following day. "State of the art. Don't worry, I'll call somebody."

But at least four somebodys had come and gone since that declaration, and still the boiler moaned on, immune to all attempts to repair it. The handymen (and one handywoman) had merely stood before it in respectful puzzlement, scratching their heads and muttering how it was "just the damndest thing." To all appearances, the boiler was in perfect working order. Of course, the technicians never charged for their visits, and they invariably departed the premises with thoughtful, humbled expressions, as if their faith in the arcane wonders of machinery had just been restored. "She's a beauty," one of them said to Allison, his eyes twinkling distantly, as if that were recompense for being troubled with this strange howling beast. "Guess she's just a bit eccentric."

Mercifully, the boiler did not make noise all the time. There were periods of blissful respite, of silence, when it felt as if the heavens had opened, when shafts of light poured through and touched ethereal fingers to the Redstones' tanned, grateful faces. The lapses varied in length; however, they were always just long enough to lull them into a false sense of security, thinking *this time* it had been fixed for real; *this time* it was finally over; *this time* they would have some peace at last. The moments of resurgence were therefore that much more disconcerting. Forks were dropped, glasses were shattered, high heels slipped while descending the stairs. Everything on the grounds darkened, just a bit, as if a filter had been placed over it. The staff became skittish. The kids fought constantly. Keith spent more evenings out with his friends (girlfriends), and Allison felt the return of that familiar sense of dread.

For now, though, she had Modesto to distract her. He had laid himself across her lap, looking upward at her, so that her dark hair hung like a heavy curtain over his face. "Allison, Allison, let down your hair." His hand brushed the tips, sweeping back and forth across them as if playing an instrument.

Allison smiled down at him. "Oh, you could never reach me. The tower's too tall. And even if you did, your eyes would be pecked out by birds. That's how those stories really go, you know."

"Then I would die remembering your beauty."

She laughed. "You wouldn't die, though; you would only be blind."

"Then I would walk the earth, begging for alms, visiting kings and paupers alike and telling everyone the story of the loveliest woman ever to live."

"You would have to learn braille."

"Then I could write exquisite poetry about your many graces."

Allison gave him a long look, stroking his forehead the way she did when one of her children had a fever. Though his attentions to her were self-evidently practiced, perfected through countless prior affairs, there was nonetheless an undercurrent of sincerity about him, an honesty of the moment, which she suspected was the case with the best seducers. *You,* she thought. *You could seduce the queen of England.* She had a sudden impulse to break from the narrative, to say something authentic for once, and though she might have resisted such an urge in the past— forbearance for the sake of their assigned roles—she found that she was no longer able to. "I used to be a poet, you know," she blurted.

He seemed surprised at her deviation from their usual banter, but quickly recovered. "You did? I didn't know that, *mi vida.* Why don't you write me a poem?"

She hesitated. "I can't."

He gave her an exaggerated pout. "Can't or won't? Don't I deserve it? I've been very loyal to you, as far as these things go."

She laughed again. "No Modesto, I mean I really can't. The ability is gone, maybe forever. Spirited away by the headless horseman," she added with a theatrical flair. "Seriously, though. Whenever I try, it's like the words are gone. No, not gone, just hidden around some far corner. They're still there, still attached to me somehow. Just always out of reach."

"I'm sure it's just like a bicycle. If you really tried, you'd remember how."

"Maybe," she said, doubtful. Then, with finality, "No." She shook her head. "No, I don't think I'll find it again. Anyway, it's my own fault for giving it away."

Modesto gave her a strange look then, propping himself up on his elbows. "What does that mean, *mi vida*? You gave it away?"

Allison was a bit startled by her own loose tongue. She had not meant to say nearly so much, but it had come spooling out of her almost without her awareness. She bent and bit his ear lightly. "Nothing, my prince. Nothing at all."

"Hmm. Well, at any rate it doesn't matter," he said. "You're so beautiful you don't need to write poems. It's enough that others write poems about you."

Just then, the boiler, which up to then had been sustaining a low, mournful hum, grew distinctly more intense. There was the faint sound of metal scraping against metal, and a loud banging began to issue from its chambers, like something large was trying to get out. Despite the heat of the room, Allison shivered.

"My God," Modesto marveled. "You really can't get that thing fixed?"

"Not so far," she said, and decided to change the subject. "I've been wondering, my secret prince. Have you done this sort of thing before? With other wives, I mean."

"Of course," he replied, then added with a coy smile: "But you are my favorite."

She sighed and kissed him. Modesto knew the script very well.

ALLISON BORE KEITH'S CHILDREN, CEMENTING THE deal. Their heads emerged like sheaves of wheat from her body. Bryn first, with her kind heart, her love for animals that was less like love and more like an instinctive alignment, a prescient recognition of what most would learn far too late: that people would always dissemble, but animals were true to what they were. Watching Bryn with the neighbor's dogs, Allison sometimes felt she was able to tap into that singular infrared, to view the animal kingdom the way her daughter did. Those wonderful, animated carcasses. Those sawhorsed sinews brightly threaded with life. Their eyes innocent yet feral, vital with the need to eat or play or reproduce or protect. Their loyalty boundless (it was most apparent with dogs, but any creature could be loyal in its way). Their existence so short you could almost watch them turning gray. Yes, they were heartbreakingly ephemeral, their whole lives passing within the span of a day. Looking at them, it was impossible to forget the deaths that would come: those quiet, humble deaths, which sat like a cross upon their foreheads, laid out for everyone but themselves to see.

The Redstones did not have animals at home. Keith was allergic, or claimed to be, but wherever Bryn found them, on the street, in the park, at her classmates' houses or even their cars, she fell over herself to embrace them, flinging her arms around them as if they were long-lost friends, burying her face deep in fur and feathers alike. For her trouble, she had been scratched, bitten, and pecked countless times, as well as peed on by as assortment of frightened reptiles, but in no way did it deter her from bounding full force into the next display of affection. She would happily risk injury or embarrassment for the chance to align herself, even for a moment, with the frenzy of their rapid heartbeats, with their elevated, unassailable souls.

Like her mother, Bryn was beautiful, and though this had been a source of growing concern for Allison, it was not for the reasons that might be imagined.

The mother was not particularly worried about being overshadowed by the daughter's looks. No, it was because she knew what being beautiful meant in this world. Allison clung to every moment of childhood that remained, counting down the years, months, minutes, until her daughter's beauty became a thing the world laid open claim to, knowing that at that point she would be unable to protect her. She could not stand against these forces forever; the coming assault was too great. Bryn was a mere eleven years, and already the wolves had started to gather. They emerged from the damp sigils of stucco walls. They descended from rain-slick stairs. They slavered in doorways, not yet approaching, oh no, not yet, but waiting, always waiting. Waiting for the inevitable ripening. Waiting with whistles and self-aware shakes of the head, as if casting off the fog of an inappropriate lust, and all of this presented as an ostensible compliment to her parents. Bryn's features were still elfin and childlike, her body little more than a lithe stalk, and yet the wolves would remark, "call me in ten years," sometimes within earshot, sometimes to the girl herself. And Allison knew that it was her fault, knew and hated herself for it, for wasn't it she who had stitched this very bomb into her daughter's tender body?—this bomb of which the girl was as yet unaware: her own doomsday clock?

When she was pregnant, Allison had said fervent prayers to the darkness. She had pleaded, bargaining in every way she could think of, even making certain sacrifices that would have horrified Bryn herself. Of all the legacies she could bequeath, she asked, let it not be this one. Let the child grow up plain. Let her bemoan her unexceptional features and lament that she was only average. In any crowd, let her fade into the background. Let her be overlooked by boys she loved. Let her envy the pretty girls and soak her pillow nightly with tears. Only spare her this hateful beauty, this burden for which there could never be adequate preparation. This beauty, which could never be ignored, which drew in everything around it like a black hole. But the darkness had laughed at her plea, and now here was Bryn, a near duplicate of her mother at that age, tethered to the same fate, that same reckless subway train going god-knows-where.

And then there was Jamie. With his cupid's face, his freckles abundant like stars, his familial inheritance was also coming to bloom. Already he was copying his father's smug smile, his imperious attitude with the staff. She had had to discipline him for his rudeness to the cook and the maids on a number of occasions, but she knew the time would come when he failed to listen; when he failed to see her as an authority worthy of his obedience; when he at last caught on to the inherent hypocrisy of her position and began to act purely on his own terms and according to his own crude morality. Before this happened, she had hoped to instill some small seed of compassion. Over the past month she had taken him with her when she volunteered: to the hospital, to the retirement home, to the soup kitchen. In each place she hoped he would be provided with a glimpse into the stubborn inequities of the world. Still, she could see the entitlement seeping into her son, a little more each day. In private moments she saw it, when he dominated a rugby game with his friends; or when he played his video games at dinner, not even trying to hide it under the table; when he huffed impatiently through his homework while sprawled like a monarch in Keith's stuffed leather chair. It was clear as day on these occasions, his privilege like a birthmark staining his skin. A brightly hued rune foretelling only success.

She did not fear for Jamie. He could do anything he wished. He might pursue finance or medicine or movie-making or law. He could be a monster and a narcissist, and he would still find no end of achievements in whatever field he chose.

But Bryn. Oh, Bryn. What of her?

Allison loved both of her children immoderately, much more than was considered reasonable by the other wives, who held themselves at a remove and let the nannies absorb all the most tender moments. A mother of her station was expected to provide everything that was wanted and more, to harpoon opportunity like a whale, to sabotage the sails of other children in order to provide even an inch of advancement for her own. For the best schools, she would gladly engage in cannibalism. For an adequate trust fund, she would fly into armed battle, massacring thousands. It was understood that, for her children's sake, she would wear 'warrior' like a gilded badge, a dazzling Cartier bauble. But she would not openly show affection.

Even the Redstone manse was not exempt from this rule. Allison did not display her adoration for her children in Keith's presence, or Babs's for that matter, for the two of them disapproved, feeling it would soften the progeny and compromise the natural dominance that was their birthright. Bryn and Jamie were made to call their father 'sir.' They called their mother 'ma'am.' They were taught to pay obeisance to their elders and internalize the rules of the realm as if it were catechism. But sometimes, when they were alone, when even the servants were not near, Allison drew them into herself as if she would reabsorb them, pulling them to her breast like chicks in a nest. Cooing her love at them. Stroking their glossy hair. Reveling in their distinctive child-scents. Creating a witch's circle that she hoped they would remember well into adulthood, that they might have a tiny seed of security housed always within them—indelible, resilient, capable of weathering any storm.

If the children were dismayed by the contrast between their mother's public and private personas, they were clever enough to not let on.

At the crossroads, so many years ago, Allison had rushed into her choice, thinking the effects of it would be assumed only by herself. Now she saw the truth of it: the curse would endure, because the constructs of the realm ensured that it would. Like vampirism, it would be passed down the bloodline, from mother to child. Bryn and Jamie, though unborn, undreamed of at the time of the deal, had never been exempt from it. In offering herself, she had offered them up as well, had given them over to the executioner's gleaming ax: not only the firstborn, as in the fairy tales, but the secondborn as well. An old-world blood offering.

At night sometimes she found herself seized by a depthless sorrow, for her children and the many now nullified paths of their futures, but especially for Bryn, sweet Bryn, imprisoned within her sleeve of beauty, bound to its many-pronged torments. And then she would weep, bitterly and without ceasing for hours at a time. Her hands would close to fists, drawing blood from her palms with the spears of her own fingernails, eight tiny points to sublimate the anguish within. She would tremble, too, with the force of her tears: an edifice on the verge of collapse. But she would do all this quietly. She would preserve at any cost the stillness of the bed, so that, other than the whalelike snoring beside her, the room remained as silent as the grave.

She would not wish to trouble her sleeping husband.

BRYN AND JAMIE ARRIVED HOME FROM SCHOOL AT the usual time, just after four, at which point the boiler had begun to clatter like a sinking freighter, the metal flexing as if under extreme pressure from the depths. There was a new odor, too, though only Allison seemed to notice it. Wafting up through the vents was a smell reminiscent of the ocean but fouler, something like brine mixed with diesel and chemicals and sweat so old it had become part of the backstory for the universe. And though she knew it was yet another byproduct of the boiler's malfunction, she could not help feeling a sense of vague terror at its emergence, a strange fancy that once engendered could not be dispelled: namely, that what wailed and moaned in the basement below was not a machine at all, but something far more sinister. Something ancient, perhaps, which had camouflaged itself as a boiler in order to infiltrate their home. Something born of pestilence, eager to press tumors like petals into her children's lungs. Something which, even if it did have an organic shape, was yet an abomination, with eyes like polestars and a brood of spiders swarming within its chest.

The smell intensified, became acrid. It burned her nose and caused her to sneeze repeatedly. It seared the delicate lining of her throat. It enveloped her like a fog, so that even within the massive rooms of her massive house, she began to succumb to the clutches of claustrophobia. Then the fancy became ascendant, and she felt her eyes harden, turning to glass, beyond whose portholes lay countless fathoms of water, and she found that she had sunk so deep, so unimaginably deep beneath the waters, that the light above was nearly gone, a mere curling wisp of it remaining. And though she protested to the universe that she was only a visitor on that vessel, that she should not be held accountable for its many failures, she knew that it would not make a scrap of difference. She would still die down there, lashed to the mast of her own body. Alone and unknown.

The next thought to take root in her mind seemed an imminently sensible one. The thing to do, she concluded, was to escape the vessel, and in this context, escape meant to remove the flawless skin that was the source of so many of her problems, her true original sin. She could just dig her nails right in and claw it away, after all, or perhaps peel it back, down to the marbled striations of muscle and bone. She saw the objective insanity of this, but the idea was so delicious she could not let it go. She could not help imagining how the flesh would look if she were to go through with it: how it might fold back on itself like an inverted sleeve, that red membrane like a husk, like a lovely sheaf of corn silk; how it might fly free in some places, gauzy, curling like paper, while in others it might simply be sloughed away, falling off her bones like a too-loose sock, like a coil of drapery at her feet. She wanted to see this, God yes, and furthermore, she wanted proof of what she suddenly suspected, that there were hidden markings on the undersides of the tissue, that below the surface, where no one could see, her skin bore the intricate patterns of maple or of lacebark pine, that despite its outward banality, her body was actually coded with meaning, with Lascaux glyphs all its own.

She felt intense relief at the prospect of taking this step, even a frisson of anticipation at the pleasure she might derive from it. Yes, this was the answer. The only way to be free from the incessant clattering, the deep-sea stench, the floating specter of the woman's hideous face. Allison's fingers twitched, aching to proceed. Knowing already the places where they would start, the ten sites of their first predations. The skin calling out to her in each of those sites, a decemvirate of cities yearning to be conquered, to be stripped away and lifted toward heaven in a grand gesture of supplication.

And yet, she had just enough sense left not do it in front of the children. *Bryn is so sensitive*, she told herself. *She shouldn't be subjected to a sight like that. I will wait till I'm alone.* With tremendous strength of will, she began to extract herself from the delirium into which she had fallen. She dragged herself slowly, as through a milky tunnel, her consciousness a limbless, fumbling beast, and when she had at last succeeded, she was cognizant of entering her beauty once again: that hateful beauty that was just where she had left it, smirking like a she-devil, just waiting to reimmerse her, to spread itself like a contagion over her body, to reclaim her.

She smoothed her hair with a shaking hand, grabbed her keys from the counter, and headed for the door. "Come on, kids," she said. "Let's get some frozen yogurt."

Amid the quotidian gaudiness of the yogurt shop, Allison felt better. The gothic sense of dread had dissipated, and she was even able to laugh at her wild flight of fancy back at the house. *I wouldn't really have done it, of course. It was just a panic attack. I've simply had too much on my plate lately.* She was still warm from her shower, her second of the day, and as she lounged in the red vinyl chair with her organic tea, her long legs felt imbued with the same sun that was bleaching the boardwalk outside. She felt the golden thread of the orb within her, flowing like amber, illuminating her organs as she crossed and recrossed her bare legs, her high-heeled wedge sandals like tiny stages for her own personal dramas ("friends, Romans, countrymen: lend me your pool boys").

The air in the shop smelled clean and pleasant, unpermeated by salt or engine oil. The pop music station playing from the speakers was blandly agreeable. There were the usual stares from strangers, the familiar side glances of lust or envy from men and women alike, the deference and the sudden hushed voices of people entering the shop, as if discovering they were in the presence of a celebrity or a nun. But rather than feeling suffocated by the attention, in the moment she felt fortified, shored up somehow, as if the world were remaking itself as it had been before.

Already, the strange episode at the house was fading from her memory, a dream in rapid retreat.

She turned to observe her children. Jamie was attacking his yogurt like a serial killer, first dangling the gummy worms over his mouth as if to torment them, moving them ever closer to that gaping maw, a centimeter at a time, before devouring them with a quick bark of laughter. Allison wrinkled her nose in disgust. She had seen him eat the real thing on more than one occasion, and once he had even bullied his friends into doing the same. She had expressed her concerns to Keith, but her husband felt it was to a boy's credit to be wild. Bryn, meanwhile, was eating her dessert much more slowly. She seemed to be distracted by a piebald cat that was shuffling just outside the glass, rubbing its patchy body against a nearby pillar. Her eyes were luminous with sympathy as she watched its progress. Her hand lifted into the air involuntarily, as if she were already stroking its fur and scratching the spot behind its pointy bat ears.

Clearly, she was not put off by the animal's pathetic appearance, by the bald spots that had been worn free by disease or mange.

Oh, Bryn.

Allison's thumb brushed a strand of hair behind Bryn's ear, framing those lovely cheekbones she was steadily growing into, those bones that rose above the surrounding landscape like twin burial mounds. Cheekbones so dramatic that many a young man would one day lie wrecked upon them, their novitiate hearts devastated, burned out by the fierce star of her beauty. And this, Allison knew, was before the inevitable happened, for it would not be long before they learned to blame her for how her face and body made them feel. They would call her cruel or frigid. Call her a bitch. Call her much worse.

Allison felt a sudden pang, a painful twinge from somewhere inside her chest, and for a moment the words *heart attack* and *stroke* flashed through her mind. But then the room began to darken, and she murmured to herself in despair. *No, please. Not again.* Still, the light continued to ebb from the shop, was squeezed out really, like liquid from a cleaning cloth. Like the light that had saturated it was only a temporary caprice and darkness was its natural state. Everything around her fell into shadow, the shapes of objects and people alike limned in charcoal gray.

And then the smell returned. The same pungent odor she had smelled at home, but this time it was somehow more expansive. It was as if before, at the house, it had been coiled tight, a chambered nautilus of rot, but now it had moved beyond the possibility of containment. It unfurled like a carpet, spreading out to encompass every available molecule of space. Like a torrent of sea, it rolled in, a great billow from the depths, its murky waters seeded with the bones of hapless sailors and teeming with sea creatures, those blind, gelatinous, bioluminescent creatures that had been sucked up from the vented trenches and were crashing for the first time into a world of sun. The smell fully overwhelmed her other senses. She could conceive of nothing else: sight dimmed, hearing hijacked, touch, even, a foggy abstraction, as if she were no longer piloting her own body. There was a wave of nausea then, like seasickness, she realized, like when she was pregnant and had a pocket ocean sheathed inside her.

"What's wrong, ma'am?" Bryn was peering at her, her elfin features pinched with worry.

Allison looked at the shape that represented her daughter, incredulous. "Are you kidding me? Do you not smell that?"

"Smell what?"

Jamie laughed in disdain. "There's nothing here but the smell of poor people."

Bryn glared at her brother, who only rolled his eyes. "Sorry. Less fortunate, I mean."

But Allison had already stopped listening, for now—though everything else was gray and lacking in crucial definition—she saw before her a full-color image of that other woman's face, like a mask hung in the air, a vivid, horrible skin. The woman outside the club, who was at once Allison's own twin, and also not, who appeared older somehow, more susceptible to the effects of aging. More haggard, really. Without the modifications Allison herself had paid so handsomely to implement. The drowned sister of myth.

Allison gaped at the image, and it gaped back, each one's countenance a mirror for the other. But it was a mirror with a filter. A mirror with alterations. A mirror attuned to the insubstantial shimmer of ghosts. She was wholly transfixed by this parallel likeness. Fascinated by the lines that stood proud, that held the years in furrows and displayed them like treasures. The wrinkled eyes like advertisements for laughter and sorrow. The nose that held its original crook, the one from her girlhood, the one she had never really minded, making a direct through line from the girl she had been to the woman she might have been, and this feature in particular was the one that Allison could not forgive. That this other woman should still be tethered to that girl when she herself was not, tethered to that beauty, yes, but also to that wildness, to that mass of contradictions, in which a fearsome physicality grew like reeds around a gossamer dream of poetry.

Soon, the color and clarity returned to the room, while the stench of rotting seaweed grew still stronger. This time it rose up from the floor, and Allison broke off her gaze in order to look down at the tiles, expecting to see them covered by at least half a foot of ocean water. Based on the smell's strength, it made sense that there would be a vast green pool of it sloshing around her designer sandals, muddying the weave of the raffia, inundating her ankles with an effluvium of bottle caps, driftwood, the corpses of jellyfish. But other than yogurt spatters and the occasional vein of ossified syrup, the floor was bone dry.

And then it struck her. None of this was real. The woman, the visual and auditory shifts—they were all part of a particularly morbid fever dream, a set of hallucinations no doubt brought on by the putrid smell that was permeating the shop. The smell itself was clearly too potent to be imaginary. It was real and it was vile, and it had to have been generated (or at least amplified) by something in the immediate environment. Having concluded this, she rose up like the fury she was and confronted the counter clerk.

"Excuse me? How do you expect people to eat in an environment like this? I demand an explanation."

The poor clerk, a teenage girl just a few years older than Bryn, was at a loss. She tilted her head to the side like a perplexed puppy. "Ma'am?"

"Don't act like you don't know what I'm talking about. The smell, my God, the smell! It's like someone emptied a vat of raw sewage in here."

The other patrons, many of them tourists, were beginning to look on with mild concern, their bodies tensing, shifting unconsciously into self-protective postures. Most were still in awe of Allison herself, so that their natural wariness was tempered by curiosity. Was this a performative act, typical of someone of her social station? Was there perhaps a hidden camera?

"I'm so sorry!" said the girl, horrified. "I hadn't noticed a smell."

Allison shook her head and emitted a mirthless laugh, as if in disbelief at this transparent lie. "It's everywhere, honey. Even a cadaver with a head cold could smell it. I need to speak to your manager immediately."

"Ma'am, I'm so sorry, but she isn't in today. I can give you her number, though! Or the number for corporate, if you'd like to make a complaint."

"What I'd *like* is for you to rectify, or at least acknowledge, the problem at hand."

A man sitting by the window, whom she hadn't noticed before, gave her a coolly appraising look. He seemed to be of her own social set, with a crisp summer suit and a watch that cost more than the clerk's annual salary. After a moment, he looked pointedly at the watch, then back at her, as if indicating that her time in the spotlight was up. Allison couldn't believe it. Could he not smell it? It made sense that the common rabble couldn't. Perhaps they lacked the necessary delicacy to sense it, as in the story of the princess and the pea. But this man thrived in the same rarefied air that she did—how could *he* not notice it? He was looking at her as if she were the crazy one. Was he, too, oblivious to what was happening?

Bryn looked frightened. She curled against Allison, having evidently made the calculation that it was safer to be within her mother's sphere than out of it.

The clerk, meanwhile, was in a panic. "Ma'am, I will talk to the manager right away, I promise. I'm so sorry about your unsatisfactory experience!" Here, she thrust a coupon in Allison's direction, which only enraged her further.

"How dare you? I'm calling the health department and having this store shut down for good. You're deliberately trying to sicken me and my children."

Jamie, who had been calmly eating his yogurt throughout this exchange and had just finished, looked up at his mother and scoffed. "What is *wrong* with you?"

Allison looked around in confusion. She found herself suddenly, painfully aware of the stares from the other customers, as well as the disapproving visage of the man by the window, who continued to peer at her in what was almost paternal disappointment, his eyes glowing red, accusing: *transgressor, transgressor.* She realized that in her zeal she had strayed still farther from the script, and this man, who with his dark hair and mask of freckles could have been a grown version of her son, had found her out. In fact, once discovered, this resemblance seemed hugely significant, for it reinforced a slippery feeling she had that the two were somehow connected, that they were both part of the same unseen network through which the realm policed itself, generation after generation. Never had she been more aware that the world she had chosen was one poised on a tightrope. It was an entire city upended like a pyramid, all its rules and governances designed to maintain that single point of contact. How easy it would be to fall to one side.

"Nothing," she muttered. "Let's go."

FOR A LONG TIME, ALLISON HADN'T MINDED THE rituals of the realm. She didn't mind because the relationships, and the words they said to one another, were not real. They were insubstantial, light as air, and at their conclusion, they would wisp up into the sky and blow away like trash. There was a blissfulness in this. A sense of Zen, almost. It was easy to live this way, to step between the days as if they were no more than lilies on a pond, while the cares of the real world lay far below, unseen and undreamed of. She wondered if it was having children that had rendered this arrangement untenable.

Whatever the reason, her serenity had been compromised. There was a fissure in it, and it was spreading, and now that it had asserted itself, she found that she could see nothing else. The film studios dotted the valley, but in reality, the entire empire in which she lived was a huge movie set. It was one endless, sprawling Potemkin Village, capable of deceiving no one. She could no longer ignore the sets crumbling to pieces around her. She was aware of the actors doing their vocal exercises each morning, rehearsing and flubbing their lines, laughing about the inevitable gag reel. She saw boom mikes everywhere she looked, bobbing just out of frame. Even her morning coffee had begun to taste like paper, as if it, too, were only a prop. Her suspension of disbelief was suddenly insupportable, the supply of fairy dust used to keep it aloft having at last petered out.

Once, though, there was a thing that had been solid and pure and real. Even now the memory of it silvered the morning before each dawn. It came to her in the drowsy moments between sleeping and waking, floating down upon her like a slow fall of leaves, like a cloud of pollen that glittered in her thoughts, a fragment at a time. She saw again the mop of unruly black hair. The set of eyelashes that were to die for. Felt the pale hand that had reached through her, inside her, that had touched all the organs she had thought to keep only for herself. Vulva. Cervix. Heart.

Like a customs agent, the boy had made careful note of each one, mapping the borders that defined her. And asking. Always asking. Sweetly asking. "May I…?" "Would you…?" "Is this all right?"

She had met Moshe, or rather not quite met him, at a nearby Orthodox synagogue where his family attended; hers was merely visiting. Allison's parents, being self-consciously liberal, had made a constant and exhausting project of broadening her and Glenn's horizons, exposing them to a variety of cultures and creeds with the goal of making them more thoughtful members of the ruling class. As such, she and her brother had been dragged through a cavalcade of instructive events, from rich-smelling twilight food fairs (Philippine, Greek, Ecuadorian, Armenian) to grassy open-air concerts (featuring Korean, Bengali, and Cuban artists), from the red-gold riots of the Chinese and Cambodian New Year parades to, once, a Pan-African film festival where they had been seated beside a B-list movie star. On the morning in question, the morning of Moshe, they had been swept into an Orthodox synagogue for a traditional Yom Kippur service.

Allison and her mother had been seated in the balcony off to the side, behind the *mechitzah*, as it was called, the barrier dividing the genders, while Glenn and her father, in their matching velvet yarmulkes, sat with the men on the main floor. Allison smoldered with resentment at this separation—she was just learning about systems of patriarchy—and she fixed her sullen gaze on the Ark, which, her mother had explained in whispers, contained the Torah scrolls. The Ark was beautiful, she had to admit. Built from a caramel-colored wood, the cabinet bore upon its doors the image of a massive tree (the Tree of Life, her mother said), the boughs of which were gorgeously inlaid with strips of lapis and something pearly, like moonstone. The stones winked in the light from the candles, like a scattering of stars, and when Allison let her eyes go out of focus, they softened and seemed to merge, creating the impression of a holy nimbus ringing the cabinet. It was like something out of a dream, like a magical installation from a children's book. The kind of thing that might not have been rendered by human hands at all, but instead plucked whole from the firmament and set down for the adoration of earth dwellers like herself. Allison liked to joke that she was a devout agnostic, but looking at the Ark, she felt she understood at least a portion of religion's appeal. It might be worth a bit of discomfort, a bit of humiliation, even, to be in the presence of such beautiful things.

She had then turned her attention to the congregants, thinking she might compose a poem in which the mostly monochrome attire at the synagogue functioned as a metaphor for spiritual yearning, when she noticed a pair of dark eyes peering shyly up at her. The boy was about her age: tall, pale, awkward, with an as yet unformed handsomeness and thick curls looping out from the brim of his yarmulke. Like most teens, he sat slightly hunched, his shoulders arced forward as if toward a kinder future, as if he hadn't yet figured out how to be present within this changed and still changing body. There was a large errant freckle, a mole perhaps, resting on the smooth plain just beside his nose, and for some reason this was the thing that drew her in, the anchor point, the single imperfection through which her sudden rush of feelings was refracted.

Mortified, the boy looked away. But in that instant, they both knew that this was only a temporary postponement, that already the wheels of fate had been set in motion. The shining hook was set, and they had been caught, each upon each. He would look to her again, and she would look back, and soon enough he did just that, and then it was Allison's turn to drop her gaze, her heart nearly bursting from her chest. Her face felt hot, as if sunburned. She stared at the program in her lap, reading the same lines again and again, until, in a feat of bravery that was surely worthy of Perseus or Hercules, she forced herself to lift her head and give the boy a small smile. He smiled back just a little, mostly with his eyes, glancing toward his father to indicate that he was not free to do more. She nodded, almost imperceptibly, and his cheeks flushed. She saw his nose twitch, a slight nervous spasm, and again she was caught by the loveliness of the mole, by its strange, wonderful expression upon an otherwise unblemished face. No doubt the mole would be his companion through all the stages of his life, from his first moments in the crib to the far future days of his old age. She imagined placing her lips on it, and then she blushed so furiously she thought it must have been obvious to everyone in the synagogue.

This is what she told her friends later: that it was as if there was already an intimate connection between them, that it was as if the tail of time had looped around and touched its own head. As if they were already lovers.

The father, at last noticing his son's inattention, nudged him sharply in the ribs. The boy kept his eyes on the cantor for the remainder of the service, though she could tell that he was not paying attention.

After the final amen, when everyone had filed out onto the sidewalk, Allison felt a sudden sense of urgency. She needed to *do* something. But what? She didn't think she could approach him in this setting without an introduction; it would be improper, possibly scandalous. She thought about asking her father to make the introductions for her, but that would require an explanation, and she was not ready to share this feeling with the world just yet. It was too new, too immense to even think of describing.

Additionally, she couldn't bear the thought of their faces when she told them, how her sincerity of feeling would be minimized by their knowing, indulgent smiles, as if her first great love were only a bit of childish nonsense. Without their involvement, however, she had few options.

Just as she was despairing of ever seeing the boy again, he walked directly and purposefully in front of her. His eyes were aimed straight ahead, as if he'd identified someone across the courtyard to whom he wished to speak, and as he passed, his fingers opened to drop something small and white at her feet. It was a piece of the program, she saw, with something scrawled on it. Quickly, she covered the paper with her foot. As he walked away, she saw how his upper body was coiled tight, his shoulders still hunched, but there was a looseness in his lower limbs that hinted at the adult he would become, a glimpse of confidence just beginning to unfurl.

Once he was a safe distance away, she picked up the note.

"Frank Fenton outfield, tomorrow at 4 – Moshe."

Moshe, she thought, savoring it.

It was as if this were the last piece of the puzzle, cementing their future together.

At the field the next day, they had sat nervously together on the grass, eating the Italian ice he'd bought from a park vendor. They talked in turn about their interests, their families, their schools, their everyday lives. He told her how he loved baseball, Prince, astronomy, science fiction novels. He told her that he wanted to be a scholar of the Kabbalah when he was older, but his parents had forbidden it, saying the whole field of study was nonsense, that it made Jews look unserious. She told him he should do it anyway. Then she told him her dream of being a poet, and how even her parents had suggested (gently) that she have a backup plan. "Well, I think it's cool," he told her. "Poetry is just mysticism of a different kind." He insisted on hearing a sample of her work and, though embarrassed, she obliged, reciting the only one of her poems she could recall from memory, an ambitious sonnet called "Bird Fountain." From time to time their arms came into contact as they talked, as if by accident, and each time she had the sensation of being irradiated, as if she were being bombarded by tiny particles that scorched and abraded the top layers of skin. It was unbearably lovely.

Before they left for their separate buses, they had shared a kiss, their tongues still numb from the Italian ice. His mouth met her mouth, and she thought how the damp grotto they formed between them was like a sacred temporal space, existing only for the duration of the kiss, how it sprung alive like a church in the middle of that green field, the doors closed to anyone but themselves. And even though they were both inexperienced it seemed to her that there was a rightness to the kiss, a sense that they were each precisely where they needed to be, that they had been irrevocably drawn through time toward each other, pulled across the shifting grid of the world toward this brief string of moments, each one bright like a pearl, like a fairy ring of mushrooms. Neither wanted to be the first to pull away.

"You're so pretty," he had said then, shaking his head in disbelief.

She looked away, irritated. "That's the worst thing about me," she said. "Seriously, I wish I weren't."

"What? Why?" he asked. He seemed surprised.

"It's just…it's like it's always in the way."

"Oh." He thought this over for a second. "No, I think I can understand that. It's like a flare that's always distracting people from what's inside, isn't it? It blinds them in a way." Their bodies having fully separated, his shyness once again overtook him. "Please. May I see you again, Allison?"

She had laughed. "So formal." When he looked embarrassed, she added, "It's okay. I like it. Yes, Moshe. You may see me again."

They had to date in secret, obviously, though Allison's parents had some idea she had a boyfriend due to the general buoyancy of her step, the proud and euphoric gleam in her eye as she passed through the entryway after each of her assignations. Allison herself would have said she felt a new sense of mastery over her life. A validation of who she was, of her garden-wild childhood, of her nascent womanhood, and of the splendid, soaring birds she knew she would one day bring forth with her pen. All these things were yoked together in her mind, inextricable, each an integral part of the shape and texture of her happiness. The sky itself was altered to her eye; the sunset hues richer and deeper than any she'd seen before, the blue of midday expressing something so profound it could not be put into words. It no longer looked like a painted ceiling, a Sistine Chapel, flatly imaged; it now appeared as it was, a limitless expanse, teeming with satellites, comets, planets, galaxies. A window to the infinite.

"I would like to hear one of Ally's new poems," her mother had announced at dinner one night, winking at her father. It was something of a routine for Allison to read new poems in the evenings, a regular bit of theater staged to encourage her creativity, but it had been months since she had agreed to such a reading. All her poems now were about Moshe.

Reluctantly, Allison had fetched her notebook and turned to the most recent page. "Okay. First, I want to tell you, this is not about anyone real. It's a distillation of personality types. And it's not even romantic, it's just symbolism about the search for love in the world."

Glenn smirked.

She read it aloud with as much dignity as she could muster, her latest paean to her love, to the boy with the black curls and the earnest heart, the heart that was always seeking, that was steeped in esoteric mysteries, devoted to uncovering that which was hidden: namely, the divinity embodied in word and flesh, which dwelled just beneath the surface of everything, both living and unliving, even herself, and it was one of her better poems she thought, so that even as her cheeks burned she felt a flicker of satisfaction at her achievement.

"That was illuminating," said her mother afterward.

"It's like Shakespeare's Dark Lady," her father said wryly. "I wonder what this imaginary young man's name might be, if he had one?"

"I've seen him, you know," Glenn said, playfully throwing his napkin across the table at Allison. "This non-specific symbol of love in the world."

"Well, I think it's a very good poem," her mother added. "Very well crafted. I just…as your mother I have to ask you if you're being careful. We can take you to our physician if you need something."

Allison marched out of the room then, her head held high, ears ringing with Glenn's raucous laughter.

It was shortly after this dinner that she saw Moshe for the last time. They had rented a canoe at the marina—he was supposed to be at a baseball game, she at tennis lessons—and together they had begun a slow paddle up the Sepulveda Basin, where the broad canopy of trees shielded them from the city's gaze, and from the flaming disc of sun, which burned like a vast omen above. But they did not notice this, so absorbed were they in the heady drug of each other's company. They seemed to dwell in the spaces between moments, reveling in the countless water droplets that were lifted with each oar stroke, each one a prismed universe; and in the languorous throb of their muscles as they rowed, which they regarded as affection's proprietary marker, as if their love itself lay ribboned within their limbs, an ache they could map.

An hour into their trip, they had pulled up to shore, tying off the craft behind a great, draping fringe of willow. Here, the trees were clustered so densely that she and Moshe were almost wholly enveloped. It was an entire world, fresh and green, belonging only to themselves.

"I should tell you at this point that I don't know how to swim," Moshe laughed.

Allison thought this was hilarious. "What? You've lived in California your whole life, and you can't swim?" She swung her oar wildly at him, teasing. "What if I upended us right now?"

"I'd drown I suppose. Tragically. Hey, keep that paddle away from me. We're not even supposed to be touching, you know."

"Oh, we're not, are we?"

"Them's the rules."

With a mischievous smile, she crawled back to where he was, making sure not to tip the boat in the process. Then, leaning forward, she placed her lips against the mole, kissing it tenderly and with great solemnity, as if it were the center of his being.

When she opened her eyes again, he was gazing back at her in total, helpless adoration. He looked so awestruck, so vulnerable—almost as if she had wounded him—that she nearly apologized. She thought she had experienced every possible permutation when it came to looks from boys (and men), those of naked lust, of tragic, romanticized yearning, of smug entitlement, of steely determination to complete a conquest, and of sulky resentment or anger at having their desires thwarted. But this look: no one had ever looked at her like that before. Truly, no one ever would again.

If she had only known.

Feeling invincible, she recited her poem. It was the same one she'd read to her family at dinner, the one that had made them all laugh.

But Moshe didn't laugh. "You're going to be so famous," he said. "I can just tell. There's something about the way you see the world. It's like you've reinvented it all."

Allison just beamed.

"Have you ever read Plato?" he asked her suddenly.

"Of course I have. Oh wait, I think I know where you're going with this. Before you embarrass yourself, you should know that I don't believe in soulmates." She threw him her best haughty glare.

"Oh totally," he said. "That's just what I was going to say. No, I definitely don't, either."

"Oh really, you don't?"

"Nope."

"Is that so?" she asked with a sly smile. She let her hand drop below his waistline. "Not even now?"

And so for the first time they moved beyond kissing, and it was like a journey of mutual discovery, a brave navigation of new waters, as they slowly, with countless questions aimed at the other's comfort, aligned themselves into complementary positions in the boat, like yin and yang, she thought, like pieces crafted in the ethereal plane to be in perfect opposition to each other, together forming something complete, something transcendent. Two halves of an intricately carved puzzle box. Like Plato, after all.

Though immersed in their explorations, they retained (on some distant, vaulted level) an awareness of ambient sounds. They heard still the plash of fish in the shallows, the buzz of dragonflies, the voices of strangers converging and diverging on the path above, and these only deepened the feeling of being insulated, of being separate from the city and its quotidian concerns; it made them feel that they were truly cocooned in a dream, where the rules of society, the rules of physics even, did not apply. In this dream, Allison's lustrous eye might dissolve into glitter in Moshe's throat; his mole might detach and float into the reliquary of her navel; their fingers might fuse and web together, forming a single hand at prayer; or they might jointly sink into the softness of each other's bodies, their cells scattered like neutrinos across eager skin, seeding it like a garden.

Because they had chosen a boat for this difficult act, their movements often resulted in a spray or two of water sloshing over the sides. To Allison's fevered mind, these amounted to tiny baptisms, or—and she thought this was the term—*mikvehs*. Each one seemed a pinpoint detonation of holiness, a signal of the rightness of the course they were on, of their preordained suitability for each other. There was only once when she thought they might tip over, and that was when the wave from a passing Jet Ski hit the boat laterally. It rocked them hard against the overhanging lip of shore and shook them like a cocktail. She and Moshe were reduced to clutching opposite sides of the canoe, hanging on for dear life and laughing riotously at the ridiculousness of their position.

After some amount of time his hips had shifted, rising like bread in a pan, and for a moment she had the absurd thought: he is levitating; I have made him fly. It took longer for her, but not by much. Though it was his first time, Moshe was assiduous.

And then they lay back, heads together this time, and with characteristic formality Moshe had presented her with a ring, inscribed with the Hebrew letters: *Ani L'Dodi V'Dodi Li. I am my beloved's, and my beloved is mine.* It was his grandmother's, he said.

It was for him to give to his bride at their wedding. And Allison, jubilant, kissing him, teasing him that he was still so shy with her, even now, accepted it.

Three days later, of course, Moshe's mother had come to their house to demand its return. "He gave it to me," Allison had protested, unable to stop the flow of tears. She had wept openly, throwing herself at his mother's feet like a Byronic heroine. But the mother, unmoved, only replied, "It was not his to give." She went on to detail her own specific and general failures, particularly how, in allowing touches of the secular to permeate her son's orbit, she had made him vulnerable to corruption. She did not blame Allison for this; she herself had been the instrument of his undoing. She pledged to rectify this. The family would be moving to New York City within the week, she said. And here she looked at Allison, really looked at her, and seeming to decide that such a step might not be enough, that the girl's beauty could easily reach that far, she modified the plan on the spot, declaring that Moshe would also be sent abroad for a time, to live with their family in Tel Aviv, so that he might rededicate himself to *Halakha*, and perhaps see the way to giving up his juvenile fascination with the Kabbalah. Allison had continued to beg, plead, and cajole, declaring her love as eloquently as she knew how. All to no avail.

Her own mother was scarcely warmer. "All this for a teenage romance?" she had exclaimed, throwing up her hands at the overwrought scene. Despairing, Allison had at last relented. She placed the ring in his mother's hand and collapsed into a nearby chair, her tears for the moment exhausted.

Moshe's mother seemed to soften now that her objective had been achieved. "You are so pretty, my dear," she said to Allison before leaving. "You will find someone."

Within the week, it was reported that Moshe's family had in fact moved across the country, and Moshe himself had been sent even farther away, sequestered in a far-off world that she knew nothing of, that might have been the Moon for all its gauzy unattainability. She wrote him countless letters, but without a specific address she didn't have much hope that they would be delivered. *Moshe Cohen, Tel Aviv.* In a city of half a million. It would be no easier for him, she knew. Living moment to moment as they had, determining only at the conclusion of each meeting the time and location of their next one, they had never exchanged addresses.

Find me.

With everyone she had ever met, her beauty had been like an unspoken passenger, a spectral presence altering the tenor and course of the interaction. It was the prong of ice that flashed above the waters, the signifier that, somewhere in her early teens, had come to eclipse the signified. It determined everything about her relationship to the world, how people treated her, their expectations. But with Moshe, it had been different. Yes, he had seen and been awed by her beauty, but he had also somehow managed to see past it. Whether because of his Kabbalistic zeal or some other innate quality, he had not been content to accept what was on the surface. He had always looked deeper. Like Diogenes, he had gone with his lantern to the darkest of places, and it was there, beneath the veil of skin, that he had at last found her.

And now he was gone.

Find me.

For days, months, years afterward, she had whispered this into her pillow each night. *Beloved of my heart: Find me, though I am hidden.*

Only later did it become clear that she should have gone after him. She need not have waited, like the damsel in a knight's tale, helpless against the oceanic forces steering her fate. She should have taken him at his word, taken his love as an article of faith and simply made it happen. Defied everyone who said it was not permitted. Left school, stolen money from her parents' account, gotten on a plane. Done whatever it took to be with him. She had a passport at the time, issued prior to a family reunion in Florence—why had she not just gone? She wondered if he had thought the same over the years, if he too was saddled with regret over failing to take that next step. Perhaps neither of them had done so because they didn't realize they could, because they couldn't see how small the world truly was, and how little it would have taken.

She had never told anyone, but she sometimes had waking visions of the children they would have had together. The room would grow dim, and then she would see them—a different version of Bryn and Jamie—nearly material beings that flickered in the air before her, their images bleeding through from a universe where she had made a different choice. Looking at them, she felt an almost physical ache. Phantom pain from a limb she'd never had. She would reach out to them, and though they never once saw her or sensed her presence, it was as if her outstretched fingers made possible a deeper a connection between the worlds. Her fingertips became receivers, converting stray electrical pulses into still-frame impressions. She saw the children at all the pivotal stages of their lives: their loves, hopes, dreams, disappointments. A thousand scattered glimpses of her alternate family. And each time, just before they faded from view, she felt the weight of Moshe's arm upon her neck, heard again his soft voice and esoteric musings.

Allison didn't believe that these episodes were real. But in her more whimsical moments, she allowed herself to imagine that they were. According to the rules of poetry, after all, a person might want something so badly that the strength of that yearning would itself bring the thing into being. Perhaps it would even fashion a brand-new reality for it, creating a parallel path to which the person would be forever anchored.

What would Moshe think of her now? Him with his lovely, inquisitive soul, his almost handsome face? No doubt he had gathered to himself a devoted wife, children, a thriving career—all the outward fullness of a life. If they were to meet again, would he see the same girl he had loved in his youth? Or would he see a monster?

UNWILLING TO RETURN TO THE HOUSE FOR DINNER, Allison placed a call to the cook and took the kids to a local sushi bistro, opened a month earlier by chef Masaharu Morimoto, of Iron Chef fame. Keith didn't arrive until just after 7—he was either working late or honoring the European tradition of cinq á sept—and this was just fine with Allison. Conversation was always easier without him present. Lately, she found herself exhausted by his alpha-male imperiousness, his condescending barbs aimed at the staff, and his stubborn insistence on dominating every topic, even those about which he knew virtually nothing. She had once heard him expound on the subject of cliff diving for nearly two hours, surely a record for him, and although he had never cliff dived himself, he felt qualified to lecture a junior executive (himself an expert cliff diver) on the best equipment and techniques for doing so. Today, Keith arrived just as the meal was concluding, so the family was only forced to endure his digression du jour (a beachable catamaran he was thinking of buying) for as long as it took him to drink an old fashioned.

After dinner, Allison dropped Bryn and Jamie off at the house, changed into her favorite party heels, and drove to a fashionable taqueria for cocktails with Jeanine and Camille. Marisa was absent. Her husband was in Tokyo, and she had taken the opportunity to hit the local clubs with her mechanic boyfriend, who just so happened to service all the cars for their friend group and was therefore an admirably conspicuous paramour. Marisa's social star being on the rise, the remaining friends only said a few critical things about her (the condition of her cuticles, her imperfect golf form) and moved on to other subjects.

This outing, too, passed without event. There was no disembodied wailing. No sewage stench rolling out like breakers from an otherwise unremarkable kitchen. The night was cool and breezy. The sky was as clear as a glass bowl, its pitched expanse infused with a thousand stars (a lot for LA), and as she lounged on the patio, drink in hand, noting and remarking on the articles of her friends' clothing that were making their debut, she breathed salt-fresh air into her lungs and felt a sense of renewal. It might have been the alcohol at work, but she was suddenly, blissfully conscious of the stricture loosening from around her throat, and the fear that had nettled her for weeks became like an absent ghost, a thing that, through the lens of memory, has lost most of its sinister quality. Allison began to suggest to herself that the previous episodes had all been in her head. The longer the cocktails went on, the more certain she was. Nothing was going to happen, because what had happened before wasn't real. Jeanine and Camille were real, as were her jewel-encrusted clutch and her Dior dress and (not coincidentally) her platinum card. As for the boiler, it was just a boiler. Utterly banal, if a bit of an aggravation. Not some overarching metaphor for the brokenness of her life. Perhaps what she'd experienced had only been some kind of midlife crisis, but even in her head that term would not stand, and so the second that thought formed, she altered it: no, a *pre*-midlife crisis. Barely more than a quarter life crisis, really. The point was, modern life had become so intensely complicated, so full of demands. How could anyone *not* go a bit crazy?

Before she knew it, Allison was on her own again. Her friends had taken cabs already, giving each other sloppy kisses good-bye, laughing about the stories they'd told and retold, all the seamy tales that held together the arabesque of the realm, when Allison, still a bit tipsy, strode down the block toward a nearby bodega. She was intending to buy a sparkling water before securing a cab of her own.

She turned the corner, her Christian Louboutin heels pivoting sharply to the left, and it was then that everything shifted, like the moment in a horror film when the colors darken, and the musical score goes into a minor key. The edges of things became soft and vaporous, revealing the slick musculature of the world. The stars swarmed like blowflies across the sky. And there was a rush of that same smell, like a sudden gust of wind. But this time it was so much worse than before, much sharper and more putrid, and it seemed to come from much deeper within the bowels of the sea, from the realm of whale bones and rotting primeval flesh. And this time, she could see it. She could see it rolling down the filthy alleyway, a spiraling gray-brown cloud, gaining strength perhaps from the junkies and the scatological emanations of dumpsters, rising and falling, sweeping down the breadth of Cahuenga Boulevard, its coils laced with dirt and detritus and the abhorrent mucus of seaweed leaves. It was a billowing scourge of an odor. A plague. She reeled where she stood, nearly falling over. Nearly vomiting. It was only through a quick recitation of a mindfulness exercise that she managed to do neither.

It would be fruitless to run, she knew, and so with resurgent dread she followed the cloud, understanding that she was nearing some inevitable confrontation and unwilling to prolong it any further. *Let it face me,* she thought wildly. *Whatever it is, let it show itself at last. Let it see what I can do.* The knot tightened about her throat once more. She began to wheeze, finding it ever more difficult to draw breath. Still, she followed it. Like a character in a cartoon she tracked its every peak and trough, her body floating through all of its convolutions, her feet perhaps lifting off the ground as she did so, for she found she was no longer cognizant of the familiar clack of her heels against pavement. Not that she could have heard it anyway. For now, above the sound of footsteps, above the angry honks and squeals of cars swerving to avoid her, above the sound of general mayhem, the cry of the boiler had begun to break through. And though the machine lay far across town, she was no longer surprised by its sinister ingenuity, by this sudden apparent mutation, which enabled it to detach from its physical location and become free-floating, like an infection. The air filled with its clanging, with the frightful sound of buckling metal. Its keening burned like a needle in her heart. And still, she followed it. Followed the fetid vapor as it coiled down Cahuenga, then Santa Monica, then through half a dozen side streets lined with palms, each somehow identical to the last, down to the paint-splattered dumpster, down to the looping red graffiti on the wall (an ominous "you are next"), down to the archipelago of rainbowed oil slicks and the single fast food bag that was ringed with silent pigeons, so that it seemed the city was multiplying itself for her alone, conjuring a menagerie of hideous new worlds.

Finally, the cloud turned into an alley she'd never seen before. It was a dead-end alley, corded with dry and leafless vines whose parallel lines started wide, then grew closer together, tapering like the point of an arrow. She had no choice but to go where it led. The alley was a long one, absurdly long really, and at first Allison couldn't make out what was waiting for her at its termination point. What she perceived was the mere suggestion of an image, a blurry, blueish flicker, as from the glow of a far-off television screen. But as she drew closer, the shape began to resolve itself into a human form. A familiar form. And Allison's stomach lurched as she continued her approach, for there, beneath a defunct neon theatre sign, was the woman. *Her* woman. Herself. The billows of brownish-gray smoke that were choking the streets poured out from this spot. From her. The primeval howls of the boiler were issuing from her lips. The odor rolling out from her body was so noxious that Allison at last succumbed, retching violently even after there was nothing left in her system to purge.

It took her several minutes to recover. Then, taking shallow breaths in order to keep the nausea at bay, she forced herself to go on, stepping forward until she was face-to-face with the specter.

The woman was transparent. She faded in and out like a projected image, like the images of the alternate children Allison sometimes saw in their alternate rooms, their curly mops strangely backlit, their skin ethereal like cellophane. Though this woman looked older, she was still quite beautiful. Her face was lined and lightly marked. A pale scar crossed one cheek, as if she had been hiking through a forest and a branch had snapped back at her. Her breasts were smaller and hung a bit lower. Natural. There was a little extra weight around the thighs, the hips, the belly—baby weight that had not been surgically erased, but had been allowed to stay. Maybe the woman didn't mind it. Or maybe she left it there as a memento, a softness to remind the children that they were wanted, that they were loved, that they would always be welcome to return to her if they were in need of nurturing.

Allison took in the woman's artsy, unfashionable clothes. The unpainted nails. The hair tied in a careless ponytail at the back. The sprawling tattoo of a feather on the right forearm. And from this last detail she knew at once that this woman was the poet Allison herself had always wanted to be, that she had persevered through hardship and rejection rather than taking the path of least resistance. When the split-yolk sun offered her a way out, she had declined its bittersweet boon. She had instead chosen to honor herself. To honor the words lying dormant in her hands. She had kept at the forge, hammering day after day, year after year, until her fingers were burned, until the tips of her hair were singed and her vision was blurred by the starbursts that scattered with every blow, so that the birds she rendered would be capable of lofty flight. And fly they did. Her very physiognomy showed it to be true; there was an ease with herself, an unflappable pride, as if she knew she had created works of such beauty they would break the heart of anyone who read them. She had done what Allison herself could not do. And Allison, overcome with regret, began to weep.

With streaming eyes, she watched her, this blessed woman with her artist's ease, who even now appeared to be seated at a laptop, composing a poem. Right there and then, framed by the squalor of this grimy alley, she was bringing a bird to life. Harvesting the clay. Piecing together the bones. Shaping and smoothing each feathered wing. Pouring salty tears into its shining eyes. Massaging its kidney-bean heart until the organ began to beat on its own, filled with its own dark rhythms, pumping hot blood through richly veined stanzas. And then, at the very end, breathing wind onto it. Saying its name.

Allison felt a surge of sense memory, recalling how it felt to do this. To be a god of sorts. To create something that had never existed before, that would not exist if it were not for her. *Sublime* was the only word for it, though even that was woefully insufficient. Visceral, maybe. It was better than the thrill of buying a Givenchy dress and wearing it in public for the first time. Better than hobnobbing with movie stars. Better than the automatic respect and deference of an entire class of people. Better than the luscious gazes of countless men and women, proving that she'd come close to attaining the current standard of feminine perfection. Better than all of it combined.

With this realization, she discovered that she hated the woman. Truly. Deeply.

Then something happened.

Turning to someone nearby, the woman tilted her head to the side, revealing delicate crow's feet that were not nearly as disfiguring as Allison had always feared they would be. And then she laughed. It was an all-consuming laugh, utterly unselfconscious, sprung from the center of her being. Her whole body shook with the joy of it. Her face lit up like a signal fire, a beacon of radiance, and in a rush of insight Allison understood who it was that was in the room with her, whose unheard words it was that had brought her such delight. She felt the magnetism of his mole, just out of view. Heard, almost, his voice. Everything drew into sharp focus around her. In this other place, the two of them were together. They had found each other as adults—of course they had—for once the constraints and taboos of childhood had been removed, what was to stop them? Perhaps she had sought him out in New York, had offered to convert. Perhaps he had seen her poems published and had gone to a reading. Perhaps he had gone that very night to her humble apartment. She followed this thread of probability, felt the ache of it, until the scene materialized before her: there they were at last reunited, their long years of yearning rewarded. His hand sliding to the small of her back. Her fingers encircling his neck, cradling them as if she could not believe he was really there, as if with that slight pressure she might prevent him from being snatched away a second time. Hips coming forward then, pelvic bones blooming like a pair of orchids, like garden frames pressed together. She, playfully kicking his foot out from under him, accelerating their descent onto the bed. He, biting at her neck while his left hand fumbled with a stubborn button on her skirt. Soon enough they would be naked and grasping, sunk fully in their passion, and then it might be that their bodies began to glow, like deep-sea fish, a stain of bioluminescence in the darkened bed. They would not even be aware of it, so immersed were they, so grateful to be entangled once more in each other's arms, drunk on the chemicals of skin, on the heat of mouths.

Him and her. His mouth on *her*.

And it was then that the wire seemed to twitch in Allison's left hand. The wire she didn't even realize she had picked up while she was stooped over, vomiting bile and pulp imbued with grenadine; the wire that had glinted like an evil thread of sunlight in the crepuscular alley, like a strand of volcanic sputum; the wire that seemed to have been placed there just for her. And filled with a spiraling rage, she reached out for the woman's collar, expecting to close on nothing but instead feeling a wisp of linen between her fingers. There was exhilaration at this small success, and somehow, concentrating her energy as she had never done before, she began to pull the woman into solidity, to wrench her out of her natural orbit in that other place and into hers. The woman's eyes went wide at this, registering shock, horror. Her body began to convulse. She seemed to be having a seizure, while Allison, emboldened by her victory thus far, yanked even harder, dragging the woman's body through the opening, drawing her as through a long, knitted tube, and the passageway was so much softer than she would have imagined, soft and pliable, like a birth canal. She would have thought it would be like hard plastic, ridged into segments, difficult to traverse. But it was easy, so easy she couldn't understand how it didn't happen all the time, how people didn't simply vanish on the street, having been plucked like a peach from their own worlds and absorbed into the next.

A voice from deep within shrieked for her to stop, but she couldn't help herself. Didn't want to help herself. The wail of the boiler had by then reached an unbearable crescendo, threatening to bring down the very bricks around her; every breath she took bore the stench of decay, of drowned sailors and fates that were even worse to contemplate; looping brown clouds hung like letters in the air, an infernal language sullying the alley. And at the center of it all was her own perfect body. Expertly toned from years of spin class and Pilates, it fairly resonated with strength, a filament bent on a single purpose.

With a thrill she felt the woman's panic. She felt the woman's silent scream ringing in the bones of her arm, and for a moment she wondered if it would leave its gnarled imprint there, like a face in a shroud, and she would either be forced to forever keep this remnant covered with bronzer or have it dermatologically resurfaced. All at once the commotion in the other place became more pronounced. Someone (she knew who) was struggling to hold onto the other version of her. Someone wanted to keep her there. But this knowledge only solidified her resolve, and so she executed one final yank, a heave of gargantuan proportions, and with a sort of snuffling sound that was to be expected when transferring from one atmosphere to another, the woman at last burst through from her world to Allison's.

There she was at last in the flesh, the best version of herself. Accomplished. Happy. Still beautiful. Blinking like an animal in the abattoir glow of the street lamp. She had come through all the indignities—the professional condescension, the gaslighting, the men claiming to be mentors long enough to gain access to her body and others who had not even waited for permission—and somehow, she had retained her resolve. She had not allowed herself to be diminished by them. This woman fairly glittered there in the alley, her skin dewy with a life of contentment, her body emitting through those putrid coils the distinctive odor of sanctity—only her eyes registering the distress of her present situation, two glass orbs shining with terror—and Allison knew at once that this woman's very existence was a judgment upon her. It was proof that the choice made on the margins of that canyon so many years ago, beneath that double-yolked sun, cataclysmic, seductive, pulsing red, had not been the only one possible, as she had come to believe in the years since. *The choice was made for me*, she had assured herself in countless, uncertain moments. *As I was made, it could not have been otherwise.*

And so, before the woman could become oriented to her surroundings, before she could even think about fighting back, Allison maneuvered herself behind her. She had to do it this way, for who could do such a thing while looking themselves in the eye? She thought it would be a kindness to do it quickly, before the woman's mind could reassert itself. (In her stunned condition, the woman was more akin to a dumb animal than a human.) Allison raised the wire, encircled the pale throat with it. *Like a halo,* she thought, nearly laughing. *So saintly now, are you? So blameless in your choices?* And in her ecstasy, she thought of all the monarchs, many of them women, who had sent their rivals to the justice of the ax, who had been unwilling to brook any threat, no matter the cost to others or themselves. And this seemed right to her, for wasn't she a queen of sorts, too? Certainly, she was. A queen of the realm.

And with tremendous strength—who would have guessed she possessed such strength? —she pulled the wire tightly, so tightly, around the woman's throat, felt the delicious squeeze of the metal strand against skin, how after a few seconds it began to cut through with a sickening sound, a huntsman from a fairytale seeking the breath of his prey, having found there were simpler ways to stop the heart than merely cutting it from its cavity. Beneath her fingertips she felt the desperate pulse of the trachea, like a snake writhing. The body spasming, too, as if she were an ocean-bound creature drowning in air.

The woman's body snapped forward and back like a rag doll. The unpolished nails clawed at her throat, and Allison had an unwelcome flash, remembering all the times in recent weeks she'd performed the exact same action, her neck throbbing with a nameless dread. But she did not let go. Her wrists felt like they were no longer part of her, like they were lengthening, hardening into gauntlets, with no further purpose but as plated conduits for her wrath. Soon after there was a suction-y sensation as the wire cut through to bone, and then a final expulsion of blood. *Like a Shakespearean epilogue,* she thought triumphantly, one last bit of moralizing after all the carnage had been enjoyed. (She had always found this funny: this dramaturgical absolution of a bloodthirsty audience.)

And through it all, the boiler moaned on like an inconsolable child, like an ancient petulant god, until Allison, spitting sea-foam from her lips, at last loosened her grip and let the body slump to the floor.

Her fury exhausted, the act she had committed began to transition blissfully into the past. She could feel it slipping away, though it seemed to drag against time as it went, struggling to remain relevant, to have the crime at its heart answered with justice. She watched as the hole to that other place grew smaller, shrinking to the size of a keyhole. Through it she thought she saw a final, panicked blur of motion, a jolt of despair, and then it sealed itself for good, snapping closed like an animal trap. Almost at once, the stench dissipated. It was still a filthy alley, but to her, the air smelled sweeter than it ever had. The whorls of vapor began to waft away, coming apart at the ligature points and gusting like tumbleweeds down the alley. And the boiler...*good Lord*. The boiler had fallen silent.

As she looked with disgust on the crumpled, lifeless body, Allison tried to comfort herself with thoughts of her childhood garden, of those carefree, sun-drenched days when the soil was as rich as royal velvet between her toes, when the earthworms crawled and the swallowtails winged by and the twilight blue hibiscus, though without eyes, seemed always to open at her approach, purely from the pleasure of being near her, as if there were something about her feral innocence that charmed it. *Once, I was a child*, she told herself. *Once, I looked at the world with awe and wonder.* But she could find no direct line between that little girl and herself. The memories might have been those of a stranger.

ALLISON RETURNED TO THE ALLEY THE NEXT DAY, drawn by some irresistible force, but no trace of the crime remained for her to brood over. No police tape, no blood splatters, no glinting wire hastily discarded in the dumpster. Nothing. She was not even certain she had found the right alley, though she sensed she had. Where had the body gone? Had it somehow been transported back to that other place? Was it suctioned up by some quantum cleaning crew? Or did it simply deliquesce, oozing over curbs and manicured lawns, past private club lots full of Bentleys till it came at last to the waters of the Pacific, where its dusky plume, for just a moment, darkened the blue?

Such questions occupied her attention for a short time, three days perhaps, and then she decided it was best to forget the whole ordeal. In a sense, she supposed, it was a crime without a victim.

From that point, the realm as she knew it was wonderfully restored. There were no more skeletal visages at brunch—no more exhaustion or resentment at the demands of her chosen role. Whenever she went out with the ladies, she spun tales of such incredible debauchery that she became a legend among them. She usurped Marisa's position as the ascendant matriarch of the group, making certain to keep the others in their place with shrewdly timed Trojan horse remarks ("You are looking *so* good for your age."). Likewise, Allison took renewed satisfaction in subjugating those of a lesser socioeconomic status, in particular those, like poor Barry, who labored on the outer fringes of her sphere. When she got them fired, she felt an unparalleled thrill, originating in the vicinity of her groin and branching outward. (She sometimes thought it was preferable to sex—the pleasure was purer somehow, and sharper.) She also made a point of humiliating Babs at every opportunity. Once, she engineered an elaborate prank to embarrass her in front of her yacht club friends, on her birthday no less, then laughed it off when Keith threatened to divorce her. In a word, she thrived.

She became a creature almost fully of the present, reckoning with the eternal only when summoning the angels for a tummy tuck or a brow lift. Both her garden-rich childhood and her ambitious younger self were largely gone. When she thought about poetry now, it was with derision; at social gatherings she often found herself ridiculing the very pursuit that had brought her so much joy in her youth. She could no longer recall a single one of her poems, any more than she could recall why she had wasted so much time composing them.

Her memories of Moshe were likewise fading. Every time she thought of him, she remembered a little less. A detail forgotten here and there. The color of the canoe. The location of their first kiss. The entire episode of the ring. One by one, they wisped away into nothingness, so that before long she could not even remember who he had been to her. A teacher, perhaps? A childhood crush or friend? Someone too distant to dwell on, at any rate. Soon she forgot even his name. His image did linger for a time, though she had lost all memories attached to it. It hung on for as long as it could, through some eccentricity of the hippocampus perhaps, insinuating itself at first light when her consciousness lay in the no-man's-land between dreams and wakefulness. He was like a ghost pressed against a windowpane, a handsome ghost, though very young, and she puzzled at the persistent mystery of his face until all that remained was the mole, her erstwhile polestar, along with a final, lovely glimmer of something she couldn't identify, some overlooked, aching thread that was lodged like a foreign body in her heart. Then that, too, was gone.

Bryn was growing so lovely that it made her proud, if a little envious. She was not worried for her anymore—the girl had everything, what was to worry about?—nor was she worried about Jamie, who had become strong enough to dominate everyone around him, even his self-important teachers. This, too, was a source of pride. Freed from her former concerns, Allison now allowed Eva to take primary responsibility for the children's care, and upon finding that there were still too many demands on her schedule, she persuaded Keith to send them to a boarding school abroad. The European experience, she explained, would give them still more of an edge over their peers.

This adjustment meant she now had ample time for social events, shopping, exercise, and the occasional volunteer opportunity (here she did just enough to meet the demands of her station), as well as for her expanded panoply of lovers, particularly Modesto.

"What if you did something terrible?" she had asked him once, long before the boiler began its reign of terror, and her fractured world became whole again. "Something illegal and immoral and all of that. Would you go to the police?"

"Of course not," he had answered, nuzzling her exposed nipple so that a shock went through her body. Modesto always knew just what to do, how to light her up like a circuit board. "My family would be deported."

"What if you were me?"

Modesto laughed, a deep throaty laugh, as if the thought were too absurd to contemplate. "If I were *you*, I could get away with anything I liked. You are rich and beautiful and white. People like you are immune from judgment, you know. You are truly free."

And so she was.

In the stronghold, everything was again as it should be. The queen was no longer restless within her chambers, no longer plucking mushrooms from the walls and piecing them into woolly trains. Instead, she blazed like a fledgling star, holding dominion as she was born to. She wielded her beauty without guilt, or sympathy, or even a single moment of melancholy reflection. All the permeable places of the city—the soft places that were like bruises on the flesh of a peach, where choices both made and unmade had flowed together like a river—these had knitted together once more, and before Allison's memory of these events faded entirely, she thought to herself that this was good and true and right. The cracks in the foundation likewise evaporated; it was as if they had never been there. The cloistered doors were barricaded shut. And if there were birds in the sky, they knew enough to abide by the oldest rule of the realm. They kept their songs to themselves.

acknowledgments

I AM FOREVER GRATEFUL TO:

Mary Ann Rivers and Ruthie Knox, my fabulous publishers at Brain Mill Press. Thank you for shepherding this eccentric little book into the world. I am so grateful for your incredible insights, unwavering support, and almost supernaturally generous spirits. You are the best there is. Thanks also for the gorgeous cover art. The aesthetic is a wonderful fever dream come true.

My husband, Nick, who is my first reader and biggest champion. Thank you for your patience, your bizarre sense of humor, and for talking me down all those times I was tempted to give over to despair. Our love deserves a Cat Stevens soundtrack.

My brilliant and beautiful daughter, Zooey, who is a fire unto themselves and an inspiration to me always.

Our schnoodle, John Quigley Quincy Adams, who has alternately frolicked and snored by my side during the writing of many of these stories. You make everything better.

My incomparable mom and dad (Mutti und Vati). Thank you for all the joyful moments and the countless ways you've believed in me through the years. You are both my heroes.

My two librarian aunts (Judy and Darla), who instilled in me a love of reading and whose book recommendations I still rely on.

Janelle and Joe, my wonderful in-laws, who are too great for such a modest title and who always have words of encouragement for me.

Brita, Paul, and Zoë, our forever family just across town. May we continue to confuse Santa for many years to come.

My many friends, my chosen weirdos, my glorious tribe, whose idiosyncrasies pair so nicely with mine and who have enriched my life in ways both large and small: Thomas ("look into your heart"), Martha, Janis, Rachael, Lori, Nicole, Melanie, Laurie (AKA Lee-loo), Susan, Emily, Grace, Eden. To Paul for being my stalwart writing buddy over the years. To Amber for her great work and for those very necessary moments of writerly commiseration.

Mrs. Dillman, my first grade teacher, for telling me I could do this.

Craig O'Hara, for the fun and insightful book, *The Philosophy of Punk*.

The late, great Shirley Jackson. You had me at "The Lottery."

And, last but not least, maybe-deity Jimi Hendrix, for guitar licks so glorious they remade the world.

about the author

KAREN M. VAUGHN LOVES READING AND WRITING UNCANNY FICTION. HER FIRST COLLECTION OF SHORT STORIES, *A Kiss for a Dead Film Star*, WAS PUBLISHED by Brain Mill Press in 2016 and was nominated for a Pushcart Prize. Her work has also appeared in *A cappella Zoo*, *Whiskey Island Magazine*, *Illya's Honey*, and *REAL: Regarding Arts & Letters*. For many years she edited for a medical journal, which might explain her fascination with evolutionary biology and the workings of the body. She loves horror and will drunkenly defend it at any dinner party you care to invite her to. In her off hours, she can often be found running long distances toward or away from things. She lives in Lawrence, Kansas, with her husband, daughter, and a highly energetic schnoodle, who is probably a pooka.

9 781948 559690